Prophet

A novel

Prophet

C. Norman Noble

I hope you enjoy!
Norm

Prophet

Copyright © 2006, 2007

C. Norman Noble, all rights reserved

No part of this book, either in part or in whole, may be reproduced, transmitted or utilized in any form or by any electronic, photographic or mechanical means, including photocopying, recording, or entry into any information storage or retrieval system, without permission in writing from the copyright owner, by way of the publisher or the publisher's agent, except for brief quotations embodied in literary articles and reviews.

ISBN 13: 978-0-9786971-4-3
ISBN 10: 0-9786971-4-6

Library of Congress Catalog Card Number: 2007929820

Book Design: Optimum Performance Associates

For permissions, serializations, condensations or adaptations, write or call the publisher's representative, Optimum Performance Associates, at

OPA, Box 1764, Chandler, AZ 85244-1764
480.275.5270 | Toll-free: 1.866.466.6643 | Fax: 480.393.1646

Published by Ironwood Publishing, Sun Lakes, Arizona

Printed in the United States of America, 2007

Table of Contents

Dedication I
Acknowledgments II
Prologue III
The Birth of an Idea 1
Invisible Radar Called PROPHET 21
Fast and Furious 35
British Crown Colony 55
Kismet? 61
Snow Like Powder 75
Gone With The Wind 81
North to Alaska And Turn Left 107
A Drunken Brawl 113
Warning Signs 117
The Deepening Liaison 143
Moles 153
A Secret No More 171
The Plot Thickens, The Knot Tightens 183
Free At Last, Free At Last 190
Confrontations With the FBI 195
Disappearing Act 225
Who Done It? 229
The Rest of the Story 233
About the Author

Dedication

This book is dedicated to my beloved wife, **DenisAnn.** Because of her, I finished this work—a manuscript I started over a decade ago and then put aside. As I say in my book, ". . . there's nothing like the support of a good woman." She is my best friend, my sustainer, and my confidant. It was her thoughtful encouragement and wise counsel that caused me to return to writing.

C. Norman Noble
Sun Lakes, Arizona
June 2007

Acknowledgments

With special thanks to **Robert Hancock** who gave me the technical ideas for the PROPHET system that are featured throughout this book. And who knows? Maybe such a system exists. Like Tom Clancy whose vivid imagination (applied abundantly to logic) has come up with uncannily accurate descriptions of American weapons systems, maybe there exists in our arsenal a terrain-avoidance/terrain-following system with these stealth-like capabilities. Would be nice.

Prologue

Gil still hadn't figured out how it happened. How could he have been so stupid? How could he have missed all the signs that were now so obvious? Had he really been that naïve?

Beautiful young women did not flirt with him. In fact, the idea was ludicrous. So ultimately, when she set her enticing trap, he was totally unwary and innocently prepared to do anything she asked, particularly with his unhappy home life as a milieu. And what she asked ultimately cost him everything.

Gil Brockton was in his forties and had been Vice President of Engineering at Pierce Electronics for several years. As a man approaching midlife, he was inadequately prepared for—and woefully unguarded against—the infamously emotional midlife crisis that faced him. His average looks, average height and receding hairline allowed him to conclude that his glory days of chasing women or even being attractive to women were behind him, if they had ever been in front of him. He had a sense of immunity from all outside threats to his well being. Besides, his passion was in the world of engineering where he could create new products of importance.

The only Eurasian he ever remembered seeing was the actress Nancy Kwan. This young woman reminded Gil of her. She had the look of a model, one who had glided down countless runways, smiling for the patrons and photographers. When he had asked how someone as young as she had risen to such a level of responsibility in her company, she hadn't lied. Her uncle owned the business, she told him.

Both her Scottish father and Chinese mother had died in a plane crash when she was twelve, and her uncle had sworn to see to her upbringing, her schooling and her financial security. He had sent her to the finest boarding school in the United States, explaining that the American experience was crucial to her future.

"But Uncle," she had protested, "all my friends, all my family are here in Hong Kong. I know no one in the United States. Please don't send me."

"It is settled. You leave the first week in September. You will not return until you have graduated." During those three weeks before leaving the British Crown Colony, she cried continuously. Sometime during the long flight from Kai Tak Airport, as the Pan American 707 lumbered northeast over the South China Sea toward Japan, the tears ended, to be replaced with a resolve that she would bring honor to her uncle; that he would be proud of her. She was, after all, Victoria Li of the House of Shek.

It was hard work, particularly the first year. Everything was new. American schools were different from English schools. American girls behaved differently than Chinese girls. Americans used different words than most English words she knew. She felt differently, too. She looked . . . well, she looked Asian. There were no other Asians in her school. In fact, everyone was Caucasian except her. When the school held dances with neighboring boys' schools, she was the curiosity. Many boys thought she was Japanese. "Naw, their eyes slant different," one had said a little too loudly. "I'll bet she's one of those Veetnams or whatever they're called."

She survived her first year. She became the top student in her 10th grade class. In her junior year, the year her enticing Eurasian beauty was confirmed, she was sought after by the boys, tolerated by the girls and still scholastically at the head of her class. When she graduated Valedictorian, there was no trace of her Hong Kong heritage. In speech, in dress, in manner, she was American. The only thing that wasn't was her passport.

Following a summer in Hong Kong, she returned to the States, this time as a freshman at Stanford University. Her uncle honored her by coming to her graduation four years later. He said it was because she had excelled Summa cum Laude. She felt it was because he was proud.

Immediately after graduation, she returned home for the final phase of her training. She was to become part of his business-consulting firm. This excited her. She didn't know much about his company because he had kept it from her. But she knew that business took him all over the world, and that clients from all over the world came to see him. She also knew that he was very successful.

She spent her first two years as a market analyst, studying the international markets of automobiles, computers and aircraft. She knew almost nothing about these when she started. She was an expert when she finished. Even so, she knew little about his business. She was about to learn.

Shek World Trading Center bought and sold product designs, serving as a broker between those who had an idea to sell and those who needed ideas. They specialized in designs with enormous product potential and charged accordingly. The idea was simple enough. Maintain a low profile, *never* reveal the details of any transaction, buy low, and sell high.

There was only one aspect that Victoria didn't understand, "Uncle, if no one knows who we are, how do the sellers know how to find us?"

"That is our task, daughter of my sister. We must find them."

"But how do we know they want to sell?"

"We do not, sometimes because they do not. Then, it is our job to persuade them." Seeing the need for more explanation, "Do you remember when I bought the sapphire ring you wanted as a graduation present?"

"Yes, it was identical with the ring owned by the wife of the Spanish ambassador. I admired it so."

"The day after you admired it, I called on the lady of the ring. I offered to purchase the ring. She said it was not for sale. I told her 'Nonsense, everything is for sale. It is just a matter of determining the price.' An hour later, we struck a bargain and you had your ring. This is how we purchase trade secrets. We find the ones we want and we buy them."

"One last question, Uncle. How do we find the ones we want?"

"We are good spies, Niece."

As in everything she had ever undertaken, Victoria was superlative in this world of espionage. It was stimulating. It was thrilling. She attended trade shows and conventions worldwide. She combined her acquired market knowledge with the technical papers and press releases she read and heard. She successfully separated the breakthroughs from the long shots from the also-rans. She accurately identified the inventors and the key designers. Then she turned her findings over to her uncle for his action.

It was only after she had participated in trade shows for a year that her uncle took her into his final confidence. "You have performed well, Victoria." He had begun using her name for business purposes, he explained when it happened the first time. "You have contributed to the profit of our company. It has not been without sacrifice, I know." He paused as if to choose his next words most carefully. "Yet, in spite of your good efforts, our joss (Chinese luck) has fallen. If we are to survive, desperate measures are to be taken."

"What can I do, Uncle?" His news worried her, not just for the threat to herself, but to her uncle and the enterprise he had worked on for so long and so hard. "There must be something I can do."

"You are young and beautiful and intelligent. You can influence, you can entice men, reluctant men who have secrets, to share with you what they will not share with me."

It was then, for the first time, that she began to use her body as well as her mind.

Chapter 1

The Birth of an Idea

1977. The University of Southern California defeated Michigan in the Rose Bowl, 14-6; Oakland defeated the Vikings in the Super Bowl, 32-14; Muhammad Ali didn't retire again and defended his heavyweight boxing crown twice; "Rocky" won the Academy Award for Best Picture of 1976; Love Canal was declared a disaster area by President Jimmy Carter; two Soviet citizens, former U.N. employees, were convicted of attempting to buy U.S. military secrets and sentenced to fifty years in prison; two U.S. citizens were convicted of supplying data on satellites and CIA codes to the USSR and sentenced to 40 years to life in prison; Seattle Slew won horse-racing's Triple Crown; and Rick Stoner joined Pierce Electronics.

A New Beginning

"Rick. No promises. The top marketing spot is not open. I don't know when it will be." Charles Strang, President of Pierce Electronics and fellow member of Rick Stoner's church, leaned back in his chair and studied Rick's facial expression from across the table. "But when it does open up, I think you're the man for the job. I've been impressed with you for some time. Your thoughts are insightful, your strategies creative, and your leadership persuasive. And best," he seemed to emphasize this, "you are honest and a strong family man.

"In the meantime, I want you as a part of our marketing team. You're the exact person we need. And when that top spot opens up, you'll be ready." He smiled that sanguine smile of his; the one that brought him so much success in business; that one that was hard to turn down.

So this was why Charlie had invited him to lunch. Rick had wondered if a job offer was going to be made. At the last church board meeting, Charlie seemed to be alluding to something like this when the two of them spoke briefly to arrange the luncheon. At fifty, Charlie was eleven years older than Rick and it didn't seem likely that he was seeking to strengthen their personal relationship, although certainly that was a side benefit.

Rick studied this gray-haired, gentle giant of a man. It wasn't just his stature and physique that impressed people. It was his deep, resonant voice. When Charlie spoke, people stopped and listened as if Moses had appeared before them with more commandments. Rick's own son Jeff had once told his dad, "When I hear Mr. Strang, I think he sounds like God must sound." It was an apt description. Rick thought the same thing.

Rick knew that Charlie's entrepreneurial spirit had founded a company that had grown into a one hundred million dollar-a-year success story. He obviously hit the mother lode, becoming a millionaire in 15 years time. Rick had liked Charlie from the start and was excited at the prospect of being a part of this organization. Still, he decided to move slowly on Charlie's offer.

"Charlie, I have been impressed with your company since I first learned about it. It's a Seattle success story. I'd be kidding if I said I wasn't interested." Charlie smiled at the report. "But," Rick continued, drawing a deep breath to stabilize his nerves, "I have an investment where I am. My company's doing well and so am I."

"I wouldn't want you under any other circumstances. I'm only interested in winners."

"Where do you see me fitting in?"

"We need someone to head up our international sales, reporting to Jim Dougherty, our VP of Marketing. You know Jim, don't you?"

"Sure. Why are you and I talking instead of Jim and me? What's he think about this?"

"He has the final say, obviously, but since I knew you well, it was agreed that I'd make the approach. If you said 'yes' in round one, he'd take over." There was silence for a moment. Then Charlie said, "What do you say? Will you talk with Jim?"

"I'll talk. When does the bell ring for round two?"

Annual sales meeting

Four months after Rick joined Pierce, the company's annual sales meeting was held at the legendary Del Monte Lodge in Pebble Beach, California. It was an incredible location for any meeting. One hundred sixty-one superbly comfortable guest rooms and suites were located in the main lodge and eleven adjacent buildings.

And then, of course, there was the golf and the celebrated golf courses of Pebble Beach—Spyglass, Spanish Bay and Del Monte. Golfers and non-golfers alike drooled at the chance of spending time at this facility. In fact, as some had observed, walking any of the courses with a camera was as exciting as walking them with a set of golf clubs. And it was a little less nerve-wracking, too. Rick speculated that some of the finest shots he would make that day would be with his Nikon.

At Del Monte, teeing off in front of the omnipresent gallery of Lodge guests on this sunny August day was no easy task. Pride made the golfer want that first drive to look good in front of spectators. Achieving this was no small task. Rick had partnered with Bruce Marcotti on this first afternoon before the start of the sales meeting. Neither one of them were in the "good golfer" category. Rick eyed the sand trap far out to the left. If he hit a monster drive, he would be in it. He had never hit a monster drive in his life, but still opted to use his 3-wood for the sake of accuracy. He needn't have bothered. He topped the ball and it rolled past the women's tee, but just barely.

"That was close," Rick said. "According to PGA rules, if I hadn't gotten past the women's tee, I would have had to take off my pants."

"There is a merciful God," Bruce rejoined.

From the outset, both Rick and Bruce realized that this course was beyond their imaginations, boasting mature stands of trees, roller coaster greens and bunkers in which they could easily hide a Ford station wagon. By the time they got to the 7th tee, they were overwhelmed by the majesty and grandness of the course. It couldn't be tougher, they concluded. Then they peered down the hill to the green far below, surrounded on three sides by a turbulent sea. It was tougher.

"It's just a little over 100 yards," Bruce said. "Think we can use our wedges?"

"Surely you jest," Rick replied. "Did you happen to notice that your bag just blew over? There's a gale coming off the ocean. Maybe a six-iron is a bit more appropriate." To add drama to the scene, waves crashed against the rocks behind the green alternately sounding like cheers and jeers. Rick studied the scene closer and pulled out his putter.

"What are you doing," Marcotti wanted to know.

"I'm putting down the hill. I have a better chance of going straight and not being blown off course." He lined up and prepared to swing. "Besides, a putter can hit a ball 100 yards. With a downhill roll, I just might make it." Seconds later, his ball bounced down the steep slope and deposited itself in the front trap. Bruce was not as lucky. His wedge shot rode the incoming wind like a kite, first straight up in the air a good 100 feet, and then back to the left, landing 50 yards down the hill in some unfriendly rough.

And so it went for the remainder of the round. They lost countless balls. They also lost count how many times they laughed over their ineptness at this game and their folly in playing this particular course.

The final hole was a fitting finish for the legend of Pebble Beach. From the tee, the fairway stretched on in a sweeping arc with a lone fairway bunker almost 200 yards out on the right. Then it was a fairway wood, an iron to the green, and two putts for a par.

Right!

It was a miserable round of golf, but it was the finest day of golf that either had ever experienced. This was a precursor of good things to come, Rick was certain.

Indoor fireworks

Sales at Pierce Electronics had been lethargic and Charles Strang had hoped that a resort location would provide a needed spark to get the company out of the doldrums. Instead, it was Rick's unscripted presentation during the first day of the meeting that provided the fireworks. The Del Monte meeting room was cavernous, capable of handling five hundred attendees with room to spare. High ceilings, massive chandeliers, plush carpeting, and comfortable chairs set up in classroom style fixed the tone for the venue. Rick's assignment at the podium was to present the five-year goals for International Sales. He did that all right, beginning with a provocative statement followed by a story.

"There are three immutable rules in marketing," Rick led off. "Unfortunately, nobody knows what they are. Ask any seasoned marketing executive; ask any Harvard Business School graduate; ask any grizzled salesperson from the trenches; no two will cite the same set of three marketing rules to live by.

"That said, I will now share the secrets of the ages with you, for I know what these rules are. And there are none to refute me, no not two. So here they are. One, marketing responsibilities begin in the womb and end in the tomb. Two, everyone thinks he or she is a marketeer. And three, one-half of all marketing efforts are wasted, but nobody knows which half." He paused and smiled at his audience.

"Now I have story to tell you. A traveling salesman was driving along a country road in Kentucky when he came upon a young boy who could have been Tom Sawyer or Huckleberry Finn. The boy, no more than twelve or thirteen, was dressed in bib overalls, no shirt, boots, and carried a rifle slung over his shoulder. The salesman pulled alongside and paced the boy. 'What are you hunting, son?'

"'Don't know,' the boy replied not looking at the salesman. 'I ain't seen it yet.'

"Sorry to say, but that's the same plan Pierce is following nationally and internationally. We'll shoot at anything that moves."

Jim Dougherty slammed his notepad on the table as he heard this assessment. A few other members of senior management, based on their expressions, were having equally difficult times with Rick's statement.

Rick continued, despite the disruption. "It's not smart to be the new kid on the block and make waves. My grandmother taught me that. But then, she also taught me to toss spilled salt over my left shoulder to avoid bad luck. She was a wonderful woman, but over the years I have found occasions to ignore her advice.

"I thought long and hard about the criticism I just leveled because I know it cuts deep into the way we do things. Worse, it cuts into those who have created or condoned the practice. My concern comes as no surprise to my department. I've voiced it at staff meetings. I've discussed it with my boss. But it needs an airing at an open forum which Charlie Strang promised this meeting would be."

Rick was beyond taking deep breaths to calm his nerves. Any more forced air and he'd hyperventilate. One hundred twenty-two meeting attendees were paying rapt attention. Rick glanced at Charles Strang. He was conferring quietly with an agitated Jim Dougherty who crouched beside him.

"We've got to stop shot-gunning. We have to only shoot at targets that fit our scenario. We have to stop allowing the dollars to dictate the decisions." He spoke softly into the microphone. "What does a fuel pressure gauge have to do with our business? Absolutely nothing. We only pursued it because the contract was worth five million bucks. It cost us thirty thousand dollars to learn that Douglas Aircraft doesn't think we should be in this business either." There were murmurings in the audience. Rick was goring someone's ox.

"Not to be outdone, we were every bit as aggressive internationally in pursuit of the potable water gauge for the new Airbus A300. A seven-foot tube with a capacitance gauge that measures the onboard drinking water is not a Pierce strong suit, nor should it be. Twenty-five thousand proposal dollars later, it wasn't.

"Gentlemen, the time for us to be focused is at hand. Our industry is coming out of a recession. Our competition is hungry. Our financial resources are not unlimited. We need to be playing to our strengths, not our weaknesses. This means we must be smart. We must scrutinize every sales opportunity. We need to devise a formal bid, no-bid process. We need to be listening to the counsel of our field sales force. No, let me amend that. We need to be hearing the counsel of our field people. They're on the scene. They know what the customer wants. They know what the competitors are doing. They know how the customer perceives us. They know what our chances are of winning.

"And speaking of chances of winning, I don't think we should give serious thought to bidding anything where our winning factor is less than twenty percent."

"Are you nuts, Stoner?" Rick couldn't pick out the spokesman, just the general location of the voice.

"I don't think so. Nervy, perhaps, but sane. I just happen to care very much for the success of this company."

"That implies the rest of us don't, I suppose." Rick now recognized the speaker as "Hump" Marryatt, Altimeter Product Manager.

"Hump, it implies no such thing. I know your passion for your job and your loyalty to the company. I know you want Pierce to grow just as much as I do. I just want you . . . I just want all of us to take a closer look at the way we're pursuing business in case there are better ways for us to proceed.

"I'd like us to undertake formal brainstorming sessions with the various components of the Marketing Department, plus Engineering and Manufacturing. I'd like us to look at every aspect of our bidding procedure. Much of it's good. But some of it can be improved. What we need is the courage to improve what needs improvement."

The undercurrent of dissension subsided as Rick drew his presentation to a close. "I think we need to apply battlefield tactics and strategies in our approach to business. No general throws every resource he has across the whole battlefront in hopes that one unit will break through. Instead, he picks his targets carefully, if possible, matching his strength against his enemy's weakness. Then he attacks with the force necessary for the task.

"I want Pierce to do no less. If possible, I want us going for the soft underbellies of business first, saving the hard-to-crack business for times when we need ego boosts. Vince Lombardi, one of the greatest football coaches ever, said, 'Show me a good loser, and I'll show you a loser.' Guys, we've been awfully good losers of late. It's time to get mean and ugly."

Rick left the podium. Modest applause greeted him as he returned to his seat. Then, it built in volume. Bruce Marcotti was the first to stand, still applauding, and turned to face Rick. Others joined his tribute, followed even by the disgruntled whose seated displeasure became uncomfortably obvious.

The morning session's scheduled coffee break was only fifteen minutes away. Charles Strang dismissed the group early, recognizing that anything else at this moment would be anti-climatic. Rick was immediately surrounded by a group of well wishers and back-patters. As they drifted off toward the coffee and pastries, Jim Dougherty signaled Rick to join him. His angry expression didn't portray him as one of Rick's well-wisher cadre.

"Rick," he started off in constrained tones. "You and I have a problem." His face was flush, blood vessels standing out along his temples. "You deliberately challenged and criticized me in front of this group. You overstepped your bounds, mister."

"Jim, I didn't say anything I haven't said to you in your office, nor did I say anything I haven't said at our staff meetings. I didn't challenge you. I challenged the system. Besides, Charlie told us to speak our minds at this meeting, remember? 'No holds barred,' I think he said."

"Too bad you don't report to your pal, Charlie. But you report to me. I hired you. I can fire you. And that's what I'm doing right now. No holds barred. You're fired!!"

Rick stood in stunned silence. He knew he was ruffling feathers. He had no idea he was destroying his own nest.

Neither Rick nor Jim had seen Charlie standing to the side, listening to their conversation. He moved quickly at Jim's pronouncement. "Jim!" His voice was harsh. "You're totally out of line. I told every man here that this was to be an open forum. An open forum it will be. If there's a fire raging in your kitchen, you know what you've got to do."

"Are you saying I'm out?"

"No, I'm saying I'm the boss."

"And I'm not free to run my department?"

"Not when you run counter to my instructions."

"Then I'm out!" Jim marched stiffly down the aisle of the conference room and out through the doors.

Charlie and Rick faced each other, at first stunned at what had just happened. Charlie regained his composure first. "Like I told you when we first talked about the job, I didn't know when the top marketing spot would be open. It appears to be open at this moment.

"If you're interested, the job is yours."

Rick felt stupid standing there with his mouth open, but things were happening too fast. He'd been fired, rehired and promoted within the space of a minute. He recovered enough to answer his new boss. "You bet I'm interested!"

"Perfect. You start right after coffee break."

***

Gil Brockton was stunned by the news that Carl Munsen shared with him. Munsen was even more distressed. He couldn't believe that his friend and ally, Jim Dougherty was gone. "You know," he told his office confidante, "I can believe that Jim was fired. He always had a mouth on him, but I can't believe that Rick Stoner has replaced him. Of all the incompetents!"

"Stoner has a degree in electrical engineering," Brockton observed.

"Yeah, but I doubt he's ever practiced his profession and couldn't design a circuit if his life depended upon it. How are we supposed to work with someone who's so technically inferior? I call him the King of Fluff. He talks a good game but I doubt there's much substance."

Dr. Gil Brockton, Pierce's Vice President of Engineering nodded in agreement. "Life's the pits, sometimes."

"Life's a bowl of pits," Carl muttered. "Someone's beatin' us to the cherries. But that's okay. I can use the pits. They make great little weapons."

"Well, thanks for letting me know. I have to go figure out how this interface with Stoner is going to work. I have to deal with him on a daily basis." He turned and walked into his office.

***

Gil's father died when he was eleven and his mother had moved the family to Portland so she could work as a teller for the Bank of Oregon. She barely earned enough to keep food on the table and the rent paid. From childhood, Gil had wanted to be an engineer, but college seemed a remote possibility because of money. His grades were high enough, but he seemed destined for junior college, at best. Gil's high school math teacher encouraged him to apply for a scholarship at Oregon State University. He didn't hold out much hope, but the application cost him only time and effort, so he made the attempt. To his amazement, he was accepted and offered a full scholarship, although it didn't provide all the financial support that he needed to subsist. Yet, by working a fulltime late afternoon-evening job in Corvallis and studying into the early morning hours, he was able to receive his undergraduate B.S.E.E. degree along with his incoming class of '57. This was followed by a master's degree from Oregon State, which took four years because of his work schedule, and a coveted Ph.D. from MIT which only came about because of a benevolent benefactor who recognized his talent.

Gil had thought he was best suited in research; the home for scientific breakthroughs. His first real-world job was with NASA in Langley, Virginia, where he felt certain he would achieve Nobel-prize performance. In fact, he was part of a research team that made significant inroads in the forerunner to microchip technology. Aside from that, he languished in his job, believing in his mind that he was better than *this*; that he should be progressing faster; that he should be appreciated more.

It was no wonder, then, that Gil leaped at the chance when he was approached by Minneapolis Honeywell Regulator Company to lead their radar systems group in Seattle, Washington. This represented a giant step forward. He was familiar with the Honeywell pulse radar altimeter. They had proposed it to Hughes for the NASA-sponsored Lunar Excursion Module. Their loss of that program was his gain, he felt. He could breathe new life into their design. Indeed, in time, the radar altimeter with its leading edge tracking became Honeywell's most successful avionics product. Gil saw to it that he received his share of the credit for its success.

A few years later, Honeywell decided to relocate its Seattle radar group to their facility outside Boston, Massachusetts. Neither Gil nor his wife Susan had a desire to move back east. So he sought another job in the Seattle area. His timing was perfect. Pierce Electronics was looking for a director of engineering.

Gil had been entrenched at Pierce for nine years when Rick joined the company.

Chamber of Commerce

"The American high technology industry, so glamorous by all outside media accounts, looks different from the inside. Born of the aerospace industry, with its equally inaccurate glamorous image, the cadre of top managers who run the high tech companies have been trained well in conservatism. Profits are not for spending on high living but for reinvestment into yet higher technology. And the world marvels at their accomplishments. With good reason. Their accomplishments have been life changing—computers, digital watches, building automation systems, telecommunications networks, men on the moon.

"The industry and the world it affects are changing rapidly. Paraphrasing *Alice in Wonderland*, 'To stay in the same place, companies must run as fast as they can.' Running equates to investment. High tech companies give the appearance of being top heavy in engineering personnel, like they might topple from the sheer weightiness of their burden. And indeed, they would if it wasn't for the austerity that marks all other phases of their operations. Their total universe is based upon staying ahead of the competition, not so easily done; and there is no choice but to invest heavily in the future, no matter how near or far it may be.

"Salaries of the high tech professionals are not high, expense accounts are not lavish, and *perks* are not commonplace. Money, frankly, is not available for those purposes."

Rick Stoner read over the opening paragraphs of his speech for the Eastside Chamber of Commerce luncheon. They summarized his viewpoint based upon almost fifteen years in aerospace electronics. The local press gave exaggerated attention to the electronics companies in the area. Theirs was a clean industry. No pollutants, no industrial waste. It was a growing industry staffed by educated, white-collar workers who brought good salaries into the suburban economies. So, the media extolled the virtues of the high technology companies, making association with them prestigious. Rick enjoyed that part. He didn't know how his ego would have handled being a part of a fertilizer company or a waste disposal company for that matter. Image was important to him. Being a key person in a celebrated industry was essential for his personal well being.

But the part of the media hype that bothered him was the stereotype rendering of a fast-paced, fast-living management infrastructure whose actions matched the dynamic movement of their industry. Rick knew things to be just the opposite, and he hoped he could get this point across during his lunchtime presentation the next day. His company, representative of most, was filled with people who worked hard, and for the most part, took pleasure in what they were doing. They were divorced, single, family-oriented, atheists, churchgoers, partiers, tea-totalers, apartment dwellers, and homeowners. In summary, portraits of middle-class America.

Rick thought of his own life. Where did he fit in life's organizational chart? What was his self-analysis? Let's see, athletically fit for a man thirty-nine years of age. He could lose a few pounds or exercise. Either one or both would make him look better. (*Darn that ice cream!*) As far as accomplishment, he'd done all right but nothing spectacular. Vice

President of Marketing for a medium-sized electronics company put him on a par with several thousand other people nationwide—hardly a "Who's Who" performance. He was happily married to Carol and had been for fifteen years, with two well-adjusted children, and a frisky Jack Russell named Roxanne. The fact that both boys were approaching puberty sending their mental faculties on a prolonged vacation was cause for some concern. Yet, once they emerged from this blackout zone, he felt confident of their potential. As for Roxanne, she was anything but well-adjusted. She was opinionated and bent on having her own way. Not only that, if she didn't want to do as instructed, she would sit on her pillow and argue with an "Ahrrr, ahrrr, ahrrr" sound that was comical.

Rick and his whole family were active in their mainstream Christian church where he was a part of the leadership. He and Carol sang in the choir. They had many good friends, all members of the church, with whom they socialized almost exclusively. He loved sports—golf and tennis in particular, although his job and his home responsibilities prevented him from indulging in either very often. When time permitted, he thoroughly enjoyed watching the Seattle Seahawks, usually on television. He and Carol had season tickets to the University of Washington Husky football games, sitting on the 40-yard line right behind the Visitors' bench. He was well respected in his community and contented with his life though he knew it fell short of perfect. Most men would be jealous of such a resume. Rick knew that and felt even better because of it.

For a brief moment, he thought about his earlier years when he didn't have everything together; his teenage marriage to Margy; his teenage divorce from Margy; his failure to finish college because of a marriage born of youthful passion. And then he thought how he had overcome those obstacles, letting them serve as his springboard for success.

Carol's voice intruded upon his thoughts "What's pleasing you so much?" she asked, observing his smile as he stared absently at the TV, the text of his speech laying in his lap. "It can't be the weather report unless you are suddenly enamored with gale force winds through the Strait of Juan de Fuca. The forecast sounds awful."

Rick sighed contentedly and smiled at his wife. "If you must know, I was just sitting here counting my blessings. I have so many, and it is so good to be able to account for them." His mind wandered back into reverie for a moment.

'Laugh' lines in Carol's face drew special attention to her blue, blue eyes. She reminded Rick of a youthful Donna Reed. There was a special presence, a gentility about her that set her apart from all other women he'd ever known. With joy, she was the woman he came home to at night.

Carol liked sensitive people; honest people. She didn't like people who put on airs, or who seemed to be what they really weren't. By her admission, she wasn't a competitive person, pointing out that she never did well in school sports because she really didn't like to compete. If she competed against anybody, it was just against herself. She always did well in individual sports, like horseback riding or swimming, but never sports like volleyball or basketball. Even tennis. She wasn't good at tennis, but she enjoyed playing with Rick in mixed doubles. "I'd probably do better if I played myself," she would tell others.

One of the things Carol didn't like was dirt. She was rather compulsive about her house and herself. She couldn't tolerate people who were unclean or a house that was the least bit dirty because she didn't think there was any excuse for it. To her, it showed the person was terribly disorganized or just didn't have any pride. So that bothered her, and as soon as her house started getting dirty, she would really get edgy; yet another wonderful thing that pleased Rick about his wife.

"Are things looking better at work?" Carol asked, her question hopeful.

"I wish!" he chuckled, shaking his head. "No, my accounting was of you and the boys. That's my real net worth. The struggle at work continues. I don't see it getting a whole lot better until twelve months after the recession ends, and so far, the recession hasn't bottomed out."

Carol's instinct for security seemed to prompt her next question. "How are you standing up to the pressure?" Unasked, but hidden below the surface was her concern for his continued employment. Only three months before, Rick and the rest of top management had taken a ten percent cut in pay. Sixty employees, three percent of the work force, had been laid off. She feared there might be more.

"I won't pretend that it's easy, 'cause it isn't," He chose his words carefully. . . "But so far, I've been able to leave my problems at the office each night."

"Is that so?" she challenged. "Then what do you bring home each night in that briefcase? And what is it that keeps you at your desk until eleven o'clock most nights?"

"Honey, I understand your reason for worry. But honest, I'm not bringing problems home." He spoke with as much resolve and sincerity as he could muster.

"What then?" She wanted to know.

"I have been badly overloaded ever since letting Mark go. He took more off my shoulders than I realized. Unfortunately, just because he's gone doesn't mean the work has. It's still there, needing attention." He shrugged his shoulders. "I'm the attendee. There's nobody else."

"There's me," Carol said softly. "I can help do something, can't I?"

"That's the best offer I've had this week," Rick smiled broadly. "Maybe the best this year!" He got up and moved across the room to his wife, bringing his speech with him. He sat next to her on the couch and pulled her head onto his shoulder. "Honey, I need your support, comfort and understanding. That's your stock in trade. That's my strength. With it, I fear no one, nor any manufactured recession."

He returned to the second part of his speech, careful to leave one arm around Carol's shoulder. International travel. This was the part his audience wanted to hear. If Rick had a dollar for every time he had heard, *Need someone to carry your suitcase*," there would be no reason to continue working for a salary.

"Traveling to another country for the first time is more than an adventure. It's perplexing. Everything is new. Nothing is familiar. If you go to Paris, what do you do at Passport Control? If you have nothing to declare at Customs, do you walk under the green sign or the red sign? If you walk under the green, do you look nonchalant? And then what? You've cleared Customs. You're in the main terminal. People are waiving signs at you. You wish you were McCarthy or Fitz or Chetrit, 'cause the people holding those signs would help you. But you aren't. You're you. You don't speak French. And you're on your own.

"A helpful friend told you to take the Metro downtown to your hotel. He said there was a bus outside the airport terminal that took you to the train station. Where is the bus? How do you find it? And when you arrive at the station, what do you do?

"Your first trip to Europe can be overwhelming. So many questions. So many unknowns. It's even worse for the first time business traveler because there are pressures borne of expectations. Of course, you know what you're doing. You're a professional. Most people don't know that only eight percent of U.S. companies export. That means that ninety-two percent do not! Unlike Europeans for whom export is an expected way of life, most Americans rarely venture across international borders.

"So when a business traveler heads across the pond for the first time, what does he do? He blunders, looks naive, and makes mistakes. He sometimes adds to the legend of the Ugly American who masks his discomfort behind a veil of disgust ('this isn't the way we do it at home!')"

He stopped. Carol's warmth, Carol's beauty beckoned to him. He put down his papers and returned his full attention to her.

The wonder of it all

Since joining Pierce Electronics, every day he was in town started like every other . . . Wonderful! The tone was set as soon as he headed up the long, winding Pierce driveway. If it weren't for the corporate sign at the entrance, no one would know that an electronics company was hidden in the midst of the dense forest that covered the hill. Stately fir, counterbalanced with alder, salted lightly with maple (no one knew where they came from) lined both sides of the road and went as deep as the eye could see. If Rick were early enough in the morning, around the time the sun came up, he could sometimes interrupt a rabbit in meditation along the centerline of the road. When it was warm enough to roll the car windows down, he would slow to a crawl, breathing deeply to draw in the fragrant aroma of the woods. It was incredible to hear the awakening calls of high perched crows. It was rejuvenating to see the blend of deciduous and evergreen. It was invigorating to feel the stirring of a breeze valiant enough to penetrate nature's towering garden. By the time Rick pulled into his assigned parking place, he was always exhilarated, charged to begin the day. *It's a thrill to be the richest man I know*, he thought as he walked toward the Pierce Electronics main entrance. "*No one else has more than I have,*" he said to himself as he entered the building.

Through the wisdom of Charles Strang, the beauty that surrounded the building permeated the inside, too. A four-story atrium, capped by a massive skylight, dominated the scene upon entering the front doors. First time visitors frequently bypassed the receptionist as they walked to the edge to marvel upwards at the spectacular beauty. Fichus trees, planted on the first level, reached past the second as they grew toward the light. A Japanese style fishpond, stocked with giant, spectacular koi (truly, the lowly carp) meandered through a lush flower garden, resplendent with begonias, gardenias and jasmine. Dotted throughout the building, in large pots, were smaller trees and clusters of azaleas. The office areas, including all the *private* offices except Charlie's and the VPs, were open to the outer wall windows, bringing even more of the outside in. There were three conference rooms that were enclosed; one just outside Charlie's office; one in Marketing; and one in Engineering. There also were two small rooms where private discussions could be held with two or three people, usually when annual reviews were given. The entire atmosphere engendered a superior work environment. And Rick was one of its strongest proponents.

***

    Rick entered the house as quietly as he could. Why was it that floors only seemed to creak late at night? He tiptoed past his sons' bedrooms, listening for sounds that might suggest one of the boys was awake. Because of his schedule, he'd scarcely seen them during the past several weeks. He would have used any excuse to go in their rooms and be with them. There were no sounds, even from Roxanne who slept with his older son Trey. She raised her head and watched him, then settled back down on her pillow. He kept moving.
    Carol had left the master bathroom light on, letting in a pale glow that gave him just enough light to avoid stumbling into the furniture. Rick undressed quietly, turned off the bathroom light, laid his watch on the nightstand, and slid under the covers. A warm hand circled his waist. Turning, he saw his wife smiling at him. At least he thought she was smiling. "Hi," she said. "I've missed you."
    She was so beautiful. Rick put his arms around her, drawing her close. "Sorry I'm so late." He kissed her neck. "I should have called."
    She laughed softly, wriggling still closer so that her body pressed against him. "It would have been nice. But I knew better." She kissed him with just a hint of passion.

The world at his feet

Rick's international sales responsibilities didn't go away just because he had assumed the reins of marketing. He got to do both jobs. The task was monumental, requiring direct interface with front line engineers for airlines and airframe manufacturers throughout the world, as well as management and administration of the whole department. New military and commercial aircraft were in various stages of design and development; Saab in Sweden; Hawker-Siddeley, de Havilland and British Aircraft in the U.K.; Fokker in Holland; Dassault and Aerospatiale in France; Messerschmitt and Dornier in West Germany; Aeritalia and Agusta in Italy. All were Rick's customers; all had unique requirements for their cockpits. These requirements had to be understood and effectively shared with the Pierce Engineering Department. That was Rick's job.

It was in this capacity that Gil had questions about Rick's competency. Carl Munsen's earlier diatribe about Rick's lack of ability added to his worry. Therefore, the news of Rick's ascendancy into the top marketing spot was of particular concern. At least, that's what Gil told himself.

***

"I am really struggling with Stoner's assignment," Gil told his confidant Carl Munsen at lunch one day. "I heard that he and Charlie are buddies at church. Sounds to me like he got the job because of that, not because he's any good."

"I heard the same thing," Munsen said. He scowled, seemingly at the thought.

"How am I supposed to work with this guy? He's expected to provide marketing guidance to Engineering? I don't think so. I don't think he knows an altimeter from a forklift. How is he going to tell us what products to develop?" Gil wiped his mouth and slammed his napkin onto the table, clearly disgusted.

"Maybe you can figya a way to show Chaalie his incompetence." A clear Boston accent emerged.

"Well, I've got to do something. Maybe you can help me."

"That I can do. Sabotage is my game."

***

"Hump, there's something about Gil that has troubled me since coming to Pierce." Rick was talking to Humphrey Marryatt who headed up his altimeter sales group. "It's not his reputation, because he's highly regarded in industry circles. His spectacular achievements at Honeywell have placed an aura around him. The fact that he has done nothing of technical note in several years seems to have applied little tarnish to his reputation. He's a good administrator who runs his department well. The engineers who work for him seem comfortable with his leadership. Yet he seems paranoid, at least to my viewing."

"This isn't something new, Rick. He's been walking on eggshells for a few years. He seems to suspect that others are trying to undermine his authority or castigate his competence."

"Are they? It isn't obvious to me."

"It's nonsense. Like you said, the guy is just paranoid. Nobody's out to get him."

"Well, I guess my assignment, then, is to help him feel better about himself. I have to work successfully with the guy, and it isn't going to happen if he is constantly looking over his shoulder, trying to see if I'm second-guessing him."

It's always helpful to know the answer

Gil felt growing concern that others were talking about his lack of performance. It seemed to come from the pit of his stomach, tightening like a knot, moving up 'til he had heartburn. It wasn't fair. The company had done well; *Hell, our growth has been spectacular since I came. Who do they think runs the Engineering Department anyway? Where did they think the new product ideas came from?* He was past the design stage in his career. Didn't they know that? He was supposed to be a manager now, not an engineer.

His greatest fear was that Charlie was thinking of replacing him; moving him out of the company altogether. He knew he had to counter any such plan by making a strong offensive move of his own. He needed to achieve a major technical triumph, something that was totally his creation, his design.

It was innocuous enough; the idea that came to him during the altimeter design review at Wright-Patterson Air Force Base. Neither terrain-following nor terrain-avoidance is for the faint-of-heart pilot. At 500 knots and at an altitude of 200 feet, the slightest twitch can convert a plane and its pilot into a Fourth of July fireworks display. Lt. Col. Matt Arant had commented during lunch that terrain-following radars, while a boon to ground-hugging maneuvers, had their liabilities, not the least of which was their advance notice to the enemy that aircraft were incoming. *Why can't our technology of today design an invisible radar system?* Gil asked himself. *Why indeed*, he mused?

At first, his project was his own. That made sense. He had no idea what the answer was to the Air Force's dilemma. He had a saying—in working toward a solution, it is always helpful to know the answer. He wasn't ready to tell anyone about this quest until he was much further along in the concept. But he had a glimmer of an idea. When he had the answer, he'd be ready to seek the solution from others.

Chapter 2

Invisible Radar Called PROPHET

The birth of an idea

The LANTIRN project, developed by Texas Instruments, gave Gil his first inspiration. LANTIRN stood for **L**ow **A**ltitude **N**avigation and **T**argeting, **I**nfra**R**ed, by **N**ight. *Man, the lengths to which some people went just to come up with a pronounceable acronym*, he thought. It was so contrived, and yet, it wasn't such a bad description of what the system did. Still, it had its technical limitations and left lots of room for improvement.

Gil began with this premise. First, he had to work out the basic Terrain-Following / Terrain-Avoidance / Threat-Avoidance algorithms. They weren't going to be easy. Then he had to decide the major system components, and what was more important, how Pierce was going to develop them. At a minimum, he knew his system would require a radome, a gimbaled antenna, an exciter/receiver, a transmitter, a pressurization unit, a processor, a power supply, a data storage unit, an air cooled main structure with fans, and of course, a radar altimeter.

The scenario he pictured was a fighter aircraft, hugging the ground at an altitude of 200 feet, traveling at a velocity of 1,000 feet per second, and pulling a maximum of 2Gs, twice body weight at sea level. Under those conditions, there was going to be precious little time for the pilot to see an obstacle, evaluate its threat to the aircraft, and maneuver out of harm's way. There had to be an electronic solution. Technology had come too far for there not to be one, he reasoned. It wasn't the technical solution that worried him the most. It was figuring out how Pierce was going to successfully design and produce the entire system when their expertise in this arena was limited to radar altimeters.

The more he concentrated on the negative aspects of active radars, the more he became convinced that this negative must be converted to a positive. But how? If only his system could use random frequencies, never the same, but spread across the spectrum. That way, no ground radar could tune in on it. But that wasn't possible. Not with a single antenna.

Then, it dawned on him. Who said it had to be a single antenna broadcasting on a single frequency? If he used phased array radars, with several small radars that were randomly pulsed at haphazard frequencies in nanosecond bursts, he could accomplish the impossible. And if these radars had narrow beams with virtually no side lobes, they would be essentially undetectable, particularly if each radar was bore-sighted and pointed along the aircraft velocity sector. A spectrum analyzer could detect them, he knew, but such were not the normal instruments of war. He didn't imagine they would be found at most ground radar sites. He became excited with his imagination. What if the system was blended with digital map data, yielding a covert penetration system with advanced terrain following, terrain avoidance and threat avoidance?

This was it! He was on to something!

Dream comes true

"Gil's idea is brilliant!" Rick had never seen Charlie so animated. Rick had been called to an impromptu meeting in the president's office. He and Gil sat in Charlie's overstuffed chairs, facing their boss who chose to sit on the couch. "Like he told me, we don't have the credentials to design this system on our own. We need outside help. But if we turn to Honeywell or Bendix or Texas Instruments, they'll do it themselves. What do they need us for? Sure, they might subcontract something to us. But they'd take most of it. And they'd be persuasive in their argument, too. 'You don't have the clout,' they'd say. 'The Air Force would never authorize a project of this size with a company like yours,' and we'd agree. After all, who are we? A company one-twentieth the size of Honeywell, that's who.

"When he first said, 'Let's do it,' I thought he was nuts." Charlie smiled at Gil. "Who of significance could we get to work with us? I never thought about using outside consultants. I drew my square and then kept myself inside the boundaries. Gil didn't acknowledge my boundaries. He didn't even see my square.

"There are a few top organizations in the country who just might want to be a part of this venture. Eiler Laboratories and Radart Arrays are two that come to mind. They are the finest in their fields.

"So here's the plan. Rick, it's your job to go out in the field with Gil. You two need to team up and get our collaborators. It's going to take all your sales skills and all Gil's technical smarts to convince these *think tanks* to work with us, particularly since we have no funding yet. Think you two can handle it?"

"Piece of cake." Rick looked at Gil and thought, *sure hope it's angel food.*

Gil was silent, appearing to wish that there was an alternative plan.

Charlie raised his hand, signifying that there was one more thing. "One more thing. I don't want anyone else in the company to know about this until we have things locked up with our partners. There is too much at stake. If Honeywell or Bendix get wind of this, they'll wipe us out. I trust all our people, but sometimes things slip out. People say things they later regret.

"For now, only the three of us know about this. When you two start your visits to the prospective team members, I don't even want your secretaries to know where you are going or who you are meeting with." He paused, realizing the implications. "That means you will have to make your own travel arrangements. Folks may wonder, but that can't be helped. Besides, this will only be for a short time."

The three men nodded in agreement. It was settled. Mum was to be the word.

***

Leaving Charlie, Gil accompanied Rick to his office next door. Rick closed the door and gestured Gil toward a chair. Both of them were silent for a moment.

Then Rick spoke. "Gil, I know we have been at odds with each other since the beginning. I'm not certain what I have done, because you have never said. Up 'til now, I have just let it go hoping that you'd come around. But that's hardly been the mature approach, and I apologize for my shortcoming.

"Now, because of your creation and Charlie's instruction, we're going to have to form an inseparable team. Inseparable teams aren't at odds with each other. Otherwise, they're not teams. I figure that if the Seattle Supersonics can do it, so can we. In fact, until we've pulled this one off, you and I are going to have to act like Gus Williams and Dennis Johnson."

Gil asked, "Am I Gus or D.J.?"

"Gus. You've got less hair than I do."

And so an unholy alliance was formed. It became the sensation and the talk of Pierce Electronics, although no one knew why it had happened.

Strategic alliances

Eiler Laboratories was an early settler along Massachusetts' Route 128, *High Tech Corridor*. A professor and a graduate student from Massachusetts Institute of Technology got the company started. The research projects followed in rapid succession. Now, no one else in the country had equivalent aircraft onboard computer expertise. They were the first on Gil's list. By his judgment, they were crucial to the success of the program.

The assignment of forming a team with Gil was a Godsend, Rick felt. The two of them had to develop a solid alliance if the company was to grow. Either that or one of them had to leave Pierce. The head of Engineering had to work well with the head of Marketing. It didn't take a whiz kid to figure that out.

They flew Northwest Orient Airlines to Minneapolis and then on to Boston. Five hours flying time with an hour layover at Minneapolis-St. Paul International Airport afforded Rick a generous amount of time to start the befriending process.

"Gil, I have been thinking," Rick said as their breakfasts arrived on the outbound Seattle flight.

"Kinda dangerous, isn't it?"

Rick looked to see if Gil was smiling. He was, so he said, "Hey, leave the humor to Marketing. No, really, I have been thinking that what you have come up with is the most exciting project I have ever been involved in. We are about to make history, not just with the coalitions of companies, but with the technical breakthroughs. I have been in and around talent my whole professional career, but this is the first time I have been with genius."

Gil put the remainder of his roll in his mouth and studied Rick's face carefully. "Thanks, Rick. That means a lot. I guess I don't know what else to say."

"You don't need to say anything. I just spoke my mind."

Later in the flight, as they were somewhere over South Dakota, Rick brought up the subject of dinner. "Seems like a lot of our days are spent planning where we are going to eat, and what. I propose that we plan where we want to eat dinner in Boston. I don't know if you have been there often enough to have a favorite, but I have a few."

"Fire away. I haven't a clue. However, I have a preference to fish."

"Good. Anthony's Pier 4 or Legal Sea Foods would be my two choices."

"You're playing with me, right? What kind of place is Legal Sea Foods?"

"Actually, it's an East Coast chain. I don't know the history behind the name, but I can tell you that the food is great. However, given the choice, I recommend that we go to Anthony's Pier 4. It's right on Boston Harbor and has great views of the city skyline."

"Sold. I can taste the lobster even as we speak."

"Me too. I know it's bad for me, but bring on the extra cup of drawn butter."

***

Dinner that night was a delight; not just because of the food but because the two men spent time getting to know each other; and discovering that they had things in common.

Meeting with Eiler

The drive north from Boston to Wakefield was easier than Rick had anticipated. It was November and cold. Happily, there was no snow and the morning rush hour traffic was headed south, opposite their route. As a result, they were fifteen minutes early for their nine o'clock appointment. "Maybe we'll get an early start!" Rick said hopefully. They waited twenty minutes in the lobby.

From the outset of the meeting, it was obvious that Gil's reputation had preceded him. While their hosts didn't kowtow to him, they did seem to accord respect for his wisdom and experience in radar. Writing papers for technical journals, something that Gil liked to do, were paying dividends.

The Pierce meeting ploy was a simple one. Present the system concept, explain the plan for funding and solicit Eiler's participation on the team. Once obtaining a commitment, reveal the more complex nature of the project. At that point, they would present a technical discussion of all facets of the program, including the radar altimeter, forward looking radar arrays, transmitters, receivers, antennas, power supplies, computers, etc.

Rick introduced the reason for the development. "We know the Air Force is working on an aircraft that can't be detected by radar. We're not privy to their success so far, but we're advocates of the saying, 'whatever the mind can conceive, mankind can achieve.' The aircraft will fly. When it does, we plan to have it equipped with a terrain avoidance radar that is invisible to ground radar."

"Tall order," Dr. Herman Truttman, former MIT professor and founder of Eiler Laboratories (named after his mother) observed. "Radars emit energy. Every time they transmit, they are subject to observation. How do you propose to make them invisible?"

Rick smiled. "Technically, we can't. The law of physics will prevail. But if we use numerous, narrow-beam, phased array radars, tuned to multiple frequencies, we think the ground will have an impossible time tracking us."

Truttman smiled in return. "Hard, yes, but not impossible. Today's ground-based radars have computational capabilities to track three or four frequencies simultaneously."

"How about five hundred miniature antennas, individually pulsing in random frequencies at nanosecond bursts?"

"That's your plan?" The professor was suddenly interested.

"That's it . . . if you think Eiler can design and build an onboard computer to process the transmit commands and the echo returns."

Collectively, the four Eiler representatives expelled their breaths and stared downward at their notes.

"Do I take it that *the sighs have it*?" Rick asked.

Dr. Truttman peered over his glasses to study Rick for a moment. Rick smiled back at him. "Sorry. I couldn't help myself. A quartet of heavy sighs prompted a stab at comic relief, if not for you, for us. We have been thorough in our research and are confident in our approach. We know it's complex and is a technical challenge. We're equally certain that it's viable. But we need Eiler or it's a 'no go'. No organization in the country can match your expertise. And it's going to take the best if we're going to pull this off."

"The funding, Mr. Stoner. It will take dollars to accomplish what you ask. Where will the money come from?" This was an important question. If Dr. Truttman were not interested a little, there would have been no reason to ask the question.

"This has been a classic 'chicken or the egg' question. Do we get the money first to interest you, or do we get you first to interest the Air Force?" Rick smiled again. "We opted to convince you in order to convince the Air Force."

"Let me speak for the group," Dr. Truttman summarized. "We're interested."

"That being the case," Gil said, taking over, "let me get into more specifics. Besides a random frequency generator, we need a fully programmable radar signal processor that will extract target and other information from received signals, and then provide this data to the aircraft's avionics in usable formats. We envision a high-speed, special purpose computer programmed in machine language. It will have a throughput of seven million complex operations per second and a two million, 24-bit word, 50-megabit bulk memory. Think you can develop such a system?"

A five-hour meeting followed, interrupted briefly by delivery of sandwiches and soft drinks. Shortly before two-thirty that afternoon, an agreement had been reached. Eiler was fully ensconced as a member of the team. What remained were hours of brainstorming sessions to prepare the way for the development efforts to follow. These would occur in the weeks ahead, both in the Seattle suburb of Kirkland and the Boston suburb of Wakefield. For now, Rick and Gil had accomplished their mission. It was time to move on to Herndon, Virginia and the next team member candidate, Radart Arrays.

Something almost as important as the accord with Eiler had taken place that day. Gil had a new and better impression of Rick. In fact, he was impressed and he told him so as they drove toward the airport.

"Rick, I had a really hard time accepting you when Jim Dougherty was fired. He was my best friend at Pierce. You were a newcomer and I felt you lacked the technical savvy needed to be head of marketing. I never gave you a chance. I didn't want to.

"But Charlie forced us to work together. And I can tell you I wasn't pleased."

"I know." Rick kept his eyes on the rush hour traffic. The approach to Logan Airport was always tricky for him because he didn't know the roads well. "It was obvious that you were suffering."

"You've got that right. Yet I knew there was no choice. You headed up marketing and you were the right person for this job; even if I didn't think you were the right person for your job." He stretched his legs up against the car's firewall and resumed. "I went home that night, crying to Susan about the assignment. She told me to grow up and deal with it."

"Listen, Gil, I want you to know that you have been an absolute pleasure to work with on this trip. In spite of your problems with me, you have been a great traveling companion."

"Quit interrupting," Gil said, now smiling. "My point was not that I followed my wife's advice and dealt with it, it's that you have proven yourself to be an outstanding marketing man who is well qualified for the position; more so than Jim Dougherty who preceded you. Furthermore, you are clearly a man with integrity and honesty. That's refreshing."

Meeting with Radart

John Hawes' large frame had once been heavily muscled. Or so it seemed, but those muscles of old had long since yielded to softer tissue. He appeared weary and pulpy. He proved anything but. Throughout the three-hour meeting, this Radart Arrays president paced from one end of the conference room to the other, launching questions in rapid-fire bursts, jiggling change in his pocket when listening to answers.

"Who's going to pay for the development of these phased arrays?" he demanded early in the discussion.

Rick responded. "The Air Force will pay for the development or there's no point in proceeding. But the concept work will be the responsibility of Radart."

"Why us?"

"Why not? If you have an investment in the project, there are greater chances you'll support it with enthusiasm."

The Radart president twisted his mouth into a smirk and said: "I see. Where a man's money is, there will be his heart also."

"You paraphrase the Bible well, Mr. Hawes." Rick smiled in return. "That's exactly what I meant."

Despite the realization that Radart money would be required to underwrite a portion of the project, interest increased to a fever pitch. Their engineering director enthusiastically brainstormed possible approaches with Gil, salted periodically by his leader's plea for restraint. "Let's not get ahead of ourselves, Art."

Art would look up momentarily at Hawes, nod his head rapidly, and then dive back into the sketch he was diagramming on a pad of paper.

Rick's initial assessment of Willy Rewalt was that he was a humorless, scrawny man, full of nervous energy. He reminded Rick of a stubby jockey with thyroid troubles. What counted, Rick figured, was that he was an expert in narrow beam radars and Gil considered him ideal for the assignment.

Before the three-hour meeting concluded, Art and Gil had the framework for the radar design. The other members of the Radart senior management team had long since leaned back in their chairs, non-contributors to the invention unfolding before them. It was clear that the genius of the company was vested fully in the engineering director. If he was sold, it was a done deal.

***

Rick and Gil celebrated their victory at dinner that night at Washington's famous Jockey Club. "We'd better watch out," Gil said over his second gin and tonic.

"What do you mean?" Rick was a little puzzled with the remark. "Watch out for what?"

"We're starting to make a formidable team. Next thing you know, I'll start to like you as well as respect you."

On the way to Dayton

Two weeks before Christmas, Charlie and Rick traveled to Wright-Patterson Air Force Base in Dayton, Ohio to meet with the Air Force to make their proposal for funding. Gil stayed home to begin an intensive development activity. Charlie and Rick purposefully refused the meal on the plane so they could enjoy a good dinner at one of Dayton's finer steak houses, the Pine Club. "You're gonna love this place, Rick," Charlie said. "It's an old establishment, all cash, and no reservations. It's always crowded so we can expect to wait about an hour. But it's worth it."

Perhaps it was because they were out of town, away from office constraints. Perhaps it was because they were drawn to each other through a relationship apart from work. Whatever, both Charlie and Rick were in philosophical moods, introspective, and wanting to share their thoughts. As they waited for dinner, Rick revealed a little of his past. "A few years ago, more than anything, I wanted to be recognized as a marketing expert. I mean, I was looking for national recognition. I spoke at a couple of American Management Association seminars and wrote a slug of articles for Data Magazine. And in the process, I planned to become rich. I figured with the recognition would come money. I had just read Napoleon Hill's book, *Think and Grow Rich*. It was a book inspired by Andrew Carnegie who did all right when it came to acquiring money.

"I was down in L.A., sitting at the airport waiting for my flight back to Seattle when I started to devise my plan. The formula was in the book. Just follow it, I reasoned. Then I realized the price that had to be paid was far greater than I was willing to give. I was not willing to trade my family to accomplish this."

Charlie looked puzzled. "Explain that last statement about trading your family. How did you figure that?"

"Well, I figured that anyone with reasonable intelligence can acquire wealth. All they have to do is work, work, work. If they were willing to work diligently six or seven days a week, ten to twelve hours a day, they can become wealthy. But if they do that, they will be trading their family to achieve their goals. That, flat out, wasn't worth it to me.

"So, I let myself off the hook. *'You could have been wealthy, Rick,'* I said to myself, *'but you optioned to find your treasure in your family, instead.'* Once I did that, I was at peace. No more pressure. No more dissatisfaction."

Charlie nodded knowingly. "Being wealthy isn't what it's cracked up to be. Oh sure, the money's nice; you can buy things; but the bottom-line is, they are just things. If you said, I can be rich if I give up my health, or give up my family, or give up my family's health, or give up my friends, would you? I don't' think so. None of those things are worth it.

"You discovered something that most people never learn in a lifetime."

Then Charlie declared it was his turn to wax a little eloquent.

"You know, Rick, when I was younger, like in my mid-twenties, I was frustrated by my youth. No one was willing to take me seriously. It was as if they were saying 'What can a kid know?' But thirty was a magical age. Suddenly, it was deemed possible that I possessed a modicum of wisdom. Perhaps I did, but for the most part, I was no smarter than when I was five years younger. I just looked older, therefore smarter. As I continued to age from that point, I'm not certain I became wiser except I began to realize that I at least knew as much as those around me."

"So much for the myth of wisdom that comes with age," Rick chuckled. "I thought that all Stanford grads were considered wise beyond their years."

"Now you know."

"Let me share a more startling personal revelation that has only recently hit me. It has to do with looks. How old do I really look? No, don't answer. That wasn't a question except to me. I'm not particularly vain. I mean, I care enough about my appearance that I seek to be as presentable and as attractive as God has endowed me to be. But I'm not caught up with the whole thing. I comb my hair in the morning and I don't worry about it again unless I'm in a windstorm. And yet, when I look in the mirror, I find myself looking out from the inside of a younger man. When someone hears my true age, I expect them to say, 'Come on. How old are you really?' I don't want them to accept the facts without a struggle.

"Then it happened. When I was in Europe a month ago, I was meeting with a Dornier buyer. She asked me if Strang was a common name in the U.S. I said, 'No, not really.' She told me she had met a Chuck Strang from Portland, Oregon and she wondered if by any chance he was my son. I told her he wasn't, and that was the end of it. But I had to face reality at last. Here was someone who didn't know my age who assumed I was old enough to have a son in business. The fact that I <u>am</u> old enough has nothing to do with it. It seems that I look as old as I am."

"Charlie, let's set the record straight. You don't look old. And you certainly don't act old. I wish I had your vitality."

"Thanks, Rick." Charlie seemed satisfied.

"Yeah, you don't look anywhere near sixty-eight to me. I just wanted you to know that." Rick laughed heartily as Charlie's mouth opened wide.

"I feel much better now that you've told me. Thanks again."

"Anytime."

"Pick up the check. Tonight's dinner is on Marketing."

Wright-Patterson Air Force Base

"Gentlemen, we have done our homework. We know the Air Force is working on a stealth tactical aircraft, one that can deliver its ordnance and be on its way home before the enemy even knows it's under attack." The Air Force officers looked at Rick with startled faces, as if saying, 'How did you know?'

The conference room where they met was typical G.I. Issue—sparsely decorated walls, window air conditioner, long, folding table and uncomfortable chairs. It was designed for short meetings.

Rick continued. "We can assume that one of this aircraft's mission scenarios will include low altitude, terrain avoidance. Under those conditions, we believe the penetrating aircraft will be in its greatest threat of discovery. In fact, the probability of survival of this aircraft decreases as the number and capability of enemy air defense systems increase. Survivable penetration can be achieved by many means, the best being covertness—the ability to penetrate without being observed or fired upon by a hostile air defense system.

"Pierce Electronics is here to offer you a solution to this threat. Our company proposes to design and develop a terrain avoidance, terrain following system that is impervious to detection. We have nicknamed this system, 'PROPHET' because of its capability to see ahead where others can't see. Further, we propose to develop this system within a timeframe that is compatible with your stealth aircraft development." Rick sat back, folded his hands in his lap and looked at each person facing him from the other side of the table.

Lieutenant Colonel James Meyers broke the silence, looking directly at Rick. "I'm not certain where you've picked up the rumor that the Air Force is working on a low-observable aircraft." His face was tense. His body language told Rick that he was right.

"I read between the lines of *Aviation Week*, Colonel," referring to the industry's 'bible,' published weekly by McGraw-Hill.

Colonel Rusty Horn, a red-haired man in his late fifties, immaculate and soft-spoken and tough by reputation, spoke. "Although your top-secret clearances preceded you, we have crossed a line of *need-to-know*. At the moment, you do not have a need to know the subject you have just introduced. Accordingly, we are in no position to share any information with you. But we are in a position to listen. If you can survive not receiving feedback from us, why don't you continue?"

Rick leaned forward. "Colonel, we understand your sensitivity and caution. We also understand *need-to-know*. It is a clearance unto itself. We are confident enough to believe what we are about to share will place us solidly inside the circle. The next time we meet, we believe the discussions will be two-way." He turned toward Charlie and nodded.

Charlie opened his briefcase, extracted a file that he lay on the table, and addressed the group. "Pierce Electronics has entered the early development stage of a covert terrain following, terrain avoidance system. Our company has teamed with Eiler Laboratories and Radart Arrays, and is negotiating with three other companies to join the project. You know our company for its precision radar altimeters. We have taken that technology and expanded it into a system that doesn't just look down but ahead as well. And the possibilities look encouraging."

During the next hour, the only sound in the conference room was the voice of Charlie Strang sharing details of the PROPHET terrain avoidance, terrain following system, and the quiet hum of an air exchange system. It was clear the Air Force was interested in what was being shared.

Chapter 3

Fast and Furious

1978. *Hubert Horatio Humphrey, former Senator from Minnesota and Vice President of the United States died on January 13th; Washington beat Michigan 27-20 in the Rose Bowl; the Love Canal area of Niagara Falls was considered to be environmentally unfit for human habitation; a midair collision over San Diego of a Southwest Airlines jet and a private plane killed all 137 people aboard the two craft and at least ten more on the ground; Affirmed won horse racing's Triple Crown; a grizzly mass suicide of 911 People's Temple members occurred in Guyana; and Rick Stoner's life took a dramatic change.*

Confrontation

It had been one month since that December meeting with the Air Force. Rick had a funny feeling about the development project. He couldn't explain his intuition, but it was there nonetheless. He knocked on Gil's office door and walked in, not waiting for a response. The dour look on his engineering partner's face confirmed his concerns. He dropped into a chair and studied Gil for a moment. "The look on your face scares me. What's up?"

"You don't want to know."

I suppose you're right. But what's up?"

"I have an interface problem that I can't seem to resolve. And for reasons I can't figure out, the altimeter won't receive."

Rick moved to Gil's round conference table and sat in one of the swivel chairs that surrounded it. "How long has this been going on?"

"Obviously since the beginning." Gil walked over and joined him. "It appears to be inherent in the design. But I only discovered the problem last week." Gil's shoulders sagged as he lowered his head into his cupped hands.

"Gil, you've got to broaden the circle."

"Meaning?"

"Meaning you need to bring in some help. In fact, you need to step back for a while and let others tackle the problem. They will be able to give it a fresh look – won't have the biases that you have." Rick knew he was on thin ice. Before Gil could reply, he added, "I know this is your baby. Nothing's going to change that. It's just that some times we need the help of others to get us through a log jam."

Gil was silent, lips pursed, staring at the wall.

After a minute, he said, "Who do you recommend I bring in on this?"

"Dirk Bogert, Tom Mathis or Pat Frankel. Maybe all three. They're your top engineering supervisors. You've groomed them for a lot of years to be the best in their field."

"And you want me to step away from this project for a while?"

"I do. I think it will recharge your batteries. Look, we have a major trade show coming up early next month in Italy. I could use your help if you'll give me the time and tag along. A week in Europe might do you good."

"Let me think about it."

"Deal. I'm headed to Hong Kong next week for a critical meeting with Cathay Pacific. As soon as I get back, we need to complete the arrangements for heading to Rome. I hope you'll go with me."

ELETROEUROPA

All trade shows require an extraordinary amount of planning and preparation. The upcoming Airlines Avionics International Assembly and ELETROEUROPA trade show in Rome was no exception; in fact, it was worse because of the details, many of them trivial, involved in shipping Pierce's booth to Italy. It was at times like these that Rick was particularly thankful for his assistant Jinnie Hayward. She had become an expert in show management technicalities, customs declarations, carnets, and more. She also took care of all hotel and flight reservations. This left Rick with the job of preparing the sales team who would work at the exhibit, organizing the lunches and dinners with key customers, and planning the sales meeting for Pierce's international representatives. It siphoned two weeks from Rick's normal routine, but the result was worth it. If it hadn't been for the special effort that also was demanded for orchestrating the PROPHET program, it would have been a welcome relief.

As it was, the stress upon Rick was enormous. And it showed. He found civility to others difficult. And because this was out of character for Rick, those who experienced his brusque behavior were caught off guard. What was wrong with Rick? Trouble at home? Did his dog bite him?

***

Carol Stoner was an extremely attractive woman, happy most of the time; sometimes just content. There were times when she was unhappy with herself, the way that Rick disappointed her, and perhaps, the passing of her youth. Now, as her sons were growing older, she wondered if she should be making plans for returning to work some day. It was a thought that gave her some pleasure, but it was not a thought she had shared with Rick. She was growing concerned about the way the two of them seemed to be drifting apart. There was nothing tangible that she could identify. It was just that sixth sense that told her not everything was perfect. She knew Rick was under pressure at work and told herself that must be the cause. Yet she wondered if there was another woman. She knew better. Still, she wondered.

Carol was a strong Christian and relied on her faith for strength to see her through all situations. Her family's involvement in church activities was also important to her. She wanted the boys raised Christian. She knew Rick did too. There were times when she could be prudish (as the world viewed such things), yet she was just remaining true to Christian teachings.

Perhaps her greatest imperfection was putting less effort into her relationship with Rick than she should. She was secure in their relationship and felt that it couldn't be breached. And so her attractiveness had waned. Oh, she had reason enough. Her sons demanded much of her time, along with household chores. Fixing her hair, getting out of sloppy clothes before his return home at night; this was just needless work for no purpose. She saw no correlation between her appearance and the subtle change in Rick that she had detected. When Carol dressed for church each Sunday, however, she was fashionable, stylish and sedate.

Under those circumstances, when she went to meet the Lord of her life, she felt the need to dress up. Clearly, in her mind, Rick was no longer lord of the house.

Arrivederci, Seattle

Rick's departure from home that Friday reflected the strain between Carol and himself. She, worrying about one thing; he, worrying about another; neither communicating the fears that beset them.

I've got to deal with this when I get home, Rick said silently to himself, as he headed toward Gil's home to take the two of them to Sea-Tac Airport for their flight to Europe. *Something is bugging her, I can tell.* He congratulated himself for being so perceptive.

***

Gil had decided to follow Rick's advice. He had brought in Dirk Bogert, Tom Mathis and Pat Frankel to attack the altimeter interface problem. And he had extricated himself from the project long enough to attend the show in Italy. He left it clear to his three supervisors that the program was *need-to-know* only. And the only person left at Pierce with a *need-to-know*, besides them, was Charlie.

If only he could resolve his problem at home. Susan had changed. She was becoming a shrew and he didn't know why. It seemed that he could do no right. All they did was argue. He couldn't remember how many times he had stayed late at work and grabbed something to eat on the way home rather than face her tirades—with no meals prepared. They were no longer friends. They certainly were no longer lovers. He figured they were on their way to divorce court unless things changed, and changed quickly.

When Susan found out he was going to Italy, she went, as some of Gil's engineers were prone to say, *ballistic*. It was the worst experience of his life. She screamed at him at home; she called and screamed at him at work. Her rage continued for three days. Gil was relieved that he hadn't given her more notice of the trip.

That third afternoon, he was sitting on his suitcase outside his front door as Rick pulled into the driveway. Rome seemed like the perfect destination and he was ready to go.

Ciao, Roma

By the time Gil and Rick got to Leonardo da Vinci airport, they were spacey. Nine hours from Seattle to London on British Airways, two hours in Heathrow's international transit lounge, and two more hours to Rome had taken their toll. As far as the Italians were concerned, it was three-thirty p.m. Saturday afternoon. But both Gil and Rick's bodies knew it was six-thirty a.m. Saturday morning.

"Rick, I am wiped out. If I don't get eight hours sleep every night, I'm pretty much a basket case."

"Let's see. We've been up 24 hours and we have 6 hours to go before hitting the hay." He smiled at his struggling companion. "Then you can have ten hours sleep if you like."

Gil grunted. "How do you figure on keeping me awake another six hours?"

"Activity. With lots and lots of activity."

"Like?"

"Like, for openers, go to Baggage Claim and find our luggage. I'm heading to a bank to exchange some traveler's cheques for Lira."

***

Half an hour later, pockets filled with thousands of Italian Lira, they made their way through Customs and were outside in search of a taxi for the long ride downtown. It was Gil's first venture to Europe and Rick looked forward to playing tour guide the next day. Perhaps he and Gil could continue mending fences.

Without any argument, Rome was Rick's favorite city in the world, and weather-permitting, he was going to share this love with this man who had become his business partner. He was determined that his former problems with Gil would be eliminated once and for all; that he would build a new relationship for the sake of the company, his piece of mind and the prospect of claiming a new friend.

The small vine-covered Hotel Raphaël exuded European charm. Neither swank nor American looking, it was hidden down a narrow, renaissance street. Their two rooms were at the end of the hall on the fifth and top floor, overlooking a tiny, tree-lined, sun-filtered patio where a small group of Italians, dressed in their Sunday best, sat around an outdoor banquet table celebrating some important family event. Rick felt revived as he reflected on the party. Their happiness became his. As Gil looked down upon the same scene from his window, he thought only that the celebrants were a little too noisy and overdressed in old-fashioned clothes.

At six p.m., bags unpacked and clothes changed, Rick and Gil met in the lobby in search of food and any events to stimulate them into continued wakefulness. The plan to stay awake was Rick's, not Gil's. His plan would have been to sleep for hours. Of course, his plan would also awaken him in the middle of the night and doom him to remain on Seattle time. So logic prevailed and he followed Rick's lead.

An immediate right turn from the hotel entrance, followed by an immediate left down an alley found them at the far end of Piazza Navona. Gil's date with history had begun. While they feasted on seafood fettuccini at an outdoor restaurant's table near the middle of the Piazza, Rick gave Gil a taste of ancient history.

"Where we're sitting," he said, "was once in the middle of a circus. Not the kind with trapeze artists and clowns," he added, "but one where horses and chariots ran races."

"Like in Ben Hur?"

"Yes, only on a smaller scale. Circus Maximus, which is nearby, was where the big races were run so that the Emperor and those of his court could watch from the top of the Palatine Hill. When the empire fell, buildings were gradually constructed along the long oval you see, giving the piazza its current, unusual shape."

Directly in front of them was the centerpiece of the piazza, the Fountain of the Four Rivers by the Baroque sculptor Bernini. Again, Rick explained, "The four statues in the fountain represent the Danube, Rio de la Plata of the New World, Ganges, and the Nile. When you get a chance, notice that the face of the Nile is hidden because its beginning was unknown during the 1600's when Bernini carved it.

A look of ecstasy was on Gil's face. He clearly was savoring each mouthful of the pasta dish he was eating as if it were ambrosia he might never get to taste again. Halfway through the meal, Rick suggested where he thought they should walk after dinner, before heading back to the hotel. "Everything is close," he said. "But it's best that we leave the

Forum and the Coliseum until tomorrow because we'll want to take our time at those spots. And the Baths of Caracalla, which are a brisk fifteen minute walk from the Coliseum, are worthy of a couple of hour's examination at least." His fettuccini was getting cold even as he was warming up. "This evening, I propose that we walk a few blocks to the Pantheon, head from there to Trevi Fountain and then double back past our hotel, cross the Tiber River and go to Saint Peter's Square for a quick look-see." He finished off the remaining shrimp on his plate, pushed back from the table with obvious satisfaction, and said, "By the time we've done all that, I know it will be time to crash and burn."

Gil, a knowledgeable aerospace authority added in aircraft parlance, "For you maybe. But I'm already in a stall condition."

Rick said to the passing waiter, "Posso avere la fattura, prego."

He pointed toward Gil. The waiter nodded and disappeared.

"What was that all about?"

"I told our waiter to bring the check."

A few minutes later, the waiter reappeared and presented the bill to Gil. Gil smirked and slid the check over to Rick so that Marketing could pay. "How long will our walking tour take?"

Rick extracted twenty thousand lira from his pocket and laid it on the check. "Probably an hour unless you dawdle."

***

Rick's run through the relatively quiet streets of Rome lasted forty-five minutes. He was back in his room, showered, shaven and dressed with ten minutes to spare before he and Gil were to meet for breakfast at 7:30. He feared the continued impact of jet lag on his associate. Rick went to the breakfast room early, wanting a head start on the coffee. To his surprise, Gil motioned to him from a table near the window.

"What brings you here so early?" Rick chuckled as he sat across from Gil. "I figured you'd still be in bed."

"What brings me to this appointed hour so early," Gil replied, "is an internal clock that continues to think it's approaching bed time. I am still screwed up. I went to bed right after leaving you last night. But I was so tired that I couldn't unwind. I finally got up and took two aspirins just to relax. They finally worked and I went to sleep. Then, around three-fifteen, my system said, 'OK. Nap time's over,' and I woke up." He yawned for effect. "I've been awake ever since."

Rick shook his head. "Pretend you're going salmon fishing. It'll be a long day, but shorter than yesterday. You'll be OK tomorrow."

"Promise?"

"No."

Sightseeing

The day that followed was amazing to both of them. Rick felt no jet lag and behaved as if he had been in Italy for a month rather than half a day. Not so with Gil. He walked and he talked. But he wasn't certain he was awake. One thing that was good was the warm, sunny sky that complemented their walking. Their picture-taking added to the adventure. Though "punchy," Gil was caught up in the history that surrounded his every step. A Caesar walked here. The Praetorian Guard stood there. Gladiators and Christians died over there. It was awesome. In spite of his announced expectation to be unimpressed, he was overwhelmed.

When the day ended, they sat eating a late dinner in a tiny restaurant down another alley from Trevi Fountain. "I'm getting used to this," Gil said. "Too bad tomorrow means work." But the trade show opened at ten a.m. and the convention gavel struck at two p.m. in the Hilton's immense auditorium. Gil knew there would be time for no more sightseeing before they headed home. The convention and trade show, after all, were why they had come.

Breakfast meeting

They transferred from the Raphaël to the Cavalieri Hilton the next morning in time for a breakfast meeting with Carlo Giacametti, the head of Pierce's Italian representative firm. Shortly after they were seated in the restaurant, a white-haired, scrawny man strode beaming toward their table. "Ricardo!" Carlo Giacametti said loudly as Rick rose to greet him. "It is so good to see you, my friend," he said, rolling the "r"s in "Ricardo" and "friend" so effectively. Carlo had never understood the fact that Rick's real first name was Derrick, not Richard.

Rick accepted and partially returned the stocky Italian's embrace. Then, standing back, said, "Carlo, I would like you to meet Gil Brockton, our Vice President of Engineering." Before completing the introduction, Carlo interrupted.

"I finally meet the famous Dr. Brockton." He held out his hand. "How do you do, Dr. Brockton?" His Italian accent was strong and colorful. "Benvenuto a mia Roma. Welcome to my Roma."

The breakfast meeting quickly brought Rick up to speed on the show, the setting up of the Pierce display booth, the competitors who were present, the preliminary list of attendees and more. Pierce's display had arrived damaged. Fortunately, Carlo's people hired a carpenter who repaired it "like a new, Ricardo" (with a rolled "r"). Everything else was as it should be.

Time to work

Rick and Gil were in the Hilton's giant display hall at 9:15 a.m. for a final check of the Pierce forty-foot display. That done, Rick went on a quick walk through the aisles to gain an overall flavor of the show. All the avionics community was there. From the USA, Honeywell, Bendix, Sperry, Texas Instruments, Westinghouse, Hughes, Litton, and of course, Pierce. From Europe, Plessey, GEC, Siemens, Racal, Crouzet, Thomson, and Diehl. From Japan, Mitsubishi, Yamatake, and Matsushita. All in all, over two hundred exhibitors vying for the attention of an expected twenty-five hundred military and civilian attendees at "ELETROEUROPA Seventy Eight." The atmosphere was charged with excitement for Rick. This turned him on. It seemed to cause the opposite response for Gil. He was at home in small groups. He played turtle in a crowd.

Rick looked up to see a swarm of people moving rapidly through the aisles. Some seemed to know where they were going. Others were less certain. But all were in search of something. It was ten o'clock and the trade show had begun. He enjoyed the exhilaration of a show. Each was an emotional high that stimulated him for days afterward. And from the looks of it, his booth was going to be busy for the next eight hours. This was going to be a real high.

Out of the corner of his eye, he saw Gil laboring with the Pierce display. He had been struggling to get it up and running for the last half-hour. Occasionally Gil would exclaim, "Eureka!" but his accomplishments were apparently minor in nature, for his feverish pace continued without letup. How was it that the equipment always worked Okay at the office? Suddenly Gil leaned back in his chair, as if satisfied with his work. He should have been. His torment was over. The display was working. This was going to be a good day, Rick decided. Gil's timely success was an omen.

The booth was inundated with customers. It was impossible to segment time to eat. It was almost impossible to go to the rest room. People were lined up all day to talk to someone from Pierce. There was no breathing room. And it was great! The next day was almost a repeat of the first. Trade shows were always hard to measure. They were somewhat like advertising. You didn't dare not participate because if you weren't there, you were making a statement that your business was bad, that money was tight; something negative. And yet there was no proof that by being there you would receive more business. But no matter what the measure, if activity was brisk, if prospective customers were seeing your products, it all seemed worth it. Besides, there was that exhilaration, that flow of adrenaline, that excitement of challenging another person to think seriously about the ideas you'd presented.

During a momentary break, Rick happened to glance down the aisle. He laughed aloud, then hurriedly muffled his humor. Why do so many Italian men wear their suit jackets over their shoulders, he wondered, without putting their arms in the sleeves? Is it the style? It has to be. The same style that dictates they cup their cigarettes inside their hand when they bring them to their lips to smoke. This is not to say he understood it. It apparently was just one of those things.

Trade show assignment

Part of the mission of a trade show was to check out the competition. Rick had assigned everyone in the booth to research one competitor. "I want to know what their new products are, how they work, and what sales volume they project. Find out how they're organized, where they plan to advertise and if they are changing or modifying their distribution methods. If you can get them, I would like technical manuals and specification sheets. In other words, get into their hip pockets and find out what makes 'em tick."

Rick knew that most of what he asked was impossible to get. And yet, the impossible sometimes had a way of happening. It was certain that if you didn't have a target to aim for, you'd be unlikely to hit it. Rick's target was to take the competitive lead in the industry and never relinquish it.

Ten members of Pierce's Italian marketing organization were at the show, and during their non-booth hours, they were out in the aisles gathering information. As Rick walked around the show, he frequently saw Carlo's people in competitive booths pursuing their assignments, and he smiled to himself. This was going to be a better show than he had hoped when he had hoped for a good show.

Rick passed Gil in the Nakamura booth. His apparent success was amazing. Gil was heavily engaged in a conversation with a Japanese engineer. A technical manual was open on the table and the engineer was explaining a block diagram. This was nothing short of amazing. Nakamura had been showing every sign of becoming Pierce's main competitor in the commercial market. What a coup!

About thirty minutes later, Gil strolled back into the Pierce booth, sporting a grin that would have put former-Georgia Governor and now President Carter to shame. He sure was pleased with himself. He moved straight over to Rick. "I can't believe it," his upper teeth bared as he slammed his fist into an open, cupped hand. "I can't believe he answered my questions. Hell, we'd never give a prospect half the details he gave me, much less a stranger." He ran his fingers through his hair, messing it up more than it was before, and then shook his head in continued disbelief.

Rick was suspicious too. It shouldn't have been that easy. "Are you certain he was giving you good information?"

"Obviously there's no way to be absolutely certain. But he sure seemed to be describing the system that was hanging on the wall."

"But why??"

"The only guess I'm willing to make is that he was the design engineer and that he was pleased to show off his ingenuity. He didn't know I was from Pierce, but he did know I could appreciate his cleverness." Gil's voice became emphatic. "I think I was feeding his ego and he loved every minute of it." Gil glanced around the booth. "Am I going to cause a problem if I disappear for a while? I have got to write down what I learned or I'll forget it."

"Take all the time you need, Gil. Nothing here is more important than what you're about to do." He patted Gil's shoulder. "Congratulations, doctor. You've struck gold."

Gil was gone with the same smile that had been on his face for the last five minutes. It was a good feeling to be a hero. It had been a long time for Gil. His fortunes at Pierce had been waning for months, despite the new TAR. But this stroke of luck might turn the tide.

What had Rick said? "You've struck gold." Maybe he had.

Cocktail party

It was her hair that Gil noticed. It was . . . it was bright vermilion, stacked on top of her head in what women called a beehive. Because of her, he saw a stunning woman seated next to her. She had the long, graceful legs of a European woman and the delicate beauty of a Chinese. Her dark brown hair was pulled back away from her forehead into a ponytail, seized by a gold beret. Her eyebrows were exaggerated in fashion-model accuracy. Her nose was straight and perfectly proportioned. Her brown eyes were large, with distinct concentric circles, dark in the center and light on the outside, giving them a look of incredible depth.

She looked steadily at him with the slightest hint of a smile playing across her lips. She wore a black, figure-hugging dress with a high collar and long sleeves. Although she was sitting, he saw enough to know that her figure was as exquisite as her face. *Who created this woman*, he wondered? She was breathtaking. She looked at him, unflinching. He couldn't maintain the eye contact and looked away. He was never the winner in such games. He glanced back. She was still looking, smiling this time. Maybe she wasn't looking at him. She probably wasn't. He judged that he was a good fifteen years older than she was. He turned to see who was behind him. Nobody. He returned to face her. Her smile was even broader this time. He smiled, albeit weakly. He still wasn't certain her friendliness was intended for him. Placing her palm on the edge of her chair, she leaned forward and beckoned to him. *This isn't happening to me*, he thought. *Maybe she thinks I work for the hotel and wants something.* "Yes, may I help you?"

"You're from Seattle, aren't you?"

There was the faintest suggestion of an accent, but Gil couldn't identify it. He regarded himself an amateur linguistic expert, but he was baffled by her mysticism. "Yes, I am. Was it the way I walked that gave me away?"

"Excuse me?"

"My webbed feet. I need them for the rain which means I need extra large shoes to cover them when I'm in public."

She laughed, her eyes still locked on his. She was making Gil nervous in a sensual way. He was certain he was misreading her, but that didn't stop the feeling.

"No, I just felt certain that I had seen you there. I hope you don't mind my boldness."

"Surely, you jest," Gil said. "When an extraordinarily beautiful woman goes out of her way to speak to me, I don't mind at all." He actually thought he saw her blush. Either that or she was a very skilled actress. "Have we met before? No, forget I asked that! I'd remember meeting you. How did you know I was from Seattle?"

"I saw you at the Washington Electronics Association meeting last month at the Olympic Hotel."

"You were there?" He couldn't believe he would have missed seeing her.

"Yes, I got there just as dinner was ending and the speaker was being introduced. You were at the next table. You had turned your chair around to face the front."

"That's right," he exclaimed. "I had. You must have been there."

"Will you rescue me from this boring party?" she asked. "I'd love to talk to someone from Seattle." She moved to the next chair, allowing him to join her; sitting cross-legged so her skirt hiked itself far up her well-formed legs." There was no way that she was oblivious to what she was doing or the effect she was having on the men in the room, not to mention Gil.

During the next forty-five minutes he discovered that her name was Victoria Li, that she was originally from Hong Kong, had been educated in the United States and now worked for her uncle's company, heading up his research division that was based in San Francisco. "My father was Scottish. My mother was Chinese," she revealed. "They died in a plane crash on their way to visit her family in Glasgow. I was only eight and they felt it best that I remain at home. My uncle became my guardian. He saw to my education, first at a private school in California, then at Stanford as an undergraduate student, and then at Cal-Berkeley for my masters. After graduation, he hired me to work for him."

She frequently came to Seattle but it was unusual that she would attend a Washington Electronics Association dinner meeting. The speaker, a man who had been her favorite professor in graduate school, had drawn her. He also discovered that she was remarkably intelligent and that for some strange reason was attracted to him.

Guests were starting to leave the reception, giving him an excuse to leave also. Gil looked around for Rick. Not finding him, he figured he must be occupied and that they would catch up with each other in the morning. "I know this is presumptuous," he said. "I mean, we've only met, and a woman like you has countless options, but would you care to join me for dinner?"

***

Following dinner, a heavy rainstorm moved into the vicinity, drenching the downtown area. Taxies, always in short supply during the evenings, were even scarcer. Victoria and Gil saw one down the street, sitting under a lamppost. They decided to run for it. Their timing couldn't have been worse. The rain got heavier. Just as they approached the idling taxi, Gil was deluged by gutter water when another cab swerved to the curb. Victoria's shoes were soaked, but Gil took the brunt. His pants were soaked. "Oh brother!" he exclaimed as they flung themselves into the car. "It's not like I have an abundance of suits with me. I'm an engineer. Engineers are lucky to have more than one suit in their entire wardrobe." He smiled whimsically. Victoria laughed heartily.

"You may dry them when we get back to the hotel. Then, I will call Housekeeping and ask them to bring an iron and an ironing board to your room where I will press them. Do not worry. I will take good care of you."

To jog or not to jog

Rick's alarm clock sounded in the middle of a remarkable dream. He reached for the lamp to confirm that it was indeed time to get up. "Yuk!" he exclaimed aloud. "It's five thirty." He threw his legs over the side of the bed, sat up and walked into the bathroom. "One of these days, I'll learn to go to bed on time when I've at a convention." As he combed his hair, he stared at his nude replica in the full length mirror. "Man, clothes sure cover a multitude of sins," he said to his reflection. *You've got that right*, he thought he heard in reply.

He walked over to the chair where he had laid his jogging suit and proceeded to get dressed. He zippered his room key into a pocket and opened his door. Movement across the hall caused him to close it quickly, leaving just a crack so he could see. A woman was backing her way out of Gil's room. She closed the door quietly, and then walked rapidly down the carpeted hallway. As she passed Rick's door, he recognized her. She was the research manager for Shek Industries. Everyone knew her. Apparently, Gil knew her a little better than most.

Rick decided not to say anything to Gil. His private life was his own. But Rick couldn't help wondering how Gil had successfully ensnared a beautiful woman like Victoria Li. That part didn't figure. He also wondered why Gil was indulging in something extracurricular. He didn't seem the type.

***

The show itself went well. Interest in Pierce's products seemed to increase with each day. Gil was chipper but non-communicative about his private activities.

***

"Why do I get the feeling that the fashion statement over here appears to be blue jeans—tight hip and leg hugging blue jeans," Gil observed as the two of them sat in an outdoor restaurant eating pasta the second day of the show.

"And" Rick added, "how come the men wear jeans with shirts and ties and the women wear jeans with cashmere sweaters . . . and dark sunglasses?" Then, looking up and down the sidewalk, he said, "On the other hand, I like what I see, so I guess I really don't have a question after all." They laughed and toasted their observations with a sip of Chianti.

"To be certain," Gil continued on the same vein, "I am no expert on Italian women, but I have observed that they have high cheekbones which I find very attractive. And they have beautiful brown and blue eyes that are intense and penetrating." He sat back, satisfied with his new role as fashion and female critic.

Their conversation drifted away from clothes to the food they were eating. "I have observed," Rick said, "pasta takes its toll on many Italians, but not as much as we Americans would believe. And certainly not as much as it seems to take on Americans." He finished the last bite of spaghetti. "Maybe it's in the Latin genes."

"I thought you had changed the subject," Gil said. "But since you mentioned it, you're right. Those Latin jeans sure look good." It was time for a last toast before returning to the hotel's convention center.

Show summary

The show ended, exceeding all the hopes that Rick had during its planning stages. They had gained valuable insights into their competition; they had successfully positioned Pierce as a company of the future; and his relationship with Gil had blossomed toward a genuine friendship.

"Great job," Gil lavished praise on Rick as they shared a taxi to the airport. "You put together a rock-solid booth at the show. We had more visitors and more interest than in my wildest dreams. And judging from the feedback we've gotten from our rep, we obtained more competitive information than ever before." He looked Rick in the eye. "I am impressed—and I didn't think I would be when we started out."

The two parted when they entered the giant departure hall. Gil was on his way back to Seattle on British Airways. Rick was on his way to Marseilles on Alitalia, and from there to Hamburg to meet with Deutsche Airbus and Lufthansa.

The ride into Hell

Crowding and jostling for position seemed to be a Mediterranean trait. There were few lines, and where there were, there were few who stood in them. It was with this prospect that Rick looked forward with disdain to check-in at the airport. His patience was always tried. But there was no other way to get to Toulouse unless he wanted to go by ship to Marseilles and then by car inland. While a cruise was an appealing idea, it was hardly a practical one.

It was Wednesday. The trade show had closed the day before, and Rick was due across the Mediterranean for a Thursday meeting with Aerospatiale in Toulouse. The meeting proved to be promotional only. There was no real prospect for business in the near future, but to ignore Aerospatiale was to ignore one of the major aerospace companies in Europe. Among other things, Aerospatiale was a principal player in the burgeoning Airbus program. And who knew what tomorrow would bring.

On Friday, Rick opted to take the train from Toulouse to Paris where he had a flight booked for Hamburg. It would be leisurely and allow him to catch up on some paperwork. He arrived at Paris' central station at five in the afternoon. Within ten minutes of arriving, he was out front of the station, in line for a taxi. His cabdriver was a woman in her thirties with thin arms, wearing a sleeveless blouse; appropriate enough for summer; out of place for mid-winter. With hope, he asked if she spoke English. "Non," was the reply. Mustering his best French, he said "Orly."

"Oui," was the response. He put his bags in the trunk, got in the back seat and settled in for the half-hour trip to the airport. Dangling from the rearview mirror was a cross on a beaded chain. A statue of a saint stood on the dashboard, seeming to assure safe travel; at least if he was the saint of safe passage.

The central station in Paris is in the center of town. Quite a concept. Streets move away from the center like the spokes of a wheel away from the hub. The first five minutes were smooth sailing. Hardly any traffic, considering it was rush hour on a Friday. *Maybe everyone is working late or attending an office party*, he thought. He shouldn't have thought. Almost immediately his cab came to a halt, blocked by a traffic snarl that looked serious. He could see the light at the next intersection. It turned green and red countless times with virtually no forward movement of the cars and trucks ahead of him. He glanced at his watch. Five forty-five. He wanted to be at Orly at six thirty. He could still make it, but they had to get moving.

Five minutes later, he began to get nervous. He couldn't talk to his driver because of the language barrier, but he could let her know that he was getting impatient. He sighed heavily and shuffled his feet on the floor, making a rasping sound. Silence from the front. He sighed louder for effect. She muttered something in French and gestured toward the other cars. "Le trafic stupide."

A while later, he repeated his frustration and she duplicated hers. At last, they were communicating. Slowly, they inched forward, now first in line at the traffic light.

The next block offered no hope. It was as obstructed as the one they were in. The light turned green. To his horror, his driver turned the cab quickly to the right down a narrow, one way street—the wrong way. Not so bad if there were no oncoming traffic, but there was. Horns blared, drivers shouted. Rick's driver honked and shouted the loudest as if she were in the right and the others in the wrong. She obviously had been to the Vince Lombardi School that taught the best defense was a strong offense. As she became more heated in her rebuttals, she became animated. Her left arm extended from her window and it appeared that rather rude gestures were being uplifted above the car, out of Rick's sight.

Just then, she maneuvered the cab further to the right to avoid a madly honking car. As she did, her right front bumper and fender scraped a parked car, raking it from front to rear. She kept going. Rick was horrified. What was his responsibility in all this? In Turkey, he would be sent to prison since he was the person who hired the taxi. *What about France*, he wondered? They approached the end of the block without further incident. Suddenly, a car turned onto the street, not expecting to encounter another vehicle exiting on a collision course. Rick's driver swerved hard to the right, catching the final parked car on the rear fender, knocking it up onto the sidewalk. From the sounds, Rick knew the taxi was damaged. The two cars they left behind weren't in such good shape either.

Once on this parallel boulevard, traffic flowed much better, and while it was now six thirty in the evening, Rick felt he had a reasonable chance of catching his seven-thirty flight if there were no further mishaps. The thing that did worry him was the mounting number on the meter. It was going to be close. He might not have enough francs.

There was a strange sound coming from the engine, but he was no expert on Peugeots. Maybe this was routine. His driver seemed unconcerned, or was the word nonchalant. Whatever. They were still in the city, but proceeding in a southeasterly direction. That was at least a comfort. Finally, they made it to the Parisian version of a motorway. It was crowded but flowing. The engine was making worse sounds now. It was definitely laboring. His driver downshifted to first gear. The noise worsened. She tried to shift up. She couldn't. He didn't understand auto mechanics but the gears seemed locked. She floor-boarded the accelerator. Cars were passing, honking their horns. She was gesturing again. Rick thought that perhaps he was in a movie, or guest starring in Candid Camera. This whole episode was so bizarre. Then smoke started billowing from the engine. It was obvious that fifty kilometers an hour in first gear was outside the design limits of the car. Still, the farce continued. Where was the "Candid" film crew, anyway?

Midst smoke and roar, his taxi finally deposited him at the doorstep of Orly Airport. A triumphant driver opened the trunk from which Rick extracted his bags. One hundred twenty francs were posted on the meter. Added to that were ten francs for the storage of his luggage. Rick had eighty francs—more than twice enough for a half-hour ride, but fifty francs short of the asking price. He had his bags. She had a smoking hulk (the right side of the taxi was so badly damaged, Rick couldn't get out that side). She had a bill of one hundred thirty francs. He had eighty. He put all his money into her hands. She screamed at him once she had counted it. "Vous êtes un voleur." She told him he was a thief. He raised his hands, telling her she had all that he once had. He inverted his pants pockets in an attempt to convince her. She screamed at him all the more. "Je suis triché."

They were drawing a small crowd, including two gendarmes who began strolling toward the commotion. Rick saw them approaching. With his apologies and futile assurances that she had all his money, he reached down, picked up his bags and hurried into the terminal. His driver ranted behind him as she stood by her former taxi. Rick knew the eighty francs wouldn't even cover the towing bill, but it was her doing, not his.

Rats, he thought as he disappeared into a sea of German tourists heading toward the Lufthansa counter. I forgot to get a receipt. Whimsy always was his strong suit, he mused.

Home and away

After awhile, there was sameness in Rick's international travels, airports in particular. London's Heathrow was sprawling and somewhat of a bother if you were in-transit and had to change terminals. Charles de Gaulle Airport in Paris was a continual hassle in clearing Passport Control. Frankfurt's Rhine-Main Airport was a model of efficiency. Sung

Shan International in Taipei was chaotic in contrast to Singapore's Paya Lebar Airport which skillfully moved thousands of arriving and departing passengers daily. The first few times in each country were always frustrating for him because of their unknown aspects and peculiarities. After a few visits came the comfort of knowing where to go and what to expect. At that point, Rick could relax because he was then on familiar turf.

Following his meeting with Lufthansa and Deutsche Airbus, Rick returned to Seattle, barely having time to get his clothes into and out of the cleaners before he had to head out again, this time to Hong Kong to put the final changes on the Cathay Pacific contract.

In the past ten months, he had traveled to Southeast Asia twice and Europe twice. Four international trips a year were on the cusp of his threshold of pain. This was his third visit to Hong Kong although it was the first time he had taken this particular routing. But business demanded that he meet with Cathay Pacific one more time before the contract was signed. So he went.

Chapter 4

British Crown Colony

As the massive door opened, four hundred passengers shuffled their way toward the exit of the 747. Rick looked longingly at the other aisle. The fortunate people in it were moving swiftly in comparison to his crawl. He evaluated the possibility of crossing over between the seats of row sixteen and seventeen. *Nah. What was the rush?* The fact that he would be walking into the arrival hall later than others didn't seem to matter that much. Furthermore, he had brought his Contracts Manager Sandy McCray with him to take care of every dot and tittle of the Cathay agreement, and she was in line behind him. He couldn't drag her across five seats to the other aisle just because he was in a rush. Still, that impatient spirit trapped inside his body urged him to go. *Those people are beating you,* it said. *They're going to get there (wherever there was) ahead of you.* He held his ground. Besides, he could see the exit door five rows ahead.

***

Sandy McCray was a rarity in her field. Not many women were in management. Her credentials included a law degree and six years in a firm that specialized in corporate law. She was uniquely qualified for the contracts position she held. Sandy was five years younger than Rick. She had the trim body of an athlete. She had been a competitive swimmer in college and still had smooth, long muscles in her arms and legs. With her brunette hair fixed in a ponytail, she had the look of a cheerleader for one of the professional sports teams. But ponytails were only worn on *casual Fridays*; not for serious work time. When meeting with customers, Sandy was dressed in tailored business suits with her shoulder length hair neatly framed around her face. She was a strikingly beautiful woman, yet oh so professional in her appearance.

Rick enjoyed being in a meeting when customers met her for the first time. 'A token woman' they clearly thought. 'Easy pickings' their expressions revealed. Rick would do nothing to dispel their notions, letting them play right into his hands. They would patronize her. She would astound them with her knowledge. They would fight back. She would parry, neatly marking each chest with a "Z." They would retreat, in awe and wonderment, enchanted by her skill and respectful of her femininity. It worked every time. But without question, bringing Sandy to Asia, where mores placed women in the home or performing menial tasks, never in meetings with men as equals, was a risk. It had the potential of exploding in his face.

It didn't.

The meeting with Cathay Pacific the next day ended with a signed contract for the ground support equipment plus altimeter spares. More than just a simple agreement, Sandy obtained a spares pricing formula almost three times the price of production units. It was a major accomplishment.

As they were leaving the Cathay Pacific building, Mr. Cho, Purchasing Manager, asked them to wait a moment while he went to his office for something. Moments later he returned with a model 747 emblazoned with the distinctive Cathay markings. He bowed as he presented it to Sandy. "You are a talented business lady. This is in honor of our meeting today."

When they had settled into their taxi for the ride to the Peninsula hotel, Rick continued the praise. "Sandy, ya done good. I was proud of you today. I thought they were going to knock our spare parts price down to two and a half times, but you got two point nine. I'm not certain anyone else could have done as well. Congratulations!"

"Rick, I appreciate the praise, but you give me more credit than I'm due." This was the first time he had ever seen her flustered. She was blushing. Or was that the Hong Kong heat? "I did the job of a contracts administrator. No more. No less."

"Methinks the lady doth protest too much." Funny how Shakespeare cropped up at the oddest moments. "You did a great job. You dazzled them with your footwork. As far as I'm concerned, you are the best secret weapon we've ever had in our arsenal. Do not, I repeat, do not sell yourself short."

"Thank you." She blushed anew.

"Tonight, we celebrate. What kind of dinner do you feel like? You name it. You got it."

"How about Chinese," she said, laughing at her cleverness.

"Haven't you had enough?"

"No, not really," she answered. "Besides, where will we find better?" She paused, thinking. "Rick, if you could only enjoy one meal in Hong Kong, what would it be?"

"That's easy. If I could only eat one meal, it would be Dim Sum. And I'd pick whichever dim sum restaurant in the neighborhood that seemed the most crowded. The Chinese know their food, and if the place is packed, it's a sure sign the menu is excellent."

Sandy frowned. "What's a 'dim soom' restaurant?"

"I thought you'd ask," he said. "Dim sum dates back to the ancient tea house days. Back then, merchants didn't have offices of their own. Instead, they sat at tables at their neighborhood teahouses and customers table-hopped to make deals. When a prospect sat, the merchant offered tea and some snacks to his guest. Waiters who circulated provided food and drink, table to table, carrying platters of dumplings, spare ribs, pork balls, and spring rolls. At the end of the day, the merchant paid up his bar and snack bills, and came back the next day for more of the same. And that's basically dim sum today."

"How do you know what to order?' Sandy asked.

"Well, it isn't from menus. There are none. Waiters and waitresses circulate, usually pushing steam carts filled with different bamboo-packaged treats, stacked four or five high; each row of baskets labeled on the front of the cart with the contents inside, in Chinese of course. You're allowed to lift lids, choose, and enjoy. Money never changes hands with each serving. Instead, the head waiter comes by when you signal you're finished, counts up all the empty snack plates at your table (which have differing color patterns denoting varying prices per course) and presents you with the tab.

"The locals recommend the fried tongues with menthol leaf, and the steamed egg white and cabbage."

"Pass." She made a face, not unlike a gargoyle.

"Pass? You don't like cabbage?"

"Funny! I have too high a regard for tongues. I'd like to learn a foreign tongue, not eat one."

"Now who's being funny?"

Yum Sing

They enjoyed a boisterous banquet in the largest restaurant she's ever seen. If it wasn't for so many individual tables, square and round, small and large, the restaurant would have seemed even larger. White tablecloths, inexpensive dishes, abundance of paper napkins and tooth picks. Small chandeliers hung throughout the room, interspersed with Chinese red light globes that matched the bright Chinese red columns that lined the room. A huge red Oriental carpet covered the floor. With the arrival of the first food baskets, Rick raised his chopsticks toward Sandy and said "YUM SING."

She laughed. "What does that mean?"

"It's the Chinese equivalent of 'Bon Appetit.'"

They ate steamed rice and grilled fish, roasted duck and steamed rice, mushrooms and peas and steamed rice, all followed by desserts of caramelized fruit and oceans of green tea. Not one tongue was found in the lot. At least not one that Sandy recognized.

During the meal, Sandy became curious about Rick's knowledge of Chinese customs as well as the language. "Rick, you have a gift for languages, I guess. I can't get over how well you seem to speak Chinese."

"It's no gift. I was born in China. My folks were missionaries in the city of Xiamen. That's not too far from here, just northeast along the coast of the mainland, directly across from Taiwan. We lived in Xiamen until the Communists took over in 1945. Then we fled for our lives. I was only 5 years old, so I don't remember a whole lot about my first home.

"I do remember an island my parents took me to on occasion," she continued. "It was called Gulang—meaning 'drum waves'—because the holes in the reefs hit by the waves made sounds like a drum. I remember having good friends, all Chinese, who I played with. My parents insisted that we be assimilated into the culture so while I heard English spoken on occasion, I was raised speaking the Mandarin dialect. My parents had always hoped to return to China, but the permanent in-vesture of Mao Tse Sung blocked that from ever happening. Still, with that as a hope, my

Chinese language lessons continued until I reached a point of proficiency. Or was it because I was eighteen and had left home? No matter. I guess that I never lost it. But that doesn't mean I can speak German or French or Spanish. I can't say much more than 'Thank you,' and 'I'm sorry.'"

"Have you ever been back to Mainland China?"

"Nope. Hong Kong is as close as I have come. To be truthful, while there is a curiosity on my part to return, I know that nothing will look familiar to me and that there will be no real point in going. But maybe some day." He diverted his eyes and signaled their hovering waiter, making a big check mark in the air with his finger, mouthing the word 'Check.' "Now, the thing I really enjoy is the advantage I can claim when I meet with businessmen in both Hong Kong and Taipei, and even Singapore where both English and Chinese are spoken. Nobody figures that I know Chinese, so when they want to hold private conversations without leaving the room, they do so with impunity. My biggest challenge is keeping a straight face while they are talking about my offer or the deal we are about to close."

"That didn't happen today in our meeting with Cathay," Sandy said.

"Nor will it with those folks. They know that I speak Mandarin."

Chapter 5

Kismet?

The past revisited

Rick was standing in the hallway talking to Peter Vandervoort, a design engineer, when Jinnie motioned that she was holding a telephone call for him. By the shrug of her shoulders, he concluded she didn't know who the caller was. He walked back into his office and reached across his desk for the phone.

"Rick Stoner," he said, moving toward his chair with the phone cord held high to avoid knocking objects off his desk.

"Guess who this is." The voice was teasing, sounding distantly familiar.

Rick leaned back in his chair and propped his feet on his desk. "I haven't the vaguest idea," he said, all the while hoping the female caller would say something he would recognize that would give him a clue. "Who is it?"

"That's what I asked you. Come on, guess."

"Look, I really don't have time for games. And I can't make out your voice although it isn't unfamiliar."

"All right for you," she said. "I would have thought you would have known who I was. After all, we used to live together."

"Margy!" he shouted into the receiver. His feet hit the floor with a thud, bringing his secretary Jinnie to the doorway of his office. He waived her off, signaling with his face that all was well. "Is this Margy?"

"Yes, and shame on you for not knowing my voice."

"Is everything OK? Why are you calling? Where are you?"

"I'm fantastic," she assured him. "I just called to surprise you and to ask you a favor."

Rick's mind was a blur. He hadn't talked to Margy in eleven years. Not since 1967. It had been nineteen years since he had seen her; that night she told him she was going to go through with the divorce. He had been devastated then. He was excited now. Yet, his excitement didn't make any sense. He wasn't in love with her. Still, a heartbeat of 300 a minute didn't seem normal. He was definitely uptight whether it made sense or not.

"Your surprise worked!" he said as he tried to recover composure. "What's the favor?"

"My phone call wasn't the surprise," she said. "The surprise is that I'm moving to Seattle. The favor is that I'd like to see you just once for old time's sake."

He listened to her voice. Now that he knew who it was, he realized that it hadn't changed. It was unmistakable, husky, and feminine.

"I still can't believe I'm talking to you," Rick said. "How did you find me? When are you moving here? Why are you moving here? And how come you sound like you're here already?"

"I found you by calling Information, getting your home phone, calling your wife and telling her that I was with an executive search firm. I got your business number from her. We're moving in about six weeks because my husband is being transferred. He's a pilot with InterContinental Airlines. He got his captaincy and will be flying 747s out of Seattle. I sound like I'm here because I <u>am</u> here, camped at the Olympic Hotel looking for a home."

Rick was somewhat at a loss for words. None of this made sense. *Why was she calling? Really?*

"It took more courage than I normally have just to call today," she said softly, pausing, then said, "Can we meet for lunch tomorrow?"

"Man, Margy, I'm married. I don't know how appropriate that would be?"

"I didn't ask if we could meet at a motel. I just asked if we could meet. Do you ever eat lunch? Couldn't we meet in a restaurant somewhere in Seattle? In public?" Her tone was playfully sarcastic.

Rick took a deep breath, feeling what he was about to do was wrong, but he was conquered by an overwhelming curiosity to see this woman. *What's wrong with me*, he wondered even as he said, "OK, how about meeting tomorrow at the Space Needle. I'll call and make the reservation for noon."

"Sounds wonderful. I'll see you then." His phone went silent.

Rick held the phone receiver in his hand, poised mid-air between his head and the cradle. What was his problem? He was married. He was passionately in love with his wife. Why was this meeting, un-thought of only moments before, suddenly acceptable? He had no idea.

"This is dumb," Rick said under his breath."

He stared across his desk at the informal family portrait Carol had framed for him. It was taken last summer when they went to the Rain Forest in Olympic National Park. He absent-mindedly stroked his chin and lower lip. A little stubble from his fast-growing beard had surfaced already, recalling the manliness he had felt the first time he'd shaved at age sixteen. That's when he started dating Margy. Hadn't he changed in twenty-three years? Could she still stir him like she once could? Didn't his fifteen years of joy with Carol and the boys count for anything? These were questions that Rick knew lacked a place in his mind. They shouldn't have been questions in the first place. And although he had committed to meeting Margy the next day, he realized that he had to exorcise his unwholesome thoughts of her before they met. Damn his libido, anyway. He glanced at his watch. Ten minutes before the staff meeting. Time for a quick walk to clear his mind.

***

Jinnie watched her boss head down the aisle and out the front door. She got up from her desk and went into his office, watching out his picture window as he walked slowly down the tree-lined path that bordered the winding driveway. Jinnie liked her boss. He was caring, thoughtful, and had a wonderful sense of humor. On top of that, his athletic body and chiseled features caused every female at Pierce to be jealous of her. Why did she get to be his secretary?

She had been Rick's secretary and, as he told her, his most valued assistant, for four years. He had picked her from the secretarial pool within a week of his joining the company. The process he had taken to hire her had been interesting. Before he would give her the job, he brought his wife into the office to meet with Jinnie. "I value her opinions and trust her judgment," he told her. "If she approves of you, you've got the job." Carol was enthusiastic. She felt Jinnie was an outstanding choice.

Jinnie knew her boss pretty well. She respected him. He was a devoted husband and father. He was committed to the company and its success. And right now, he was troubled. That much was evident. And it was more than the loss of the F-14 Radar Altimeter program. That much was evident, too. The phone call he had just received was somehow at the bottom of his newfound stress.

Grady Morgan stood in the doorway of Rick's office, looking at Jinnie. Jinnie was tall, willowy and seductive with California blond hair that fell loose, framing wide green eyes that were so alive. She was good looking. She seemed to understand this without vanity. Her friend Grady was almost an opposite, short and plump, with mousy brown, closely cropped hair that made her horn-rimmed glasses seem to jump off her face. Grady "ahem-ed" and Jinnie turned around.

"What's he really like, Jinnie?" Grady looked past her at the retreating figure of Rick.

"I was mesmerized by him when I first met him. I mean, I'm still awed by him, but I know him now. Not that this precludes veneration, but it puts a little dust on it."

"That's no answer. What's Rick like? Has he made a play for you?"

"Grady!"

"No, I mean it. Has he made a play for you? You're so pretty and he's so good looking. Certainly, you've fantasized about it."

"I have not!" Pausing. "He's happily married."

Lunch with Margy

What time was it? It seemed later than eleven, but it wasn't. Rick figured that if he left the office by eleven fifteen, he could be at the Seattle Center in twenty minutes; perhaps thirty under the worst of conditions. Finding a place to park and riding the elevator to the restaurant should consume no more than five minutes, getting him there at least ten minutes early. He didn't like the thought of anyone having to wait because of him. It seemed better that he be the one to arrive early and he was satisfied with his plan. He walked up the stairs toward Manufacturing.

"Rick, glad I caught you." Mark Minster ran up the stairs behind him. "We're having problems with our pricing on the General Dynamics proposal. Think you can share some wisdom with us?"

"When?"

"We just took a five minute potty break. We're about to restart."

"Your timing's rotten. I've got to leave in fifteen minutes."

"No problem. We'll have you out in ten."

Finally!

The promise of having him on his way in ten minutes proved to be just a little off the mark. As he drove down the road from Pierce, he wondered if he could make Seattle Center in five minutes. Not likely. He hated being late to anything. This was worse. He could feel his body's reaction as adrenaline raced through his bloodstream. He was anxious and irritable, excited and impatient. This had been building all morning. Now, in the final moments, it was almost unbearable.

Rick wished it wasn't raining. That hardly supported the image of the Pacific Northwest that he wanted shared with visitors. Besides, there was a distinct possibility that he would get wet when he ran from his car to the Space Needle. Then it would be <u>his</u> image that would be jeopardized.

He searched the glove compartment for his collapsible umbrella. He didn't own a raincoat; it didn't rain hard enough in Seattle to justify one; except maybe for today. He found the bumbershoot and popped it open as he got out of his car. Rain drummed on the taut fabric as he ran for the entrance to the Needle.

A not-too-wet Rick left the glass elevator that had brought him to the revolving restaurant 500 feet above the ground. He headed across the foyer toward the smiling young lady at the reservation desk. "My name is Stoner. I have a reservation at noon for a party of two."

"Oh yes, Mr. Stoner. Mrs. Stoner is already here." She turned away from Rick efficiently and started onto the moving platform that was the dining room, then paused and motioned Rick to follow her.

At the mention of his wife's name, Rick paled. Then he realized how the hostess must have assumed that Margy was Carol. His heart raced madly. He could not control his excitement. What did Margy look like? Would he recognize her? He'd changed. Surely, so had she. Some people didn't grow older gracefully. Was Margy a matron now? The hostess stopped beside a table next to the window and waited for Rick to seat himself. Instead, he stood there transfixed. It was Margy, and she was more beautiful than he remembered her as a girl of nineteen. Margy was smiling broadly at him.

"You're handsomer than you have a right to be." She extended her hand. "I can't really believe that you could look so good after so many years."

Rick took the offered hand as he seated himself across from her. Her dress was immaculate, like something out of *Vogue*. He absorbed the beauty of this woman who was once his wife.

"Hey, stop right there. I'm a good fifteen pounds heavier than when you last saw me, my waist is three inches thicker, and my hair is receding a little and graying some. You, on the other hand, look absolutely sensational!!"

Then, pointing toward her head, he observed, "I'm not certain I would have recognized you with blond hair, but I sure would have looked." He pushed back away from the table, arms locked at the elbows, giving himself a wider-angle look. "Wow! I can't get over how great you look! How have you stayed in such great shape?"

She tossed her head and smiled in receipt of his admiration. "I play lots of tennis. I swim and I don't eat." She smiled at him radiantly, and a highly charged excitement flowed actively between them. Both of them were aware of the electricity in the room, yet each pretended there was none.

"So tell me," Rick took a different tack in the conversation, "what you've done with your life since I last saw you. What has Margy been up to?"

"Wow," she exhaled almost with a sigh. "I have a feeling I'm falling thirty stories in an elevator and my life is about to flash before me. I'll try to give you the highlights without boring you to tears." She paused as the waitress arrived to take their order. "Just coffee for me, please."

"Make it two," Rick said, and the waitress left, looking somewhat disgusted at the size of their order. "Margy, we're supposed to be having lunch, not coffee. Let's take time out to look at the menu and order something." Rick appealed to her.

"You go ahead and order, Rick. This is part of my daily routine. Fruit and coffee for breakfast, coffee for lunch and a decent dinner when Jim's in town. Otherwise, I just fix something simple for me and whatever the kids feel like."

"Well, I'm certainly not going to eat in front of you. And if I don't want to add to my weight, I guess I can go without lunch too. Now, on with your story." He made a sweeping gesture with his hand ala Ed Sullivan.

"OK. Let's see. Where was I?" Margy rolled her eyes upward as if in deep thought. "Oh yes," she said musically. "I hadn't begun yet.

"I met Jim about nine or ten months after our divorce. He had just completed a six-year hitch with the Air Force as a KC-135 pilot. He loved flying but wasn't so keen about the military. Back in the late Fifties, there was a great demand for ex-military pilots with four-engine jet experience. With the almost parallel introductions of the 707 and DC-8, all the commercial airlines were following the wave of the future. Transitioning prop pilots to jets was not as easy as hiring pilots with thousands of jet hours under their belts already. So he saw his chance to build a career, and he took it. He had just completed training and was assigned by InterContinental Airlines as a flight engineer, flying out of Washington, D.C. when I met him at a party. I needed someone like him about then. He was mature, older than me, and experienced in the ways of the world. He'd been around and was ready for domestic responsibility, I figured. So I latched onto him.

"We were married on Groundhog Day in 1961, making me Margy Guerber. I had hoped for Valentine's Day, but Jim was going to be in Minneapolis that day so we took our opportunity when it presented itself. Our honeymoon consisted of a long weekend in Virginia Beach before Jim had to go back to work. It rained the entire three days we were there. In 1963, our daughter, Cathi was born and eighteen months later, our son, Steve was born. Both of them have turned out to be healthy, normal kids and we consider ourselves to be very lucky. Because Jim's income has been good throughout our married life, the kids have not lacked for much, although we have tried to keep extravagances in check. I don't think they've been too badly distorted because of our upper middle class status. I've not worked since we were married. Jim has always felt that I needed to be at home where the kids could rely on me. My life has not been filled with anything momentous. I have enjoyed it. I have been pampered and provided for. I can play tennis summer and winter because of a club membership. I've travel a lot; really, whenever the mood has overtaken me, thanks to Jim's airline passes. I guess I've tasted some of the better parts of life and have much to be thankful for.

"Now, is that summary enough?"

Rick smiled. "I feel like we're playing tennis and suddenly the ball's in my court." They grinned at each other. "I'll try to be as succinct as you were as I recount my high adventures since the parting of our ways.

"I began as a child . . ."

Margy screwed up her face. "Not that far back, please!"

"No, you misunderstand me. After our divorce, I began as a child. I was hardly mature. I had no clue what I was going to do with the rest of my life and not a semblance of an idea of how to go about it. I ruled out becoming a cowboy or a fireman. I hadn't wanted to be either of those since I was ten. And I knew I didn't want to be a doctor. It seemed reasonable to me that I should have a job that carried with it prestige. So I went to work in a bank in New York City. It was a low level job since I lacked experience and had no college degree behind me. I started going to school at night, taking core curriculum subjects, still without a specific career goal in mind. I wasn't certain banking was to be my life's work, but I figured I had time. And with time, I saw a great attraction to the field of engineering. It would give me the opportunity to have community respect, and a good salary.

"I took a heavy load at night school because I wanted to accelerate the program. It took four years of hard work, added to the two years I had before you and I were married, and I got my degree with honors. I was ready. All I needed was the right company to come along and make me rich and famous. An ad in the Wall Street Journal by an electronics company in Seattle drew a response from me. I didn't know who the advertiser was because I was directed to write to a P. O. Box. I hate those kinds of ads. Since then, I have always been tempted to write to them anonymously, giving them my P. O. Box without my name in return, but I haven't. In any event, TELCOM, a major supplier to the aviation industry, was the name behind the P. O. Box, and following letters and telephone conversations, they flew me out here for an interview. I got the job. I couldn't believe my good luck. I couldn't believe that they'd move me clear across the country, but they did. Perhaps the fact that I had hardly any belongings entered into their decision." Rick paused to see if he was boring Margy. Her eyes shone and her interest seemed high, so he continued.

"I met my wife Carol at TELCOM. She didn't work there. She came to a Christmas party as the date of one of the other guys in the office. We hit it off immediately and within four months, we were married. Carol was a fashion designer, working for a local Seattle firm. From all indications, she had a brilliant career ahead of her. She was born and raised in Seattle. Her father is a purchasing manager for Boeing's Commercial Airplane Company in Renton.

"The first of our two kids arrived four years after we were married. They came in more rapid succession than yours. Trey is eleven and his brother Jeff is ten. As you can see, I specialized in boys. Our kids, just like yours . . ."

"Rick, excuse me for interrupting, but I've never heard the name Trey. How did you come up with that?"

"Easy. It's a nickname. His real name is Derrick Harris Stoner, the Third. Trey, for short. It could have been Tres or Drei, both of which also translate into the word 'three'. We just thought that Trey was clever enough." Then, chuckling at his cleverness, he said, "We knew we didn't want to call him 'Three.'

"Anyway, Carol gave up her promising career when Trey was born, and I don't think she's regretted it since. She's been a great mother and has really invested her life into those boys. Their success as children seems to prove that.

"After three years with TELCOM, I got a great opportunity to move up the business ladder as far as experience was concerned, and certainly as far as salary was concerned when I was offered a product manager's position with Flightline. That was too good to pass up. I stayed with them for eight and a half years, the last three as national sales manager. Then I came to Pierce Electronics where you found me, and where I am Vice President of Marketing.

"It's been a pretty good life. I've achieved just about everything I've set out to achieve. I really don't have any regrets. I suppose I would do some things differently, given the opportunity to repeat them, yet from each mistake, I've been the winner; the better for each. I don't drive a Mercedes, but I do have a top of the line Olds. I don't have a swimming pool, but I do have an incredible view of Lake Washington and the Seattle skyline. I have enough money in reserve to put my boys through college and I'm surrounded by a great circle of friends. I really feel fortunate." He looked at Margy, obviously trying to think of something else pertinent, finding nothing, shrugged his shoulders slightly and said, "I guess that's it."

He signaled the waitress for a refill of their coffees and said, "I don't mind telling you that I was apprehensive about this meeting. Your voice on the phone brought back so many memories; so many good memories." His voice lowered. "A couple of bad memories." His enthusiasm resumed. "I was anxious to see what you looked like. I was interested in knowing what had happened in your life. And I guess, being a sort of nostalgic fellow, I was looking forward to doing some reminiscing with you."

The rest of the lunchtime passed all too quickly. Rick had a meeting at two o'clock that he couldn't be late for, and it was past time for Margy to leave also. Still, they lingered. "Do you remember the New Year's Eve when we were seventeen? We vowed to stay awake all night," Rick said.

"And Pete got into my father's treasured, twenty-year old Scotch, killed the bottle and nearly himself with it," Margy added. "Oh, I remember it all too well." They both laughed.

She slid from her chair and stood up abruptly. "I must go! I expected to be back at the hotel at least half an hour ago."

Rick rose and followed her to the elevator. They rode in silence to the ground and walked to her rented car.

Margy opened her car door and paused before getting in. "I hate to call this to an end. I don't know when I'll see you again." She turned to face Rick and then moved quickly toward him, giving him a kiss on the cheek. She turned as quickly again and got into her car. Rick closed the door behind her and she rolled down the window. "I'll be in touch, Rick. Suddenly, seeing you again is important to me." She backed her car from the stall and drove away.

Rick knew that he shouldn't have come. Curiosity, indeed, must have killed the cat.

Personal and Confidential

An envelope marked "Personal and Confidential" lay unopened on Rick's desk when he returned to his office from lunch, several days after his lunch with Margy. It had been placed prominently atop the day's mail. It was postmarked Arlington, Virginia. It was scribed in a woman's handwriting. He paused before opening it, trying to think who he knew in Arlington. *Margy!* It was from Margy!

He wanted to open it immediately, but noting that he was in view of Jinnie, he thumbed through the rest of the mail as if looking for something of equal importance. His quest satisfied, he felt justified in reading his "personal and confidential" letter. Jinnie would have been disarmed into believing it was not anything special. A job application, maybe. He received many of these "personal and confidential" unsolicited inquiries each month.

Prophet

Dear Rick,

I really can't believe I'm writing this letter. It's out of character for me. But I don't know how else to let you know I'm back in Arlington, that I've found a home on Mercer Island, and that seeing you was more exciting than even my fantasies allowed me to dream. I would have called you, but Jim would have wondered about the call when the bill came in. So I decided a letter to your office was the safest.

I'd tell you that you looked wonderful, but you know what I thought because my eyes revealed everything. How have you kept in such good shape? Except for your salt and pepper hair, you look the same as you did twenty years ago. Maybe even better. I'm impressed . . . and jealous of your wife. Does she know how good you look? Does she know how desirable her husband is? Is she taking full advantage of you?

Well, enough of this. We will be moving to the Pacific Northwest in 6 weeks. Jim will be coming out sooner because his assignment starts the first of next month. I get to pack the household and ship the dog. Doesn't that sound like fun? I'll fly into Seattle on the 15th. Want to meet my flight? Jim will be on a trip. (Only kidding, of course . . . about meeting me. Jim will really be on a trip but you have no reason to meet my flight. Besides, how would I explain you to my kids?)

I have relived our coffee-flavored lunch probably 50 times. It wasn't long enough. There is so much about you that I still want to know. But no problem. All I have to do is wait. Then we can spend all the time we need being reacquainted.

Oh yes, my new home address is 12549 Mercer Park Lane, Mercer Island. That's where we'll be settling. It's a beautiful English Tudor with four-bedrooms. I've always loved English Tudor but never thought I'd live in one. I hope you'll visit someday. Maybe you could drive by before we move out, just so you'll know where it is. It overlooks Lake Washington, facing the north. We can even see some of the Seattle skyline. We couldn't have afforded anything half as nice in Arlington. I'm so glad we're moving to the Northwest. But the house and the view are only a fraction of the reason . . . !

Please write if you have time. I need to hear from you.

Love,

Margy

Rick sighed heavily as he replaced Margy's letter in its envelope. What was her agenda? He thought he knew and he grew uncomfortable. He wanted to tell her he would not be answering her letter.

Was he going to tell Carol about this? Not on his life! Yet his silence was breaking his own rule . . . to hide nothing from Carol.

He tore the envelope and its contents into small pieces.

***

Rick walked into Carl Munsen's office and closed the door. "We've got to talk," he said, sitting at Carl's small conference table.

"Don't have the time," Carl said, reaching for a folder on his desk.

"Make time."

Munsen looked up from his work and studied Rick's face. It was flush, the muscles of his jaw hard. He got up and moved reluctantly to the table.

"I don't have time for marketing discussions."

"You bet you don't. From what I can observe, you've got more than your hands full in manufacturing."

"What the hell are ya talking about?"

"I'm talking about a design that's three months behind schedule being production-engineered. I'm talking about an absence of communication with the rest of the company. I'm talking about failure . . . ."

"Butt out, Stoner! I resent your insinuations. You're not qualified to make them. In fact, I don't think you're qualified to do your own job, much less mine."

"A strong offense is the best defense, right Carl?" Rick was surprised at the anger that had built up inside him. "We're at risk of losing this contract that we've worked so hard to get, and you want to pretend it isn't happening. And you're the key. This is your project now. If you fail, we all fail."

"I'm not failing. I've run into some snags, that's all. Technological breakthroughs, like the impossible, take a little bit longer."

"No one thinks differently. But the fact remains that we're bordering on default on our contract. We've got to do something and we've got to do it fast." Carl pulled on each finger of his left hand until its knuckle cracked, then shifted to his right hand. It was a telltale sign of his nervousness; a barometer that Rick had learned to use with some skill.

"Look," Rick continued, softening his voice. "This is a load you're under. You can use some help. You're not the Lone Ranger."

"And you're sure not Tonto."

Rick stood up abruptly. "This conversation is going nowhere. But it's not over. When Charlie's back tomorrow, we'll discuss it with him."

***

"Christianity is just so much spiritual hogwash that's better relegated to the realm of mythology than to reality." Carl's face was defiant.

"What brings on this?" Phil Talbot looked confused. This was supposed to be a meeting to discuss personnel benefits.

"Stoner. He walks around with a holier-than-thou attitude."

"That's a stretch and you know it, Carl. Just 'cause he plays by the rules and doesn't use foul language, he's hardly sanctimonious. For one, I think it's refreshing. He's a straight-shooter."

"To you, maybe. To me he's a hypocrite."

"Because?"

"Because he's faking. Underneath all that piety lives a guy just like you and me. All religions are phony. I know it, and so does he."

"Where do you come up with this stuff?"

"The school of hard knocks. I have never met a Christian who lived the so-called Christian life. He either cheated on his wife, or swore, or drank too much, or stretched the truth if not down-right lied."

"You do all those things, Carl."

"Yeah, but I'm not a Christian and never claimed to be."

"So even when you see someone living the Christian life, you figure he isn't; which accounts for how you claim to have never seen one." Talbot frowned at this conclusion. "Your logic escapes me."

"Yeah? Well I have it on good authority that he was having a romantic lunch today with a beautiful woman, not his wife. How much more of a hypocrite can that be?"

"How do you know that?"

"I have my sources."

Chapter 6

Snow Like Powder

"Come on, boys. The longer you take, the more the snow's gonna be packed down." Rick finally steered his two boys out the door and headed to nearby Snoqualmie Pass for a day of skiing. This was their special time together; father and sons only; no females allowed. Besides, Carol didn't like the cold and the snow, so leaving her at home was no problem. She'd just head for Bellevue Square; her special time; no males allowed; unlimited shopping.

A State Patrol roadblock just east of North Bend delayed their drive up to the pass. All cars were being checked for snow tires or chains. There had been a heavy snow the previous night and without proper equipment, no one was being allowed any further. They arrived at the summit half an hour later, found a place to park next to a particularly large snow pile and were on the intermediate slope within half an hour. It was March, it was Tuesday, and not many people were there. It was nothing like the weekends when the fanatics showed up before the snow disappeared until the following November. The skies were a dark blue, contrasting in picture-book fashion against the white blankets of snow on the mountains.

Rick purposefully chose the Summit at Snoqualmie because its slopes weren't as difficult as nearby Alpental, yet it still had a vertical drop of 765 feet and almost 200 acres of ski-able terrain. There were six chairlifts and two rope tows which gave novice and intermediate skiers wonderful opportunities to learn and to practice their skills.

The horseplay between the boys began almost immediately. Sibling rivalry was something to behold, Rick mused. On occasion, he was drawn into the fray, usually with the boys ganging up on him. They seemed to like the odds. One time, after a particularly rough exchange, Jeff skied over to Trey and hugged him as if to reassure him that he had only been kidding. He shouldn't have made the effort. It was an awkward embrace and threw both Jeff and Trey off balance. They ended up in a heap on the snow. Rick skied over to see if they were alright and found them sprawled on the ground, laughing.

A short time later, the boys came up with a new stunt. Rick overheard the plot. "We'll ski side-by-side with our arms around our shoulders. I'll hold up my right leg and you hold up your left leg," Trey said. "We'll ski right toward that big fir tree. Just when we get there, we will let go of each other and ski around the tree, still holding our legs up. The tracks in the fresh snow will look like one person skied around the tree—on both sides." They both laughed. "It will be great!"

And they did as planned, making perfect tracks up to and around both sides of the tree and back together on the other side. It was a stunt worthy of "Candid Camera."

When they rode the chairlift back up the mountain, they saw a crowd gathered near the tree. "This is better than we hoped," Jeff told his dad. "Look," he said pointing, "nobody knows how it was done." The boys had another good laugh.

The day passed quickly for all three of them. There was considerable shouting back and forth between the boys at technique or lack of it. On occasions, there was a reference to the inability of one or the other to make it gracefully down the mountain. Both boys started ski lessons the same year. Trey, perhaps had an edge (as they say in skiing parlance) over Jeff, but both had fairly equivalent skills. As was typical with brothers, there was rivalry. It was because of that rivalry that the accident happened.

"Jeff, I'll give you a head start. Bet I beat you to the lodge." The challenge was extended. Rick knew it would be accepted.

"You guys take it easy," he admonished. "Don't take stupid chances."

They were off, Trey giving Jeff no more than a five-second advantage. Rick followed, watching as the boys stretched their skills, pushing themselves for bragging rights that would carry through the week. They were approaching the bottom of the run. Trey had narrowed the gap but he was still behind. It looked like he would need a miracle to beat his younger brother. Suddenly, what had appeared to be a mound of snow ahead moved. A woman skier, who had fallen, struggled to get up. She was dressed totally in white. Jeff saw her too late. He hit her head-on just as Trey swept past, laughing lustily at his obvious victory. Rick skied quickly to his son and the woman he had hit. The woman was sitting, holding her ankle that had twisted under her other leg.

Jeff was not moving.

The Ski Patrol came quickly and transported Jeff to the lodge. Half an hour later, Trey and Rick followed the ambulance as it rushed on the long ride to Bellevue's Overlake Hospital. They were silent, neither one knowing what to say with this tragedy. Finally, an anxious Trey asked, "What's wrong with him, Dad?"

"They don't know, Trey. It's a head injury but until the doctors at the hospital can examine him, we won't know."

"Will he be okay?" Trey began to cry, and Rick reached his hand across the seat to comfort him.

"He'll be okay. I've been praying to God since it happened. He'll be okay."

Hospital

Rick was consumed with thoughts about Jeff. He realized, perhaps for the first time, the extent of the love for his son; how much he relied upon him for love, for humor, for joy. Jeff was the antithesis of the description Rick had once heard for boys. 'Do you know the difference between boys and girls?' his friend had asked. Rick said he thought so. "No, not that difference," he was chided. "I mean the difference between little boys and little girls."

"Oh," Rick had said. "No, why don't you tell me."

"I plan to," his friend went on. "You pull into your driveway after a hard day at the office. Your son is in the front yard having a catch with a friend. You get out of your car, he says 'Hi, Dad,' and throws the ball to you. You catch it, say, 'Hi, Son,' and toss it back. Then the front door opens and a little girl comes running down the walk, jumps in your arms, and gives you a hug and a kiss. *That's* the difference between little boys and little girls."

Perhaps that was the difference between most little boys and girls, but it hardly described his boys . . . and Jeff in particular. Jeff was so loving, so demonstrative. He was the one member of the family who could always make Rick laugh—with a look, a gesture or a saying. He was the one who still hugged and kissed.

Now he lay unconscious in a hospital bed with an uncertain prognosis. He had injured his neck in the collision and while there was some response of his arms and legs to stimuli, the doctors said it was inconclusive. They hoped to know more tomorrow. Meanwhile, why didn't Rick and Carol go home and get some rest.

Sure. As if rest were possible.

***

It was the middle of the second night after the accident. Carol sat on one side of the bed, Rick on the other. He looked at his son and squeezed his hand. Rick imagined seeing Jeff smile that special, brave smile that was uniquely his. His breathing seemed so labored and raspy. Rick looked at his son. "You and Trey are the most perfect things I've ever done in my life." He looked at Carol. There were tears in her eyes.

Later, Rick fell asleep with one hand on Jeff's stomach. When he awoke, he realized that his hand was no longer rising and falling with Jeff's breathing. Jeff's eyes and mouth were open, his body completely still.

***

Their loss was apocalyptic. Everything was dark. There was no sun. Joy had left the family and with its departure, a bankruptcy of feelings took hold. Trey stayed home from school; Rick stayed home from work; Carol found no place to retreat.

When does the grieving end?

Rick was beyond grief. He was numb, yet felt the sharp stab of guilt. *The sins of the father are visited on the son.* An Old Testament scripture came to his mind. For a brief moment, he had lusted for a woman not his wife. Now his precious son was dead.

Rick had never known so much pain and anguish. He had cried when his beloved grandfather had died. His was a passing Rick found difficult to accept. At the same time, while *GrandDad* was relatively young – in his mid-sixties – he was certainly at the point in life where death was not unexpected. But Jeff was only ten years old. He had his whole life in front of him. Was this a God-caused punishment for something Rick had done? *Am I the reason my precious son is dead,* he wondered? At the same time, he knew better. The God he worshipped was not a god of retribution, but a God of love; a God of mercy. He was a forgiving God.

Still, Rick had thought *thoughts* about a woman not his wife. And he knew the punishment inflicted on King David of Israel for his act of adultery. *I haven't done anything with Margy*, he reasoned. *I mean, I accepted her kiss, but it's not like we've been to bed.* Still, he knew the thoughts he was suppressing were adulterous, and didn't the Bible teach that was the same thing? His guilt was overwhelming, and his grieving all the greater.

In memory

Jeff's memorial service had the largest attendance of any held at the church. The 600-seat sanctuary was filled with people lining the aisles and the back wall. Rick and Carol sat with Trey between them. Rick's parents, Derrick and Dorothy Stoner from Pawling, New York sat to their left and Carol's parents, Garrett and Kathy Morgan, from Seattle sat to their right. Carol's eyes were tightly closed. Rick bit his lip and stared at the floor. Trey watched vacuously at a ceiling fan as it spun, driving warm air back down toward the pews.

Jeff's Youth Minister, Bob Crowe, presided over the service. Though not much past his teenage years himself, he was a gifted speaker and a caring man. "There are no words that will sufficiently comfort us at this time," he said. "Jeff was so vibrant, so special . . . so young. He gave us so much, and had so much more to give. But God's wisdom and will are beyond our knowing. He called Jeff home. And He called for us to carry on." His voice trembled with emotion and he paused to regain composure.

"I heard a story about a five-year old boy who had worked for some time, with his Mom's help, to make a surprise Christmas gift for his Dad. It was a ceramic vase for his office. The vase was completed, wrapped and carefully placed beneath the Christmas tree. The little boy was filled with excitement. Finally Christmas morning arrived. The child reached for the vase and carefully picked it up, but as he carried it to his father he tripped, shattering the vase as he fell to the floor. With that, the boy began to cry uncontrollably. His father, attempting to give the child some consolation, thanked his son and said, 'It's OK. It's not worth crying about. Don't let it upset you.'

"But the boy's mother was much wiser, and she held the little one in her arms and said, 'It is important. We worked so hard on this gift, and it meant so much to him.' And she wept with the boy. And finally, when the tears had subsided, she said, 'Son, let's pick up the pieces and make something of them.'

"Rick and Carol and Trey, it's all right to cry. In fact, it's important to weep. But when your tears cease, you must pick up the pieces and make something out of what is left—life must go on.

"So, after the pain of this loss, may God help you not to go to pieces, but instead to pick them up." He stepped away from the podium and down from the platform, walking to the Stoners, putting his arms around them. They remained standing together in a tight circle, heads bowed, as the youth minister prayed quietly with them. The service was over, but like he had said, *life must go on.*

Following the service, many of the mourners adjourned to the church's fellowship hall where sandwiches, fruit plates and beverages were served. It was a time for personal condolences to be expressed by friends to friends. It was not an easy time for the Stoner family because their grief was still fervent and all consuming. But they endured it, accepting the well-meaning words from folks who didn't really know what to say. Rick's parents remained in Bellevue for two days after the memorial. They wanted to provide as much emotional and spiritual support as they could during this stressful time. Since returning from the mission field where they had taught English to the Chinese in Xiamen, they both had gone to work for Norman Vincent Peale's *Guidepost* publication, working out of his Pawling, New York headquarters. But there was a need for them to return soon to oversee the next edition so they were unable to stay as long as they would have liked.

That was OK. While Rick and Carol appreciated their kindness and intent, they really needed to be alone with their sorrow, and they were relieved when Rick drove his folks to the airport on that Saturday morning.

***

Margy had seen Rick's name in the *Families* section of the Seattle Times. The article told of his family's tragedy on the ski slopes of Snoqualmie Pass. She grieved for him and his loss. She wanted to call, but decided to wait for a few weeks. This was not the time to be aggressive.

Chapter 7

Gone With The Wind

The breakthrough

The walnut conference table was lined with Pierce's entire management group, including the four district sales managers from Atlanta, Washington, D.C., Los Angeles and St. Louis. The paneled walls helped suppress the noise level that often filled the large room. Today, it wasn't necessary. They all knew they had been gathered for a major announcement. Everyone went silent as Gil Brockton rose to speak.

"It's a breakthrough!" Gil was breathing hard, his ruddy face flushed with excitement as he made his presentation. "We've talked about this for years. We always figured there was a way to reduce or eliminate a radar's telltale signature. We use radars to find targets on the ground and the targets on the ground use the emissions of our radars to locate us. Not an enviable situation for the flight crew. Every time one of our radars is turned on, it's like making a public address announcement. 'Here we are guys. Why don't you see if you can shoot us down?' All the enemy needs to do is sit there passively and wait for us to broadcast. On top of that, the bad guys have powerful radar transmitters of their own that actively search the skies for incoming unfriendlies.

"Several years ago, the Air Force conducted an unclassified study of stealth that they labeled 'Project Harvey.' 'Harvey' was named after the invisible rabbit in the Broadway stage play of the same name. Three years ago, the Air Force and Defense Advanced Research Projects Agency, DARPA for short, began a series of classified studies, code-named 'HAVE BLUE' to figure out ways of reducing aircraft radar cross sections, called RCS. Before that year was up, their studies produced enough results that they requested proposals from Boeing, LTV, Grumman, Northrop,

Lockheed and Douglas for a prototype aircraft they called the 'XST'—Experimental Stealth Tactical. Northrop and Lockheed were finalists and built prototypes for competitive flyoffs. Last year, Lockheed's "Skunk Works" won the production contract.

"Gil," Paul Grove spoke up. "Define stealth."

"Fair question. In the case of this aircraft, stealth is basically employing techniques to lower the electromagnetic signature, both radar and heat, of an aircraft. It's a means to minimize the distance a plane can be detected by ear and by eye. Minimizing the radar cross-section and the heat signature are the two most important factors that end up driving the design process. But it's tough. For example, to cut the radar detection range in half, you have to lower the RCS by a factor of sixteen—the fourth root. To lower the IR signature in any meaningful manner, you must give up the afterburners for your engines and bury the engines inside the airplane to cool the exhaust gases, the sum total of which is less thrust. It's a world of design compromises.

"Lockheed's job is to build an airplane that doesn't show up on radar. Last year, we negotiated a contract from Wright-Patterson Air Force Base to develop a terrain-avoidance radar for the XST that won't show up on radar either." He paused. Carl Munsen interrupted his private whisperings with Ollie Hunter and the room became silent.

Gil resumed once he seemed certain the attention was all his. "We've had this project under wraps since then. Thousands of Pierce's dollars have been spent; nowhere near as much as Hughes, Westinghouse, General Dynamics, Texas Instruments, Norden, and Sperry, but by our standards, a sizable portion of our hard-earned R & D dollars."

Jim Nyberg, Pierce's Vice President of Finance interrupted. "Wait a minute, Gil. I've never heard of this project. We've never talked about it at staff meetings, it doesn't show up in our annual report, it's not a budget line item. My department has never processed any charge numbers that tied to an unknown program." He seemed irritated. "You mean to tell me that we've spent maybe a hundred thousand dollars on something none of us has heard of?"

"More." Charlie Strang joined the discussion, rising to stand next to Gil.

"More what?"

"We've spent more like three hundred thousand dollars of our money and that much more of the Air Forces'." The president looked directly at

Jim Nyberg, then slowly at the others around the table. The floor was now his.

"Jim, we are in an incredibly competitive market. What's worse, we're up against the big boys. One slip of what we're doing can remove any edge we might hope to have in the next generation system. For fifteen years, our lifeblood has been radar altimeters. But for some time, we've known that this business was going to pass us by; that our subsystems were going to be replaced by superior, all-inclusive systems. We just decided that if anyone was going to replace us, it was going to be us."

"But what the hell do we know about terrain-avoidance radars?" Jim persisted. "Like you said, radar altimeters are our niche; nice, low-to-the ground pulse radar altimeters. I remember in particular the little speech that Rick gave at the Pebble Beach meeting. 'Know your place and stay there,' I think he said."

"Look, Jim," Charlie persisted, "radar altimeters are one component of a terrain-avoidance or nap-of-the-earth system. Conventional military aircraft have been using low-level flying techniques to avoid hostile radars for years, Back in nineteen sixty-one, I worked with General Dynamics Electronics on a system. We successfully demonstrated it in a B-25 that flew for hours over the mountains east of San Diego at an altitude of four hundred feet. The system was great unless you ran into a thousand-foot sheer cliff that didn't give you enough warning time to climb.

"It was Gil who developed the idea of using our specialty as a building block and catapulting us into this whole new arena where nobody had a successful system."

"What are we doing that's so different?" Carl Munsen wanted to know. Some times his Boston accent was stronger than other times. This was one of the soft times.

"We're developing a covert radar that allows an aircraft to hug the ground at an altitude under four hundred feet, climb over hills and mountains, and drop rapidly into valleys at exceptionally high speeds. We will flight test it on an F4 Phantom in three months. We anticipate incredible results. If the Phantom's radar cross-section is anything like the XST, the air-defense radar range at Tonopah will never see us."

"So how does the system work?" Munsen continued his questioning.

Charlie moved to the chalkboard. He drew a simple diagram; first, a horizontal line with high and low bumps running along its length. On the lower left outer edge of the line, he drew a small vertical dish. Extending away from the dish, he drew two lines, one at an upward, sixty five-degree angle, and one, more horizontal, about ten degrees above the bumps. Last, he drew two airplanes, one marked "A" between the two lines; one marked "B" below the lines and just above the bumps.

He pointed to the vertical dish. "This is an early warning radar installation. Between these two lines," he gestured to the chalk marks extending from the dish, "is the radar's field of view. The radar easily detects a non-stealth aircraft like a B-52 or F-4 if it's in the radar's field of view. A B-52 has an RCS of one thousand square meters. An F-4 has an RCS of one hundred square meters." He chuckled, "Man, what targets! By the way, in comparison, the stealth is slated to ultimately have a cross-section of point zero one square meters that would make the aircraft appear smaller that a hummingbird. For today's aircraft, to be missed by the ground radar, they would have to be under or over its search pattern," he said, pointing to the "B" aircraft.

Charlie drew a second diagram, simpler than the first. At the center was an aircraft flying above his bumpy, horizontal line. Emanating from the nose of the aircraft was a straight line. It intersected one of the bumps that protruded from the "ground." Another line dropped vertically down from the aircraft to the "ground" below.

"It's a simple math equation," Charlie said. "One radar looks forward and one looks down. The one looking down provides precise altitude information. The one looking ahead provides obstacle warning. The two inputs permit the necessary calculations so that the central computer knows when to pitch up, pitch down or maintain straight and level. Simple, huh?"

Shaking his head, he continued. "It's so simple, it's deadly. A terrain-following system relies on a continuously operating, high powered forward looking radar like I've just described. This radiation makes these systems susceptible to detection by enemy intercept receivers. Further, the use of radar data creates a problem when the radar is jammed. Jamming causes these systems to generate pull-up commands, exposing the aircraft to hostile fire. So our challenge has been to come up with a covert system that avoids detection. Not so simple."

"You got me scared, Charlie," Carl Munsen persisted. "If our system is the enemy's best early warning system, what good is it? It sounds like money down a rat hole," he seemed to enjoy the assenting murmur of others around the conference table.

"You didn't let me finish." Charlie sounded just a little irritated. "The system that we've developed is capable of computer-controlled terrain following, terrain-avoidance and threat-avoidance. There are times when terrain-following systems contribute to aircraft survival, but they are more likely to be used during escape. During initial penetration, the most secure way in to the target is with terrain-avoidance and threat-avoidance systems. Right now, threat-avoidance is being achieved only on a gross scale. The Air Force knows where the SAM sites are supposed to be, and mission planning produces routes . . . actually, corridors several miles wide . . . that guide the aircraft around the threat sites. But onboard computers have a ways to go before threat-avoidance will become a major factor. However, our system is being designed to accept the inputs as soon as they are available. Gil is designing it that way.

"The days of the crop dusters have passed. Used to be that you could fly an airplane slow enough that you could maneuver around any obstacle. Of course, you could only do this during daylight hours. But good pilots could fly at treetop level and not be detected until they had passed overhead. Nowadays, we're asking our pilots to fly at treetop levels going five hundred miles an hour. Manual terrain-avoidance is impossible. If it's going to be done, day or night, it must be done automatically.

"We knew that the radar had to be operated in non-standard modes so that its emissions wouldn't be detected. So, we've developed a K_u-band radar system that uses small, multiple, electronically steered arrays, flush-mounted in the wing's leading edges. K_u-band gives higher resolution than X-band, and, for a given antenna size, smaller sidelobes. Its sidelobe signals, which are often guilty of betraying radar's presence, are also more quickly attenuated in the atmosphere than X-band emissions. In addition, narrow beam radars have virtually no sidelobes. With the inherently higher resolution of K_u-band, the radar should be capable of resolution in the same class as infrared devices, even in the presence of clouds or obscurants.

"The aircraft should detect the radiation from ground radars long before the radar detects the aircraft—a simple matter of physics—and avoid the threat, then destroy the threat with IR missiles.

"The other details of the system are classified Top Secret, and if I start to get into system functions and the various supporting algorithms, I'll be saying more than I'm authorized to reveal."

"Swell." Ollie Hunter, Operations Manager, joined in, changing the subject back to the initial contention. "I can understand the need for government secrecy, but why wasn't your management team trusted enough to at least know the overall plan? For God's sake, Charlie, we're not the enemy!" His pride was hurt and he let it show.

Charlie shook his head. "No, Phil, you're not the enemy . . . today. Yesterday, Frank Ahearn wasn't the enemy, either. He was a principal engineer working in research. Today he's working for Bendix. If he had known, he would have talked. The schematics may be classified, but the concept isn't."

Charlie was silent for a few moments, even as he opened his mouth and motioned with his forefinger. Everyone knew he still held the floor, so no one interrupted. Finally, he said, "We're in a war for the life of this company. In the nineteen forties, there was a slogan that said: 'Loose lips sink ships.' In the military community, classified information is only shared with those who have a '*need-to-know*.' When Gil came to me with his proposal, I was the one who decided who would know . . . and who wouldn't."

"So, who knew?" asked Gary Wentworth, Gil's right hand man.

"On the management team, there were only three," Charlie answered. "Gil, Rick and me."

"Your answer implies there were others," observed Bill Felt.

"There were. Inside Pierce, there were Dirk Bogert, Tom Mathis and Pat Frankel."

"Those are three of our top engineering supervisors," Chris Tey commented, "but it sounds like there were others along with them. In fact, if we've spent a few hundred thousand dollars in one year, there were a whole lot of others."

"Right again. Except for Jodi White, who served as security administrator, the others were all outside the company."

"How's that?"

"We subcontracted the three major design tasks to three of the country's best consulting firms. None of them knew what the total package was and, in fact, none of them knew about the other. Each thought they were supplementing the work we were doing inside. They had no idea that we were only serving as systems integrator and that other than the interface and the altimeter, they were doing all the design work."

"Charlie, how does this level of effort outside Pierce make sense?" Bill Felt sought to penetrate deeper.

"We weren't certain that it did," Charlie answered. "But the Air Force liked the idea so much that they matched our efforts with their funds for proof of concept."

"What about rights in data?" Ollie Hunter sounded concerned.

"Fully preserved. We told the Avionics Lab at Wright-Patterson Air Force Base that we'd go it alone at our own pace before giving up our rights. They bought it."

"What's next?" Hunter persisted.

"We have a preliminary design review at Wright-Pat in two weeks. I'm hoping Rick will be back in time to be a part of the presenting team."

Back on the job

A week after the memorial service, Rick returned to work. His responsibilities at Pierce were significant and he knew he was needed. The time for grieving was over, at least the official part. There was the upcoming design review at Wright Patterson, for one thing. Furthermore, he needed the diversion from his narcissistic thoughts before he went mad.

He hadn't been in his office five minutes when his phone rang.

"Rick, how are you?" Margy's voice was soothing, seemingly filled with compassion. "I have been so worried, ever since I heard about the accident and the tragic loss of your son."

Rick stood and walked around his desk so he could close his office door. The telephone cord stretched behind him. "I'm learning to deal with it," he said. "But I have never hurt so much in my life."

"Is there anything I can do?"

"I wish there was, but I've got to sort things out for myself." He gripped the receiver tightly. "I never should have let the boys race."

"You can't blame yourself."

"I blame me for everything. Maybe if I hadn't met you for lunch, maybe none of this would have happened."

She gasped for air. "Rick, you can't mean that."

"Oh, I sure do. The sins of the father are visited on the children." Then, seeming to be anxious to end a painful conversation, he said, "Margy, this isn't something I want to talk about right now. For the time being, I need to live with my pain alone." He shifted the phone to his other ear. "I'll call you."

She listened as the connection terminated.

Raising his son correctly?

Rick thought about those sins of his and began to worry about his son Trey, the way he was bending, perhaps the way he was bent. Was he choosing Rick's values in life? Were his values even known by Trey? He was gone so much these days . . . to Hong Kong, Atlanta, Chicago, Rome. When was the last time he had even shared with him something deeper than, "How was school today?" or "Why does your room always have to be such a mess?" Did Trey know what Rick thought about cheating on your income tax, or the war in Vietnam or smoking pot? What about lying or seeing "R" rated movies? To this point, he seemed to lead by example, and a distant one at that. This was one of those philosophical musings that Rick seemed to have whenever he was alone, usually in a restaurant thousands of miles from home. Never mind that he rarely followed up on his thoughts. It was enough that he thought them. Some were certain to come though by osmosis.

Sure.

Trouble at home

Work was not the solution he had hoped for. Everything irritated Rick. And when he went home, he brought his troubles with him. Carol tried her best to comfort him and to bring him out of his deep depression, but he accepted no consolation. Eventually, she snapped too.

"You know, Rick, you're not the only one grief-stricken," she said one evening as the two of them sat staring at the TV. "I lost a son, too."

"And your point is?"

"My point is that we have to keep on living. We have a son who needs us. We have each other in need. I can't do it alone."

The pressure was taking its toll.

"Rick, you've got to talk to me. What's wrong between us?"

"Nothing." Rick might have been the great communicator at work, but she was right; he didn't want to talk at home.

"I know there's something wrong. You've been acting detached for weeks, as if neither Trey nor I were important to you." She stood in front of his chair, blocking his view of the television set. "I'm more important than 'Mary Hartman. Mary Hartman.' I want you to talk to me." And speaking with added emphasis, "Now!"

"I don't know what you're talking about. Nothing's wrong." He tried to look past her.

"Credit me with some intelligence, Rick."

"I do. Only you're wrong." He glanced up in time to see tears start flowing down her cheeks.

He glared at her. "I thought that I would be more at peace at home than at the office. But it looks like I was wrong. This is pure hell." He lunged from his chair and stormed out of the room.

"Don't you walk out on me," she called after him.

Two minutes later, Carol heard the garage door open and Rick's car drive out.

When he returned two hours later, Carol was folding clothes in the laundry. She didn't look up as he entered the room. It was obvious that she had been crying. He walked up behind her and put his arms around her. "I am so sorry," he said. "My only thought was selfish. It was all about me." He pulled her closer. "I went away and parked opposite Nordstrom's at Bellevue Square. I just sat in the car, in the dark, and thought. I wasn't pleased with my thoughts, either. I love you with all my heart. And I hurt you beyond measure. Can you forgive me?" He peeked around her face, trying to determine her feelings. "No, let me rephrase that. I know you can forgive me. My question really is, will you forgive me?"

She turned with his arms still encircling her. She tilted her head upward and softly kissed his lips. "I forgive you."

Deep in the heart of Dixie

Rick had no sooner arrived in his office on Monday morning than his phone rang. It was Bruce Carrozzo, district manager in Atlanta. The Southern Aerospace order was being threatened by a surprise low bid from an Italian firm, GHIA Elettronica, who was obviously trying to buy in. "We're going to lose this one if we don't counter-propose by tomorrow afternoon," Bruce said with obvious alarm.

"What makes you say that?" Rick tested.

"The Purchasing Agent, who really wants to buy from us, told me that his hands were tied. Management has decided to go ahead with GHIA or us tomorrow. They're not going to delay any longer. Low bidder wins because both systems have received design proposal approval."

"OK," Rick said. "Stay in your office. I'll be back to you by noon your time." He hung up and headed for Charlie's office.

He intercepted Charlie in the hall. "Charlie, we've got a problem. Can we talk right now?"

"Monday's are not supposed to begin with problems, Rick," the company president smiled. "Problems are reserved for Tuesdays through Thursdays. You know the company policy." Then he observed Rick's concern. "Come into my office. Do we need anyone else?"

Answer from on high

Rick boarded his flight, claimed his seat and quickly settled behind a sheath of paperwork. He felt the 727 back away from the gate, was mildly aware of the emergency in-flight announcements, mostly because a stewardess was dangling a model oxygen mask off his right shoulder, and was nearly oblivious to the actual takeoff. And, he figured, being engrossed in the work he'd spread before him would help take his mind off his own troubles. He wasn't in the mood for conversation and politely rebuffed the attractive lady sitting by the window who was on her way home following a visit with her sister and three nieces. She'd always wanted a family of her own but she and her husband couldn't have children. How about Rick? Did he have children? Oh, he did. What kind? A son. He specialized? That was funny! What kind of work did he do? A manager of an electronics company. Why was he going to Atlanta? Oh, he was meeting with the president of Southern Aerospace. And he still had work to do before the meeting. She would leave him alone.

Rick unlatched the tray table in front of the unoccupied middle seat. He spread his paperwork out and the barrier between him and his fellow traveler was established. He figured he had a good hour and a half of work time before lunch. That was more uninterrupted time than a full day at the office and he wanted to take advantage of it. Besides, the busier he was, the less he thought of the loss of his son. And right now, he needed to get his mind off him.

He was pleased that Bruce Carrozzo had gotten a one-day delay in the Southern decision. A face-to-face meeting would give Pierce a fighting chance to overcome its opposition. Charlie had given him carte blanche to come up with a winning bid. "Whatever it takes, Rick, so long as it's break-even or above." Rick started looking at the angles. How could he come out the winner without giving away the store? There had to be something creative that would set them apart from GHIA. He puzzled over that until a friendly flight attendant inquired if he wanted fish, short ribs or the lamb stew. It was lunchtime. He needed a mental break anyway since he certainly wasn't making much progress.

He put his papers into a single pile, stretched his legs, and lay his head back against the headrest. That was all it took. He started thinking of Jeff and the pain returned. His lamb stew arrived.

"How's your project going?" his window seat companion inquired between mouthfuls. "You've sure been busy," she added, evidently hoping to stimulate some conversation.

Rick looked over at her and smiled faintly. "Busy, but non-productive. I'm not having much success in achieving my goal." He tasted the stew to see if he had made a good choice.

"What's your goal?" Her face seemed to glow with joy over his verbal diarrhea.

"Between now and tomorrow morning at nine, I have to figure out a way to win a large contract from another company that has just underbid us. And I'm trying to do it without lowering our price more than I have to."

She buttered a roll. "Is that the only way you can win?"

"It's competitive," he acknowledged. "Price is the bottom line." Her roll looked good. He contemplated eating his; then decided the calories weren't worth it.

"What a shame that you can't give them something they'd want yet something that wouldn't cost you much." She looked at him for a response.

"I wish we could, but there's nothing that falls into that category. Everything we make costs money and we're not too keen on giving it away. That's not our reason for being in business." He returned his attention to his lunch. The lamb was getting cool and the conversation was not proving helpful . . . rather, reinforcing his frustration, which was hardly an aid to digestion.

"Is your equipment complicated to use?" Rick began to wonder about her questions.

"Yes . . . well, not so much to use, but it's complicated to maintain."

"How do they learn to maintain it, whatever it is?"

"They spend a lot of time reading manuals . . . and pestering us on the phone." She was asking more than your average, run-of-the-mill questions.

She shifted in her seat and looked directly at Rick. "Why don't you offer to put on in-depth training seminars for them to learn your product? Would that cost much more than you're planning to spend on manuals and answering questions over the phone?" Her eyes lost contact with Rick, as she seemed to become suddenly self-conscious.

Rick, who had been playing with his uneaten roll, rather than focusing on her, abruptly sat up in his seat and looked at her in amazement. That was the answer! She had come up with the ploy that would win the job for Pierce Electronics!

He breathed and exhaled audibly a few times before responding. "That's absolutely incredible!" he said, a smile crossing his lips even as his forehead furrowed in disbelief. "That's a perfect tactic! They'll love it and we'll be heroes!" He looked at her until she returned his gaze. "What made you think of it?"

She returned his smile, minus the look of incredulity. "My husband is the president of Southern." She watched Rick's expression transform into even greater disbelief. "A week ago, he came home from work muttering how he wished his major suppliers would offer training seminars without it costing an arm and a leg. He said it would make Southern just that much more effective in its sales efforts." She adjusted her seat into a deeper reclining position. "So when you told me why you were going to Atlanta and the frustration you were having, I just thought that maybe my husband's needs and your desires were compatible."

"I can't believe this is happening to me. I never get to sit next to pretty women on airplanes; I never meet customers on airplanes; I never have marketing ideas handed to me on a platter." He reclined his seat to match hers. "And now, all three of these things have happened at once." He extended his hand to shake hers. "Thank you, Mrs. Friesen."

"How did you . . .? Oh, I told you my husband is the president of Southern, didn't I." She took his hand and smiled. "You're welcome."

The contract is won

"I wish that I could take credit for coming up with the winning formula, but I can't." Rick was briefing the Pierce staff when he got back to Washington. "It was Mrs. Friesen, the president's wife. She was the one who suggested that we offer to throw in the training program to sweeten the offer. I merely expanded on her idea."

"How come you knew her?" Carl Munsen wanted to know.

"She sat next to me on the flight to Atlanta. She kept asking me questions about our company, why I was going to Atlanta, who I was meeting with, and how I expected to win the program. I told her that I had hit a stone wall. I was trying to beat another company that had offered a price slightly lower than ours, yet I didn't know how to do it. Finally, she suggested that I propose to put on intensive training seminars at no cost. It was only then that I found out who she was."

He knew a stalk when he saw one

The first time he saw Margy since their lunch was in the foyer at church. Rick was certain he was seeing an illusion. It couldn't be her. He told Carol he was going to talk to Mike Neva, one of the deacons and that he would be right back. Mike was standing close to Margy. As he approached Mike, Margy was smiling broadly at him. She said nothing, but with a slight nod of her head, said everything. He turned nervously away from her. *What was she thinking of? Why was she here? How did she know this was my church?* Then he realized that she read it in the newspaper.

"Mike," he said, trying to draw himself away from this fresh development, "what progress are we making with the city on the new building approval?"

Carol broke up his impromptu meeting five minutes later when she told Rick she was going into the sanctuary as the service was going to start soon. He looked for Margy as they walked into the large auditorium, but he didn't see her.

Rick didn't hear much of the church service that day. He worried about Margy's presence at *his* church. He knew it wasn't coincidence. He knew she had something in mind and he worried about it. It was almost as if he was being stalked.

Then he realized that he was, and he went numb.

***

Weekends were designed for relaxation—R & R, as Gil looked at it. But he found little peace or rest at home. Nowadays, he was always tense and walking on egg shells. Susan's nagging was continual. Nothing he did pleased her. Nothing he did satisfied her. He was always in the wrong; always incompetent. This weekend was no different.

He was an early riser and could usually count on two hours of quiet before her day began. Not today.

"Gil!" her shrill scream from the bedroom interrupted his solitude. "Get in here!"

He glanced at his watch. It was only six-thirty. *What is she doing up at this hour?*

He appeared at the bedroom door. "What?" There was disgust in his voice.

"You're rattling that damn newspaper. I can't sleep." Her back was turned to him as she lay on the bed. "What the hell's your problem?"

"Aside from you, I can't imagine what," he snapped in reply.

"What's that supposed to mean?"

"You're the genius in this family. You figure it out." He disappeared from the doorway.

"Close the damn door," she yelled after him.

The temptation to slam it was too great. He pulled the door violently toward him, causing the wall to vibrate with the impact. It was childish, he knew, but he felt better.

He knew that his day was off to a bad start. He went to the hall closet, put on a coat and headed to the garage. Anywhere was better than here. He drove to the office.

PROPHET update

Cigarette smoke clouded the small conference room, permeating the clothing of every participant. Rick, his eyes watering, wondered why so many people in the United States still smoked. Certainly the government's campaign against the practice was powerful. He hated to go home after meetings like this. Carol always had something negative to say about how badly he smelled. Fortunately, the meeting was drawing to a close, and fresh air was not far away. It was just a status meeting to bring the staff up to speed on the PROPHET project. Rick was chairing the meeting in Charlie's absence.

"The whole idea's stupid!"

No matter what Rick said, no matter what his position, Carl Munsen always took the opposite viewpoint. He was an arrogant man, which made absolutely no sense since he was clearly inferior in Rick's opinion.

"Why are we chasing a program that's clearly over our heads? Seems to me that someone's smokin somethin funny." Carl's eyes bore in on Rick's. It was as if there was a competition between the two of them with Carl determined to be the winner. Rick would start to speak; Carl would interrupt. Rick would express a viewpoint; Carl would declare the opposite. Save for Carl's reverence of Gil, there was no reason that would explain this contrary attitude.

And so, when Carl lashed out this time, Rick counter-attacked for the first time. "Carl, I have never figured out what it is between us, but the chemistry has always been bad. I have never said anything that you didn't take issue with." He leaned on his forearms, seeming to draw himself closer across the conference table to his stocky antagonist. "There is no issue here," he said with deliberate enunciation, wanting every word to be understood. "There can be no issue. We have clear, pre-set, and previously agreed upon marching orders. The time for debate is long past. Either you join the parade or you move to the sidelines. But get out of the way."

Carl stared at Rick, glassy eyed, seemingly without breathing. Then, he snapped his neck. Carl lacked a visible neck. He was built somewhat like a bulldog. Three or four times a day, he would turn his head to the left, and then violently twist it to the right to the accompanying cracking sounds of vertebrae popping or whatever went on internally. It was a sickening sound, one that had all the potential of rendering Carl a quadriplegic, and his listeners screaming-mimis. He answered Rick with his favorite cliché. "Who died and left you king?" He settled back in his chair, seeming comfortable with his deathblow retort.

"Anyone else have an input before we close this meeting?" Rick looked around the table.

The meeting attendees shook their heads, gathered up their notes and filed out of the room. Rick glanced at Carl before heading to Gil's office. Rick knew Carl came from lower class Boston neighborhood where the Italians fought with the Irish, and that Carl was half Italian and half

Irish. He was considered a half-breed – not accepted by the Italians and not accepted by the Irish. That must have been where he had learned to scrap and fight so much. In Rick's opinion, Carl was the type of man who climbed over friends and co-workers who were in his way. Apparently, it had worked for him in the Army, except as an enlisted man, he could go only just so far. In the business world, it seemed to be better. He had won a succession of promotions, first to supervisor, and later, to production manager. He fooled the people who trusted him with his ready smiles, solid handshakes, and his solicitous behavior. The bosses bought it. The people he stepped on discovered too late the fallacy of trusting first impressions.

Carl caught Rick just as he was about to knock on Gil's office door. "When can you give me a thorough briefing on the program?" His incessant jiggling of coins in his pocket was yet another irritant that Rick found intolerable.

Rick shook his head. "I can't. It's *need-to-know*. You don't." He turned and entered Gil's office, leaving Carl standing alone in the aisle, jiggling his coins even harder.

Surprise call

Gil reached for his office phone at the first ring, but before he could answer it, the caller hung up. "Changed your mind, didn't you," he muttered at the mouthpiece, waving Rick to take a seat. "I don't need these interruptions. I think I'm going to start having my calls screened."

"It wouldn't hurt, particularly while you are so involved with PROPHET."

"What's up?" Gil asked just as his phone rang again. "Excuse me," he said, picking up the bane of his existence. "Gil Brockton," he said matter-of-factly.

His expression visibly changed as he responded to the person on the other end of the line. "Sure, I remember," he said. "How are you?" His voice lowered as if trying to screen Rick from the conversation. Then he said, "Listen, I'm in a meeting. Is there a number where I can reach you?" He nodded and jotted down a number. "OK, I'll call you in a few minutes."

"Sorry about that," he said to Rick. "That's an old friend I haven't heard from since Honeywell days. She's . . . "he corrected himself, "he's in town and was hoping we could get together." Gil's face was flushed.

"No problem. I only stopped by to update you on that little meeting I just hosted."

"Yeah, sorry I couldn't make it. Anything happen that I should know about?"

"Nope, just the usual. Carl is upset that we are working on this program—feels we are throwing good money after bad. That's about it."

"I need to talk to him so he'll get the big picture. I think he's mostly just bent out of shape because he wasn't a part of the inner circle."

"It would help. I'd really like to get him off my back."

Dinner

As soon as Rick left, Gil picked up his phone to return the earlier call.

"Victoria?" he asked as the connection was made.

"Is this Dr. Brockton?"

"It is, only it's Gil, not Dr. Brockton."

"Gil, it is. I am so pleased that I was able to reach you. I have thought a lot about when we met in Rome. I have hoped that circumstances would bring me to Seattle again so that we might meet again."

"I confess I wasn't so optimistic. I didn't think I would hear from you."

"Well, you have. I have a favor to ask."

"Name it."

"Could we meet after your work today – maybe for a drink or dinner? I need to ask your advice on something. I promise to not keep you out late."

The air seemed to leave Gil's lungs, forced out, no doubt, by the excessive pounding of his heart. "I will have to make some excuses, but I think I can meet you for dinner. Do you have a place in mind?"

"Actually, I do. Are you familiar with the ferry dock in Mukilteo?"

"Sure. Are you thinking of Toni's Restaurant?"

"Yes. I had dinner there last year. I just loved it. And it's enough out of the way that we shouldn't run into people you know."

"Thanks for thinking about me. I don't need to stir up trouble, particularly the kind of trouble that would result from being seen with a beautiful woman. What time do you want me there?"

"How about seven? Is that too late?"

"It's perfect. I'll be there."

Mukilteo never looked so good

Gil tried to hold his speed to the fifty-five miles per hour limit, but it was difficult. He had told Victoria that he would meet her in Toni's cocktail lounge at seven, and because he had missed the turnoff on Interstate Five, he was five minutes late. Hardly a major problem, but Gil liked to be punctual and he hated missing one extra minute with this woman. He pulled into Toni's partially filled parking lot.

As he expected, she was already there, waiting at a window table. Moments after being seated beside her, he ordered a bottle of his favorite Washington wine – Chateau Ste. Michelle's Johannesburg Riesling. When it arrived, he lifted his glass to hers in a toast. "I don't know what prompts this occasion, but I am thankful to the gods for it." They touched glasses and smiled at each other.

She tasted the wine. "It's fragrant," she said. "I was always told Riesling was too sweet, but it isn't." She held the stem of the glass below the bowl and swirled the wine as if to spread its fragrance about the table. "It's fruity, but wonderful."

"I hoped you would like it."

"I do." Her voice was as sweet as the wine and had a similar effect on him.

They settled for *small* talk for the next hour. He was in no rush to learn why she wanted to meet with him; he was just thankful that she did. He mentally reminisced over that night in Rome when the most beautiful woman he had ever met spent the night in his room. It was a once-only fling, he was certain. She was lonely and for some unknown reason chose to use him to fill a void. Beggars couldn't be choosers, he reasoned. He figured he would never hear from Victoria again. So any excuse to meet with her again was good enough.

Finally, during dinner, Victoria got to the point of her invitation. "Gil, I wanted to talk with you to see if you had any suggestions of how I might go about making contact with a small electronics company in the Seattle area who we understand is thinking of selling a product they've developed but now don't want to market."

"I know some of the community thanks to the Washington Electronics Association, so maybe I can point you in the right direction. What company?"

"Airmarc. They have a new 50-watt single sideband radiotelephone that apparently doesn't fit their marketing profile. We think we can help broker it to a company in Virginia."

"I know them. Last year I served on a WEA committee with Jim McEniry who heads up their engineering department. He was excited about that development." He paused, looking quizzically at Victoria. "Are you sure they are looking to dump the unit?"

"That's my understanding."

"Wow, that's a switch. I thought it fit perfectly into their product line."

She smiled and shrugged her shoulders. "Situations change things, I guess." She leaned forward across the table. "Do you think you could introduce me to Mr. McEniry?"

"Sure, assuming he's still at Airmarc. I haven't talked to him in months."

"What sort of man is he?"

"A former Marine pilot. A Major, I think. Even flew some missions for the CIA in Central America. Blunt and to the point. Yet, uncharacteristically with that image, he's a talented pianist with a bent toward jazz. It's hard to picture a take-no-prisoners kind of guy sitting at a piano playing anything but *Chopsticks*."

"He sounds interesting. Do you think he would talk to me?"

"I can't imagine why not. I'll give him a call tomorrow. Will you still be in town?"

"I'll be here." She looked wistfully at him. "And maybe after I talk with him, you and I could get together and I could brief you on what happened."

"You're kidding!" This was beyond all his expectations. "Why would you want to do that?"

"Gil, I like you. I would just like to spend more time with you. Do you think you could get away?"

"You had better believe it. There's nothing for me to go home to."

He thought about Susan. She was probably drunk by now and had no idea that he wasn't home. It would be the same the next night, too. The prospect of spending even more time with this exotic woman was beyond the telling. He didn't want this night to end, but he couldn't wait for the next night to begin.

Then looking deep into her eyes, he muttered almost involuntarily, "I never seem to breathe properly when I'm near you. You literally take my breath away."

"Gil, what a sweet thing to say."

"I'm not the sweet kind of guy."

She smiled, saying nothing except with her eyes, which were fixed on him; then reached across the table and placed her hands on his. "Yes, you are."

The hook was set. And the evening ended all too soon for Gil.

For Victoria, it didn't end until she returned to her hotel and placed a phone call to Hong Kong.

***

The next day dragged by slowly for Gil. He tried to purge his thoughts of Victoria, but he couldn't stop thinking of her, much less remove the pictures of her from his mind—that incredible smile, those deep brown eyes, the perfection of her flawless body.

He got up from his desk and closed the door to his office. He needed a few moments alone before reentering the mainstream of the afternoon's activities. He stared at the phone messages laid neatly on his desk. He picked up one message and put it down without reading it. He walked over to the window, looking out at the trees and their autumn foliage, seeing nothing. *It's as if I'm possessed*, he thought. *I love my wife, or at least I used to. I don't really want things to change at home. What am I doing? Why am I treating Susan this way?* Then he paused. *"Better yet, why is Susan treating me this way?"*

His deep sigh was met with a knock at his door.

"Yes?" Then, knowing it was his secretary, "Come on in, Agnes." The last half of his day was about to resume whether he was ready or not.

***

Rick's phone rang in the middle of his meeting with Gary Wentworth. He glanced past Gil's right-hand man to see where Jinnie was. She always answered his phone when he was in a meeting. She wasn't at her desk.

"Excuse me, Gary. I'd better get this."

He picked up the phone and greeted the caller. "This is Rick Stoner."

"Rick?" Margy's now familiar voice whispered in intimate tones. "Can you talk?"

"As a matter of fact, I'm in a meeting just now." His body stiffened and his jaw squared. "I'll have to call you back." He had no intentions of doing so.

"You've said that before, but you never have."

He grimaced. "Well, believe it or not, I have been busy. Right now, I'm in a meeting going over plans for my trip to Rome tomorrow. I'll have to call when I get back."

"You're going to Rome?"

"Yes," he said impassively. "Look, sorry for cutting this short, but I have to go."

He hung up the phone and sat staring at it for a moment. Margy was beginning to make him nervous. There was no longer any question. Margy was pursuing him.

He returned his attention to the matter at hand. "Have you been to Rome?" he asked.

"I have never been to Europe, so no, I have never been to Rome."

"I wish that we had time for you to sightsee. It is the most incredible city I have ever visited. You can't turn a corner without running into antiquity. There are ruins and historical sites everywhere."

"Yeah, I've heard." There was a look of disappointment on his face.

"Well, cheer up a little. I've booked us at a hotel in downtown, even though our meetings will be out at the airport. This will allow us to tour a little the day we arrive and during the evenings. So you'll get to see some of the sights."

Rick sees a sight in Rome

Alitalia had a crisis with their altimeter; one that couldn't be resolved over the phone. Hump Marryatt, Altimeter Sales Manager, was visiting Lockheed-Georgia, so Rick was elected. He had a whole day to prepare for the trip. Because the discussions were to be technical, he brought Gary Wentworth with him to shore up anything he might say that was off target. Gary had backed up Gil for several years, seemingly content with his role as Deputy Engineering Manager. Rick liked Gary and was pleased at this opportunity to know him better. The two of them boarded the evening British Airways' over-the-pole flight to London's Heathrow

Airport with a two hour layover before heading on to Leonardo da Vinci Airport in Rome.

Because of late departure of their BA flight from London, they didn't arrive in Rome until mid-afternoon. That was fine with the two of them since there was nothing planned for that day other than to transition through the nine-hour time change.

The airport yielded its usual cacophony of voices—Swedish, or was it Danish or maybe Norwegian, French, German, and the inescapable Italian, occasionally English, and some tongues Rick couldn't identify. Based on their garb, some were African, but what nationality he didn't have a clue. The same held true for the Arabs. They could have been Saudis, Jordanians, or whatever.

Once in town and settled in their hotel, the Grand Hotel Hermitage, they headed out toward the nearby Tiber River to stretch their legs and to kill time until dinner. Carlo Giacametti had made the arrangements for this hotel because it was in the elegant Parioli quarter of Rome, one of the quietest areas of the city, not far from the city center, and close to his apartment.

As they walked, Rick found himself thinking about his lunch with Margy, seeing her again at church, and then her phone call the day before. He was worried. Clearly, she was after him. As much as he condemned himself for thinking any thoughts, they kept invading his mind. He was flattered by the attention even as it had become the bane of his life. Something F. Scott Fitzgerald wrote in a short story came to his mind. It said, in effect, that there are many kinds of love in the world, but never the same love twice. He had thought about that a lot and concluded that Fitzgerald was right. When he and Margy married as teenagers, it was puppy love, fueled by teenage passion. But that was then. This was now. He was not a puppy any more.

Rick suddenly caught his breath. More correctly, he stopped breathing. There, about twenty feet ahead of them, was Margy. She was walking with another woman along the shop-lined pedestrian street leading away from the Spanish Steps, in the same direction as he and Gary were heading. Rick's heart raced. Without explaining to Gary why, he picked up the pace to narrow the gap. He didn't want to shout out her name on the off-chance that it wasn't her. But he was certain it was. The same walk. The same great body. The same hair and shape of head. He thought he heard her laugh.

What is she doing here? Rick and Gary were within three feet of the two women. Rick's heart was pounding. She was stalking him. He reached out and touched *Margy's* arm. She turned and looked at him.

"I'm sorry, Ma'am," Rick said, stunned. "I thought that you were a friend of mine from Seattle." He was embarrassed. He was devastated.

She was Italian . . . and protested his familiarity with a stream of words he didn't understand. "Arresto o io denominerà la polizia." She looked furious and walked off angrily at a fast pace, waving her arms and shouting, "Americani! Chi li pensano sono?"

I have got to get a hold of myself, Rick thought, *before the Devil overwhelms me.* "Come on. Let's get out of here," he said urgently.

"What was that all about?" Gary asked.

Rick shrugged his shoulders. "It was weird. I honestly thought that woman was a friend of mine from Seattle."

"Lucky thing she only yelled at you. For a minute, I thought she was going to pop you one, or call a cop."

"I did too. I heard the word, *polizia,* and that was enough to scare me. And the way she was waving her arm, I was ready to jump behind you at the first sign of a swing."

Nothing as traumatic occurred during the sessions with Alitalia and within two days, the problem was solved and Rick and Gary were on their way back to Seattle.

But Rick's problem persisted, and he was haunted with the thought.

A concern shared

How long have Art Cassidy and I been friends, Rick wondered? *Probably fourteen years.* They'd started out as hotshot design engineers together at TELCOM. Rick and Carol used to spend many hours with Art and Becky back in those days. Hardly a weekend passed when they weren't doing something together. It was an unusual bond. The two couples used to talk about it a lot. "Of all men and women, we're the most to be envied," Becky used to boast. And it was true. Their relationship was special. Then something happened to Becky. Her personality changed drastically and suddenly. Nothing ever seemed right to her. She complained about everything. She always seemed angry. And it was unpleasant to be around her. It was as if she were chemically unbalanced. Rick and Carol gradually found excuses against spending time with her—

business conflicts, church activities. And so, the friendship was reduced to occasional lunches between Rick and Art.

Art said that he regarded Rick as a comic relief and spirit lifter. They enjoyed each other's company. Rick called Art, "Hip-Along Cassidy" because of an old injury that had impaired his walk. They were a pair of good buddies. For men, who didn't often form close friendships, their relationship was special.

Rick had called Art, asking that they meet for lunch at the nearby Azteca, his favorite Mexican restaurant. He asked Art to be punctual because he was under a time crunch. He asked because it was as if Art's internal clock was unalterably set fifteen minutes behind everyone else's. "I'm not as concerned with time, and even though you consider punctuality as thoughtful consideration of others," Art told Rick one time, "I find it a needless bother." Yet they showed up at the restaurant almost simultaneously, much to Rick's surprise.

They had no sooner been seated then Rick poured his heart out. "Art, I've got to tell someone. I'm in trouble."

"What kind of trouble?"

"Female."

"No way. Not you. You're the original straight-arrow."

"The shaft broke."

"What happened?"

"I've never told you this, but I was married before Carol. It was a teenage thing, filled with hormones run amuck. She was beautiful and she got pregnant, thanks to me. So we got married. I dropped out of college. Then, in her fourth month, she had a miscarriage. The thing that brought us together, separated us. We were divorced within a year. I didn't see her again . . . until three months ago. She called me at work, told me that she and her family were moving here from Washington, D.C., and wanted to see me for old time's sake. We met for lunch the next day.

"Art, she looked incredible. I mean, her face and figure turned heads at the restaurant; male and female. If I had been available or on the hunt, she would have been my target."

"So, what happened?"

"She bought a home on Mercer Island, flew back east to settle things there, and then moved here two months ago. Her husband flies 747s for InterContinental . . ."

"No, I mean why are you in trouble?"

"She keeps calling. And now she's attending our church. I think I'm being stalked."

"Have you given her any encouragement?"

"Not in the slightest; well, I didn't discourage her when we had lunch. But she wasn't coming after me then. It was just a lunch."

"What are you going to do about it now that it's more than just a lunch?"

"I haven't a clue. I don't know what to do. Suggestions?"

"Well, for openers, does Carol know about this?"

Rick shook his head and gave Art a look as if he was crazy. "No way."

"Well, I think you should tell her. If you don't and she somehow finds out, it will look like you were keeping it a secret. Then the next place her mind will jump is to wondering why it was a secret." Art leaned across the table to Rick. "You don't want that to happen. Women think funny; different than men. Women have an uncanny sense about them. They know how to deal with other women. Men don't have a clue. Right about now I'd say Carol is your best weapon to counteract this stalker, as you call her."

"I don't know if I have the guts to tell her. What if she thinks the wrong thing?"

"What if she does? She's definitely going to think the wrong thing if she finds out on her own. Your argument has to be that you have nothing to hide and that you need her help. After she has thought about it for a little while, she will see that your argument makes sense."

Art's Chicken Fajitas and Rick's Chile Colorado arrived just in time for Rick to eat and do some serious thinking. Between two mouthfuls he said, "I'll go back to the office and practice my speech. When I tell her, I want to be ready."

"Good plan. Vince Lombardi was right: the best defense is a good offense."

"Did he say that? I thought it was the other way around."

"It was. I was just trying to make a point."

"Point made."

Chapter 8

North to Alaska
And Turn Left

It was a smooth flight most of the way. If it hadn't been for a forty-minute late departure, Rick would have classified it as nearly perfect.

Clouds covered the North Pacific except for a brief respite as they passed over Anchorage. The mountains below were rugged and covered with snow. The ice-free water along the coastline was the only thing that let Rick realize that he was flying over Alaska and not Greenland. It was a sight, and the man in the window seat pressed himself back so Rick could take a few pictures.

Hours later, the Captain announced that they were one hundred miles from Tokyo, the temperature was sixty-five degrees, and the skies were partly cloudy. That suited Rick just fine. When he left Seattle, it was forty-seven degrees and raining.

The landing was as smooth as the flight. "My compliments to the captain," Rick said to no one in particular. He listened without interest as the hostess welcomed everyone to Tokyo where the local time was four thirty seven in the afternoon, April tenth. Don't forget, it's tomorrow here," she observed. Then she went on, "On behalf of Captain James Guerber and his entire crew, we want to thank you for flying the golden skies of InterContinental Air Lines. Rick sat still and tried to reconstruct what she had just said. "Captain James Guerber?" Had he heard correctly? Margy's husband?

Rick had never seen Jim Guerber. He decided now was as good a time as any. He wanted to size this man up. So he was purposefully slow in exiting the aircraft. Only a few stragglers were left when he made his way down the aisle. The Captain was leaning against a seat in the First Class section, acknowledging the passengers as they left and joking with the crew. He was Rick's height but maybe thirty-five pounds heavier, with a substantial middle-age pouch. He probably isn't as old as he looks, Rick thought, but that excess weight isn't doing him any favors.

"Captain Guerber?" Rick asked with uncertainty.

"Yes." The pilot moved away from his resting-place and toward the man who was addressing him.

"I wasn't sure I understood your name correctly when I heard it. I just wanted to say, "Nice landing. After ten hours in the air, you showed a mighty steady hand." Rick watched the man, whose wife has once been his, smile.

"Well, thanks," he gestured toward the cockpit. "Most of the credit goes to a triply-redundant autopilot, and a phenomenal performing onboard computer system. For nine of the ten hours we were in the air, I did precious little." Then, wishing to shift the conversation away from himself, he asked: "Do you travel with us on this run frequently?"

Rick started to get nervous. What he did not want was a conversation that led toward an exchange of names, yet this one was getting personal fast. "Oh, I come over here about every three months. Most of my flying is to Europe." Then moving his briefcase to his left hand and extending his right toward Jim Guerber, "Well, Captain, I've got people meeting me, and I've got to go find out what your ground crew has done with my luggage. Thanks again for a great flight." They shook hands and Rick made a hasty exit from the aircraft. No one was meeting Rick. He was in transit. But the excuse got him away.

As he headed toward the transit lounge, he marveled that Jim Guerber was the pilot on *this* flight. Was it coincidence or was God talking to him? He figured he would never know. Meanwhile, he had two hours to kill until his flight for Hong Kong was scheduled to depart. Sleepy or not, he had to keep going. Browsing through the duty-free shops would help.

Hong Kong

The ride from Hong Kong's Kai Tak airport to the Sheraton Hotel took longer than it should have for this time of night. There were taxis everywhere, filling the streets. He was disappointed when Jinnie was unable to get him a room at the Peninsula. She joked that she could get him a room on either side of the Peninsula . . . at the Sheraton or the YMCA. He opted for the former. There was a better chance that he wouldn't have to share a room. He liked the location on Salisbury Road because it was an easy morning walk to the Star Ferry, on which he could enjoy a fifteen-minute water ride across the harbor to the Central District on Hong Kong Island. Pierce's Asian representative, Queensway Engineering, was a ten-minute walk up the hill to the Hilton Hotel.

***

The next morning, Rick bought his ticket and boarded the Star. He enjoyed sitting in the second class section of the ferry because of its closeness to the water and the commotion of the Chinese throngs. He would hear them protesting his presence. "Why does this foreigner insult us? Look how he is dressed. He is here to look down upon us." But he would tune out his antagonists and concentrate, instead, on the contrasts of old and new spectacles that lay across the water. This morning, before the imposing backdrop of banks and company buildings, junks passed rapidly along the Pearl River bringing goods into the city. Ahead, a new skyscraper was rising. Its architecture was modern, even futuristic, but bamboo was still used for the scaffolding. More contrasts of old and new. For Rick, this interlude always ended too soon. But he was here on business, not as a tourist. If he wanted a pleasure boat ride, he would go to Aberdeen. The idea of a cruise at sunset appealed to him. *Perhaps, if I have time tonight. No, I can't.* He remembered his dinner appointment with Brian Bergson that would prevent this.

As he walked up the ramp from the boat, a Chinese man muttered: "Bruddy Hairo!" Rick wondered if this was an ancient Chinese incantation. He said it over and over in his mind, puzzling over its meaning. *Bruddy Hairo, Bruddy Hairo*. It defied his knowledge of Chinese. When he reached the street, he laughed as he realized what the man had been saying. It was his version of modern English. *Bloody Hell*. It was his protest to a Caucasian who didn't know his place.

Hong Kong Island

Hong Kong. A British Crown Colony, on the coast of China's southern province of Canton. British rule, English spoken, Chinese through and through. Rick walked away from the ferry. It was lunchtime and he was hungry. He had time for a meal on the street before his meeting. He stopped at a crowded stand, and in Cantonese, the dialect of Hong Kong, ordered a small ravioli-like pocket of pasta that contained a meat he couldn't identify, and some tea. "Shay Shay," he said to the vendor who wondered at the European's command of the language.

He moved to a nearby bench and consumed his meal. Although Chinese was his second language, he hadn't practiced his skill in some time. As he had told his Contracts Manager when they were in Hong Kong earlier in the year, he found it to be an enormous secret weapon when he eavesdropped on conversations, particularly when he would barter with a shopkeeper over the price of a camera or silk pajamas for his wife. "Aiee, you deprive my children of their food!" (Translation: "This will be my best sale of the day.") He would leave the merchant with rice for his family, but never roast duck. There were times when his knowledge was useful in business too, although not as much as on the street.

Dinner delicacy

A woman's scream pierced the din of the crowded restaurant, followed by hysterical sobbing, the excited shouting of a man speaking French, and a waiter speaking Chinese. Rick listened intently, but it was hard to follow. The commotion continued for a full five minutes before an elderly European couple slowly stood and the man, with his arm around the woman's shoulders, moved slowly out of the restaurant. The woman's sobs could still be heard after they had left the room. Gradually, the restaurant returned to its normal noise level. A few minutes later, Rick asked his waiter in Chinese what the problem was. His dinner companion Brian Bergson, a friend who worked for Honeywell and just happened to be in Hong Kong at the same time, waited for the translation.

After the waiter left, Rick revealed an incredible story. "It seems that couple was from Paris," he reported. "They brought their poodle puppy with them to the restaurant. I guess bringing one's dog to a restaurant is *de rigueur* in Paris." Rick shook his head. "Anyway, they suggested to the maitre de in their best pidgin English that he arrange to give their leashed pet a meal while they ate. A waiter took the dog back to the kitchen. Several courses later, the pièce de résistance of their banquet arrived. When the lid of the serving dish was lifted, there was their pet, suitably steamed, sauced and garnished. The rest of the story you know."

Brian gasped. "That's awful!" How could something like this happen?"

"You've got to understand that the Chinese are ecstatic about the taste of young dog meat. The maitre de thought he was complying with their request."

***

The next day, Rick met with the Pierce representative in their Kowloon branch office. He had been asked to brief others on the staff about company engineering projects as well as update them on recent sales activities with Cathay Pacific and Taiwan's China Airlines. There wasn't much sales effort that could be expended by Queensway Engineering since the primary activities came from the Pierce home office. On the other hand, airline spares represented a good portion of the total sales from these airlines and in this area, the local people needed to be on top of each situation. This was where they earned their commissions.

As he got on the elevator, he glanced at the signboard on the opposite wall that listed the building's principal occupants. The name Shek International stood out. In turn, this made him recall the beautiful Victoria Li and her presumed liaison with Gil in Rome. *I wonder if he ever saw her again,* Rick wondered. *Probably not*, he concluded. It wasn't a match made in heaven.

***

Later that afternoon, Rick flew to Kuala Lumpur for a meeting the following day with Malaysia Air. Then it was on to Singapore for two days of meetings with Singapore Airlines before returning to Seattle. The travel was beginning to weigh heavy on Rick. He needed to be home with Carol and Trey. He needed to be working on the marketing of PROPHET. He needed to be anywhere but on an airplane or in an airline terminal.

Chapter 9

A Drunken Brawl

There is nothing like the support of a good woman. Conversely, there is little worse than the strife of a contentious spouse. Susan had ridiculed Gil's technical abilities for months. She used to be his succor, his strength, and his encourager. Now, he couldn't remember the last time she had praised him or even showed the least bit of interest in his work. Once, he could bounce ideas off her and although she lacked the technical expertise, she was able to offer logical thoughts and reasoning. Now, he avoided discussions with her on most topics. She wasn't the most reliable conversationalist after seven o'clock in the evening; or five o'clock in the afternoon, for that matter.

That left Gil with no counselor, and right now, he was desperate for help. The PROPHET design was not going well. More precisely, the systems integration was not going well, and systems integration was solely Gil's responsibility. He had staked out that territory as his at the beginning of the project. He had made certain that full credit for the design would be his. He hadn't counted upon failure. He hadn't foreseen obstacles of this magnitude. But now that they were upon him, his paranoid feeling of vulnerability precluded consultation with anyone else. He would lose all credibility with his peers. He probably would lose his job. He became a recluse, sheltered by his secretary either in his office or behind the closed door of the small office in the Engineering Lab that he had proclaimed his private think tank. "Gil's finalizing the design. He's not to be disturbed." He heard those words on the other side of the door more than once. But he was bluffing. And he was frightened.

Longing for things now past

Gil longed for the days now past when he could go home to the comfort and joy of being with his wife, just spending a quiet evening together. They used to read biographies. They would purchase two copies and read them simultaneously, then discuss their thoughts about what they had just read before going to bed. It was a challenging time because even though they read the same words, they didn't always form the same conclusions. "How can you sit there and tell me you thought that he didn't have ulterior motives," she would chide him. "It was obvious the way he reacted."

"Well, I didn't see it that way," he would differ with her. "You women always seem to think there's some hidden agenda whenever a guy acts in a way that fails to meet your criterion for male behavior. You seem to think you flawlessly understand the male psyche—and you don't. Sometimes you're wrong, and this is one of those times."

Their sporting debates every now and then would extend past bedtime, with neither convincing the other but both feeling victorious. It was exhilarating and at the same time beneficial because it allowed Gil to leave his work-related problems at work. He would always return to work the next day rejuvenated and ready for new challenges.

But those days were gone. Susan had changed.

Battle over booze

"You've had enough, Susan," Gil spoke through clenched teeth with unusual force, "and so have I!" They stared coldly at each other.

Susan held her glass motionless, resting against her lower lip. She couldn't believe that her timid husband had spoken to her that way. She studied the face that scowled at her. She hesitated, and then deliberately raised the bottom of her glass slowly, watching Gil's expression as the last of the bourbon drained into her mouth. The warmth that the liquid spread as she swallowed was the best satisfaction of all. *To hell with Gil Brockton and his new found courage*, she thought. *This is all I need. This is all I've ever needed.* Her tongue licked a drop that clung to the rim of the glass. She leaned forward and set the glass down on the coffee table, never taking her eyes off him.

"To hell with you, Gil," she hissed the words passed her teeth. "To hell with you and your disapproval! If you showed me the least bit of attention, if you spent time at home, if you were more of a husband, I might not need this." She gestured abruptly, hitting the glass by accident, sending it careening across the table and onto the carpet. A brief look of embarrassment flickered in her eyes, replaced quickly by anger. "Don't think that means I'm drunk," she sneered. "I just brought the glass down to your level so you could get me another drink."

Gil turned and walked out of the room. "No ice, lover," her voice trailed behind him. As he mounted the stairs to the bedroom, two at a time, she shouted one more time. "Make it a double." Then he heard her laugh.

It was quiet in the bedroom once the door was closed. If she was still talking, still mocking, he couldn't hear, and that suited Gil just fine.

Her drinking was constant now. He almost never saw her without a drink in her hand. And as each day progressed, as the alcohol poisoned her mind, she became an intolerable drunk, a real bitch. Was it her drunkenness that kept him away from home, or was it his work habits that drove her to drink? He sat on the edge of the bed staring into the darkness outside the window. "Damn!" His loud exclamation startled even him. "My life is out of control. It's all screwed up!"

He leaned forward, head in hands, and began to sob.

Slow pitch

"Rick, got a minute?" Hump Marryatt called after his boss.

"Sure, what's up?" Rick turned toward his Altimeter Product Manager.

"This isn't work related, but a few of us were wondering if we could talk you into joining our slow pitch team. Bill Felt said that you were a pretty good shortstop in high school."

"Yeah, but that was high school. I'm a tad bit older now." Rick chuckled. "Besides, I was never in your league. Weren't you the starting catcher at Grambling?"

"Sure, but Grambling was just a small black college in Louisiana."

"Don't give me that, Marryatt. Your football and baseball teams played as good as the best colleges in the country."

"Well, we still need a shortstop and someone said you were good."

"Who is this anonymous person?"

"I don't remember, but he seemed to have the straight scoop."

"Did he? Well did he also tell you that I am really overloaded with work?"

"We all are. That's why playing slow pitch makes sense. It helps us let off steam and stress. And, here is the clincher, it lets us beat up on folks like Sundstrand, Honeywell and Boeing. They're all in the same division with us. They figure that since we're little, we are a soft touch."

"How have you done so far?"

"We've only played one game. Beat the tar out of Boeing's Renton group."

"Well, let me think about it. Since it's after hours, it affects my home life. So Carol has to be in on it."

Hate runs deep

"I hate the man," Carl's face was turning crimson. "I can't tell you why. Maybe it's his smugness or his cocksure attitude." He flailed his arms a little, making a hopeless gesture. "Maybe it's the way he says things, or that he is a goody-goody Christian. Maybe it's the fact that he's Chaalie's friend."

"Take it easy, Carl. You're going to burst a blood vessel." Gary Wentworth obviously was trying to be a calming agent. "This isn't getting you anywhere."

"Not right now, maybe, but I'm sure as hell gonna torment the life out of him until he can't take it anymore. He's gonna hate the sight of me."

"Well, on that score, I think you're close to achieving your goal. You know, I can't stop you, but if it were me, I sure would take it easy on Rick. Like you said, he's Charlie's friend. Crossing swords with Charlie wouldn't be the smartest thing you have ever done."

"I don't plan on crossing any swords with Chaalie. But I'm gonna find some way to discredit Stoner. Maybe he's having an affair. I haven't forgotten about that lunch he had at the Space Needle. Then it will be Chaalie who cans him all on his own. I won't be any paat of it."

Wentworth shook his head. "Carl, I'm standing clear of this one. When you go down, I don't want to be anywhere near you." He looked at Munsen with a perplexed expression.

"Don't worry about it. I'm a survivor. Ain't no one going down but Stoner."

Chapter 10

Warning Signs

Carol wasn't growing. Trey was. Initially, when both boys were infants, they talked, well she talked; and they walked, well she walked; and they filled uncountable pails of diapers, and spewed out immeasurable amounts of cereal and bananas and milk. Then they ran, they played, and went through countless shoes, socks, pants, and Band-Aids®. She loved them with enormous joy and faced their years of growth with happiness for each new experience. The thousands of hours, hundreds of weeks, scores of months that she had devoted to her husband had been replaced by the all-day, everyday needs of her children.

And then it all began to slip away. Slowly, at first.

The school day was the initial shock. Pleasant to begin with—the abrupt cessation of the high-pitched, demanding voices. The silence, the peace; the wonderful first aloneness. Then the silence, the peace and the aloneness took their toll. She missed the challenges of dealing with five and six year olds. She missed the noise and activity that they produced.

Rick was more often away than at home; it was necessary, she understood that, too. But the combination of things – the kids in school and Rick out of town—left her without a functioning world of her own.

Then she climbed aboard a roller coaster the day Jeff died.

***

Carol knew better. It was late. She was tired and so was Rick. When she got tired, she knew she became cranky, and when he got tired, she knew he became defensive. Still, she chose this time to let him know that things weren't perfect in her world; that she was weary of his late hours; that she needed his help with Trey; that she longed for the companionship of her husband. It started off low-key enough.

"Hi, Hon." The front door closing emphasized his return home. "Sorry I'm late." He walked into the living room where Carol was sitting. He reached down to pet Roxanne who had gotten up to greet him.

"You've been sorry a lot, recently," was her rejoinder as she glanced up from her book, then resumed her reading as if uninterested in his return home.

"What's that supposed to mean?" Rick was on guard. From the kitchen came the dwindling smell of a meal prepared earlier, now cold, undoubtedly.

She put her book in her lap. "It's supposed to mean that you haven't been around here much. And it's supposed to mean that I don't understand why suddenly your work is more important than your family. And it's supposed to mean that I'm tired of us living two separate lives, you exclusively with adults, and me exclusively with our son."

"I don't understand what you're telling me," Rick said. He apparently decided it was best to move cautiously.

"You're not really that slow at work, are you?" Carol's pent-up emotions seethed through. "You are perceptive in business matters, aren't you?" The battle line had been drawn.

"Carol, you know this hasn't been a particularly fun day, not that it sounds like you give two hoots." He set his briefcase down on the edge of their new Oriental rug, but continued standing. "Besides, why am I suddenly a bad guy because I'm working hard? I haven't heard you complain about the benefits it brings!" Confrontation was not his specialty.

But Carol was not to be denied. Rick wasn't hearing her and it was time that he did. "Back before you were so important; when you were home every night in time for dinner," she paused and glanced toward the kitchen, "when you had time for your son and for me; when we didn't have all these benefits that you think are so wonderful; we were happy. We had fun together. We did things together." She stared toward the picture window and the dark nothingness beyond. Her eyes became red and tears spilled down her cheeks. "Now, there's no tenderness; no caring; no time. Trey and I are alone. You sleep here. But you no longer live here." Her eyes turned in despair toward him.

Rick was angry, yet frightened by the words that spoke of his insensitivity to her. He could never handle her tears, and just now, her tears were flowing. He was uncertain what to say next. He started to move toward her, then, changing his mind, reached instead for his briefcase and abruptly left the room, his heals clicking emphatically across the hardwood floor.

As he undressed for bed, he listened to her crying downstairs. He so wanted to hold her in his arms and comfort her, but he didn't want to yield in their argument. He knew she was wrong and was certain that if he did seek to appease her, there would be changes in his life that he wasn't ready to make. His resolve stiffened. This was something that Carol would have to work out for herself.

When the clock radio turned on the next morning, Rick realized that Carol hadn't been in bed all night. On his way to the bathroom for his morning brushing, shaving, bathing routine, he toured the house looking for her. He found her in the living room, asleep in the chair where he'd left her seven hours earlier. He figured she was still upset with him and decided not to start the day where he'd left off the previous night. He withdrew to begin his morning ritual. He couldn't afford to be late to work.

As he shaved, he stared at his reflection in the bathroom mirror. He was scared. His relationship with his wife and his son were at risk. Carol was his wife. She was his lover. Until as recently as last night, she had been his friend; his best friend. How much of their problem was his fault? None of it, he reasoned. But he knew better. Things had been different since Jeff had died. He had been different as a result.

He found Carol in the kitchen. He walked up and drew her into his arms. She started to speak, but he silenced her, placing a finger against her lips. "I need a hug," he said. "I desperately need a hug." They embraced, albeit tentatively, in silence. "I am so, so sorry. I don't know what's going on in my head. I don't know why I am treating you this way. You have done nothing to deserve it." He drew her closer, her stiff body slowly softening.

After a while, he said, "I've been a fool. Still love me?"

She chuckled in his ear. "Yes."

"A little or a lot?"

"I'm thinking."

***

Rick spread his papers in front of him on the conference table. He wondered why it was that he was always the first to arrive. Was he the only one who was punctual? Maybe he was the only one who was a clock-watcher. In any event, he was a little discouraged that his time was continually being wasted because of the tardiness of others. He leaned back in the chair and waited. Gil Brockton's head suddenly appeared in the open doorway. Missing was his stocky body. Rick amused himself by wondering what could have happened to it.

"Rick, are we meeting in here? I thought we were going to use the boss' conference room."

"Jinnie told me it had been moved in here, and if anyone has the straight scoop, my secretary's sure to be the one."

"Right! I'll go get my stuff out of Charlie's conference room and be right back." Gil's bodiless head disappeared.

Charlie Strang walked into the room and stood at the end of the conference table. "Rick, would you run this meeting for me? Tell the others something has come up that has higher priority. And that I doubt I'll be done before you are. If I am, I'll come in for the tail-end."

Rick nodded his assent. "Anything special you want brought up at the meeting?" He looked at his fifty nine-year old boss. He's a performer, he thought. Tough, hard-driven, shrewd, brilliant strategist, refreshingly honest and fair. Those who were jealous of his achievements credited them to his rugged good looks, athletic build and charming personality. Never mind his other credentials. He got where he was going through luck and timing. That's what they wanted to believe and that's what they espoused.

"Just keep the meeting on track, and don't let Engineering slide the schedule again."

"Thanks a bunch!" Rick laughed. "Any other dreams you want dealt with?"

Charlie just smiled and left the room, passing Gil as he reentered with Carl Munsen and Frank Morrow, Assistant Controller. As they were taking places around the table along with the others, Carl asked, "Where's Chaalie headed? Isn't he gonna be in he-a?"

"Nope. He said something about an item of higher priority and that he'd make the tail-end of this one if he could."

Hump Marryatt leaned over to Rick and whispered, "What the hell is that smell?"

Rick motioned toward Carl with his head.

"Carl?" Hump whispered even quieter.

"Yup. Why do you think no one wants to sit next to him?"

"I thought it was his sparkling personality. What's the story?"

"About a month ago, he became convinced that showering reduced his resistance to disease – something about opening his pores to invasion. At least, that's the way I understand it."

"Is that the reason he shaved his head?"

"I guess so. He must have thought his hair harbored germs."

"Well someone has got to tell him to bathe. This is awful."

"This sounds like a perfect assignment for you."

"In a pig's eye. This calls for top management intervention." He looked squarely at Rick who sidestepped the suggestion by starting the meeting.

Rick leaned forward. "OK, guys, let's get this going. Charlie can't be here and told me that I was to run the meeting . . . and that I was not to allow Engineering to make another time overrun on this project."

Gil looked up from the papers he was laying out on the table and studied Rick carefully to see if a joke was hidden in the words. Seeing none, he returned to his paper shuffling, although this time he appeared to be looking for one document in particular. Finding it, he placed it on top of his stack. "Now's as good a time as any to talk about schedules," he said. "Rick has revealed the hope. I am about to reveal the real world, and play the heavy in the process."

He looked around the room to make certain everyone was paying attention. He needn't have bothered. They were. He continued: "We have run into problems that no one anticipated as little as a week ago. If you asked me then, and you did, I would have said that our troubles were behind us, and that we needed only four more weeks before turning the project over to Production Engineering. But a lot has happened in a week, or more properly perhaps I should say, a lot hasn't happened in a week."

Genuine concern was on everyone's face. Every delay was affecting Pierce's ability to meet the schedule laid down by McDonnell Douglas. Worse than that, it could mean that someone else would end up with the business. Gil was not responding well to the pressure.

"I'll be damned if I'll accept your acid looks! We're busting our butts, maxing out on overtime!" He looked with anger at each man. "Nobody's deliberately trying to screw things up! We're doing things no one's done before. There's no blazed trail for us to follow, you know."

"Take it easy, Gil," Carl Munsen uncharacteristically tried to play peacemaker. "Nobody's accusing you or any one of screwing up. What you're sensing is fear that if this project suffers any more delays, everything may be down the tubes! And since none of us can help you out in Engineering, all we can do is stand on the sidelines." There was a jiggling of coins. Munsen was at it again, even sitting down.

"If you're going to stand on the sidelines, why don't you try playing cheerleader instead of critic," Gil snapped. His eyes held no one's. He glared instead at his clenched fist.

Only Rick knew that there was more to Gil's tirade than just frustration. Things must be worse at home, he thought.

Trouble identified

Rick knocked on Gil's office door to announce his arrival and walked in. Gil had his back to the door, hunched over his work desk. He glanced up at the interruption. "Your timing is crummy, Rick. I really don't have time right now."

"I know you don't. That's why I'm here."

Gil swiveled his chair to face Rick. "You're here because I don't have time to talk to you?" He shook his head. "That makes absolutely no sense."

"I'm here, Gil, because you seem to have no time for anything. I sense that you are at the end of your rope, and although I know we're not the best of friends, I feel we made good headway when we were in Rome, and I want to know if you want someone to talk to." He sat in the sofa by the window. "I make a pretty good sounding board."

Gil studied Rick contemplatively as if searching for some evil intent. The furrowed brow and the pursed lips showed that he was deep in thought. He ran his forefinger across his protruding bottom lip in further reflection. He began slowly. "To extend your metaphor, there are two ropes dangling in front of me, and I am at the end of both. And no, we're not the best of friends, but I learned to trust you when we were in Europe. Right now, I need someone I can trust." His tongue replaced his finger tracing his bottom lip. His contemplation continued and silence resumed.

"OK," Gil finally said. "Here goes. My marriage is disintegrating. My wife has become an alcoholic and is making my life a complete hell. I don't want to go home at night, but I do, and when I get there, I want to run away. We do nothing but argue and fight – to the point of almost being physical. She screams at me. She hurls insults; castigates my manhood. I yell back, hurl insults and rebuke her drinking."

"Gil, I . . ."

"There's more." Gil held up his hand in a stopping motion. "Things aren't going much better here, either. Maybe my home life is the cause. I would like to think that was my excuse, but I don't know that it is.

"What do you mean?"

"You remember that stone wall on PROPHET's altimeter design that I hit just before we went to Rome? Well, the altimeter still fails to communicate with the rest of the system. It doesn't make sense, but there is a snag somewhere that's blocking transfer of information."

"Dirk Bogert, Tom Mathis, and Pat Frankel haven't been able to shed light on it?"

"Not yet. They're as baffled as me. We've kept it to ourselves because we haven't wanted to set off alarms without cause. We remain convinced that we will figure it out, but in the meantime, it is driving us nuts.

"And now, on top of this, we have the problem with the McDonnell Douglas project."

"It's time to bring in Charlie." Rick stood up. "There's a lot of his money tied into this. One more good mind working the problem is certain to help."

Gil fell silent once again, seeming to ponder this latest suggestion. He sighed and said, "I have wanted to avoid this, but you're right. Charlie needs to be told. Bearing this burden is almost more than I can handle, particularly with my other problem."

"And speaking of that other problem," Rick said, "would you and Susan be willing to go to counseling?"

"Ha! That will be the day. Susan doesn't have a problem, she says, except with me."

"That's precisely the reason people go to counseling."

"In her state, she isn't to be reasoned with, I'm afraid. She was fine before she started drinking. First she has to stop the booze."

"Can you cut off her supply?"

"I've thought about it, but she can still go to the store and get more – or even have it delivered."

"So, you'll have to go on a witch hunt every night."

"Thanks, Rick. That's at least a start.

"Now, let's go see Charlie."

***

"What's up, guys?" Charlie looked up from his desk as Gil and Rick walked into his office. "You look a little worse for wear."

Rick looked at Gil who seemed reluctant to respond. "We've got a problem on PROPHET," Rick said. "Gil and I were just talking about it and figured we'd better bring you in." He decided to leave the McDonnell Douglas project alone for the moment.

"What sort of problem?"

Gil was no stranger to cold sweat. This was not the first time he had been over his head on an engineering project. In the past, he had been able to fall back on others who lifted his burden. Not this time. It was time to confess. "The altimeter design has bogged down," he said. My circuits aren't interfacing with each other. The altimeter is transmitting but it isn't receiving." He paused and expelled air in an attempt to relieve his internal pressure.

"Worse, the altimeter is not interfacing with the overall terrain avoidance system. The forward-looking radar and radar altimeter algorithms, though loosely coupled, have to operate over the terrain that the lateral algorithm has selected. All the while, the lateral algorithm has to consider the vertical dimension so that it doesn't generate flight paths that the aircraft is unable to negotiate. This isn't happening. I don't know where I've screwed up."

"Are you working the problem alone?"

"Nope. Rick urged me to bring in Dirk, Tom and Pat. They've been on it for a week. They're baffled too."

"That was not the answer I was hoping for."

Rick chimed in. "Don't call this a brainstorm, because I don't know that it is. What if we go have a sit-down with Herman Truttman at Eiler Labs? The guy is a genius, just like Gil. Maybe the two of them can figure this out. After all, at this point, Eiler has as much a vested interest as we do."

Both men stared at Rick, then Charlie said, "Set it up. The sooner the better. If he can only do it over the weekend, Gil, I want you in Massachusetts at his convenience."

"I'll go call him right now," Gil said as he headed out the door. He sounded almost giddy.

Trouble confronted

Gil was the happiest he had been in weeks. His meeting with Truttman was scheduled in two days. He didn't reveal the reason for the meeting other than to say that he needed some counsel and advice. He figured Susan would be a little miffed at his sudden trip out of town, but she would get over it.

The front door was ajar when he arrived home. It was late, and sensing the worst, Gil entered the house cautiously. There was no smell of dinner. There were no sounds anywhere. Something was wrong. Where was Susan? Why was the door open? He moved from room to room, his heart racing. He puzzled over an empty Scotch bottle he found in the kitchen. Why was it there? Susan hated Scotch and he only kept it for guests. He'd opened that bottle a week ago when Carl Munsen dropped by. He'd only had one drink. Who had the rest?

As he walked by the laundry room, he heard talking, not loud, not excited, just talking. He opened the door. Susan sat on the floor on top of a pile of clothes, mumbling to herself. She was alone and seemed startled by Gil's intrusion. Tilting her head sideways onto her shoulder, she squinted as if trying to see him better. He dropped down beside her. "Are you Okay?" He felt silly with his question. Clearly, she was anything but Okay.

Gil picked up the phone and dialed Rick. As soon as he answered, Gil apologized. "I didn't know where else to turn for help," he explained.

"Susan is in trouble. She's drunk out of her mind."

"Where is Susan right now?"

"She's sitting in the middle of the laundry room with an empty whiskey bottle."

"I'll be right over." The phone line went dead.

***

It took Rick ten minutes to drive from his home in Bellevue to Gil's in Clyde Hill. If it weren't for the 25 mile per hour speed limit in Clyde Hill, he would have been there a few minutes earlier. But the cops in that little township made their living off folks going 30 and above and Rick wasn't about to contribute to their retirement fund.

Gil opened the door before Rick could knock. "I'm sorry to drag you out like this," he said, motioning Rick toward the living room. "I know you can't do anything, but I needed someone to talk to."

"Sometimes that's all someone can do—just listen." Rick sat sideways on the couch, facing Gil who sat at the other end. "And sometimes there is more. Gil, I'm a Christian and when Christians face tough situations, they pray. If you don't mind, that's what I would like to do right now."

Gil studied Rick's face before answering, then said, "It for sure can't hurt," and bowed his head.

Rick's words were short and pointed. "Lord, my friend and his wife are hurting and I'm asking You to intercede—help them through this stressful time. Let them feel Your presence. And I'm asking this in Your Son's name."

Then, looking at Gil he said, "You know, God doesn't give us guarantees if we aren't in His will. He does say in the Old Testament— *'If My people who are called by My Name will humble themselves and pray and seek My face and turn from their wicked ways, then will I hear from heaven, and will forgive their sin and will heal their land.'* So just asking for help may not be enough if He doesn't see some evidence that you and Susan are turning your lives around. You both need to make a commitment to Him.

"I'm not an evangelist and there are others who are better equipped to share the Gospel with you, but if you want to know more about what I believe, I'm ready to talk."

Then Rick stood. "It's late, Gil, and I need to get home. If there's anything else I can do, call me. Like I said, if you need to talk, let's talk."

With a reassuring pat on the shoulder, Rick was gone.

Boston bound

In spite of Susan's problems, Gil had committed to fly to Boston the next day. He had scheduled a noon flight that connected through Minneapolis. That would give him time for a final briefing with his engineering team before heading to Sea-Tac Airport. Although he felt guilty for leaving Susan in her current state, he felt relief for getting away. This would be his first break since going to Rome. It was therapy that he knew he needed. And the prospect of plunging into an engineering problem with a top scientist like Truttman was all he needed to emerge from his blue funk.

***

It took three days of almost non-stop work, but Herman (as he insisted he be called despite Gil's protest) and Gil unlocked the puzzle of the non-communicating altimeter. Gil returned to Seattle Sunday afternoon, singing the praises of this technical genius, his new-found friend and mentor. He could hardly wait to come into the office the next morning and give his report on the results. But first, he had to face Susan.

"I'm home," he called as he entered from the garage. "Is anybody here?"

His calls were met with silence. He walked through the house, peeking into each room, including the laundry room, but there was no sign of Susan anywhere. She knew he was coming home. He had called her earlier in the day from Boston's Logan Airport shortly before he boarded his flight home. She sounded sober then. She even sounded halfway glad he was coming home. Her car was in the garage. So where was she?

He went into the kitchen and got out a can of Campbell's Bean with Bacon soup. Northwest didn't serve the best meal on the flight. The soup was steaming as the phone rang. He answered it and stirred the concoction simultaneously. He froze when he heard the caller identify himself as Sergeant Phil Tuggle of the Bellevue Police Department. "May I speak to Mr. Brockton?"

"I'm Dr. Brockton," Gil answered.

"Sir, I'm sorry to tell you that your wife has been in an automobile accident."

"How can that be? Her car is here in the garage."

"No, sir, she was walking along the road and was struck by a hit-and-run driver."

"My God, how is she?"

"The medics are transporting her to Harborview Hospital right now. She should be there within a few minutes."

"Why didn't they take her to Overlake Hospital?"

"They felt the trauma unit at Harborview was better equipped to handle her injuries."

Gil spent no further time with the officer. He thanked him, turned off the stove, grabbed his car keys, and headed for the garage. Fifteen minutes later, he pulled into a parking lot across the street from the hospital and raced for the Emergency Room entrance.

***

"Your wife is in serious but stable condition, Dr. Brockton," the person at the counter told him. "Her left ankle is shattered. She bruised some ribs and has a gash on her forehead. A medical team is working with her right now. If you'll wait over there," she said, pointing to a set of chairs in the next room, "someone will let you know when you can see her."

***

Susan was not in the best shape to talk to Gil when he was finally able to see her. They had put her in a private room, at least for the first night. She would have been in a lot of pain except for the drugs she had been given. As it was, she was sleepy and was having difficulty speaking without slurring her words. Gil couldn't help wondering if she was really just drunk, but the nurse told him Susan was acting normally under the circumstances.

He pulled his chair up close to the bed. "What happened?" he asked. "Where were you going?"

She looked at him but seemed to have trouble focusing on his face. She raised her eyebrows and tilted her head back, as if trying to see him better. "I jussh wanted to get shom fresh air," she said. She closed her eyes, breathed heavily and fell into a deep sleep.

Gil rose and went to the nurse's station. "What's the prognosis," he asked. "How long will she be in here and how long will her recovery take?"

"This will depend in part on her," the matronly R.N. said. "Most people with similar injuries are out of here within two days.

"Even if they have had multiple pins inserted in their ankles?"

"Even then. It's a long recovery process, but she can do it at home. She will have to remain in bed for a week or so. Is there anyone at home who can watch over her?"

"No, we have no children." Gil was pensive for a moment, and then asked, "Is there some kind of visiting nurse service that I could hire?"

"There sure is," she replied, "but we aren't permitted to make recommendations." She paused. "Do I understand you live in Bellevue?"

"Yes."

"Well, if it was me, and I'm not recommending, you understand because I'm not allowed to . . ." her eyes twinkled . . . "I would call Home Healthcare. They're located in Bellevue, near Overlake Hospital. They are caring and highly qualified."

The next day, before heading to work, Gil followed that lead and hired Home Healthcare to provide eight-hour a day service during the week. He figured he could handle the weekends. He would continue the service as long as it looked like Susan needed the help.

***

Gill decided to keep Susan's accident quiet for no particular reason other than he was a private person and really didn't want all the fuss that undoubtedly would ensue. At least, that was what he told himself, when in truth, he didn't want her accident to take away from his news about the altimeter.

"Charlie," Gil reported to his president, "I'm not going to say it was a piece of cake. It took us working 14 hours a day, Thursday, Friday, and Saturday to come up with the solution. Dr. Truttman is an absolute mastermind. He is methodical and careful and precise. He refused to jump to the end, looking for a quick solution. He dissected the enigma from the beginning of the design and worked his way through, one circuit at a time. Before we sent out for lunch on Saturday, he pretty much had it figured out and by dinner time, the altimeter was sending and receiving. We celebrated that night with a lobster feast at the No-Name Restaurant on the Boston Pier. Have you eaten there?"

"Once, several years ago. Doesn't it have two dining areas, one upstairs and one down?"

"Yup, we ate upstairs because the harbor and airport views were great. I also liked the décor—the heavy dark timbers, Formica® tables and tile floors—something like it must have appeared when fishermen ate there." He licked his lips. "And that seafood chowder! Man, was that good. I almost canceled the lobster, but I had ordered it sautéed with shrimp and scallops. I wasn't about to miss that."

"Well, congratulations, Gil, on a job well done. Be sure to thank Rick for the idea. If he hadn't come up with it, you might still be sitting and sweating in your office."

"That's where I'm headed next."

***

"I owe you lunch," Gil said as he walked up to Rick who was down the hall talking to Hump Marryatt.

"For what?"

"For suggesting I make a little trip." He purposefully avoided specifics so that Hump wouldn't know too much.

"Oh, well that was my pleasure. You looked like you needed a break." Rick nodded at Hump, letting him know that their conversation was over, adding, "Hump, I'll check with McDonnell Douglas to see if they can meet with you next week."

Then he turned back to Gil. "Tell me, what happened? I figure your trip was successful or else you wouldn't be buying my lunch."

"It was a total success. Truttman solved the problem. The old guy is phenomenal. I hope I have half his smarts when I'm his age."

"So we're back on track?"

"We're back on track."

***

Rick had never figured out why Carl Munsen disliked him. It was more typical to find a barrier between Engineering and Manufacturing, not one between Marketing and Manufacturing. It must have been something beyond their professional relationship. Every opportunity he had to take a shot at Rick, Munsen took it. And his aim was exceptionally good, improving with practice over time.

That there appeared to be no love lost between the two was common knowledge. Carl Munsen was considered tough, crude and cantankerous, a product of his long climb from warehouseman to manager of Pierce's entire assembly and purchasing operations. His formal education ended in tenth grade, followed by nine years service in the Army, never rising above corporal. By actual count, he earned his corporal stripes four separate times, but always managed to lose them through one military misdemeanor or another, more times than not because of his mouth. He always thought he'd retire after putting in his twenty. He never thought he'd quit because of suspicions, never substantiated, that he was a security risk.

***

Carl opened the door to his office and ran headlong into Rick's blazing eyes; it was not unlike staring down the barrel of a menacing .38 caliber Police Special. He stopped dead in his tracks.

"I've had it!" Rick shouted, bolting upright from Carl's chair, where he had been sitting, waiting. "I've had it with you and your innuendos and your gossiping behind my back."

"I beg your pardon?" Carl recoiled as if he had walked into a buzz saw. "What the hell are you talking about?" He adopted an instantly defensive posture, physically and verbally.

"I'm talking about the lies you are circulating about me having an affair. I'm talking about your snide remarks. I'm talking about the way you constantly challenge and question my every move. I'm talking about your unwillingness to be a Pierce team player."

"I'm not saying anything that others aren't saying."

"The only folks who are talking are those you've prompted. You lit the fires. And they blaze on with the aid of your wind."

"Very poetic, Stoner. But I'm not saying anything that ain't true."

"You're saying nothing that's true and it's going to stop now." Rick moved menacingly toward Munsen, who backed out the door and fled down the hallway.

"We'll see, Stoner," he called over his shoulder in full retreat. "We'll see."

Outpatient

A phone call to Harborview Medical Center revealed that Susan was ready to be released and seemed anxious for him to come pick her up. Gil left work at 2:30 that afternoon, telling his secretary that he was heading home. He didn't add that his trip was by way of Seattle.

When he walked into Susan's room, she was dressed and sitting in a wheelchair, with her leg elevated. Never mind that she was wearing the same clothes she had worn the night before when she was hit. They had been laundered and didn't look too much worse for wear.

Her left leg was in a soft cast from the knee down. The doctor had told Gil earlier when he had called that he didn't want to put on a "real" cast until the swelling in her leg had gone down, probably in a week. There was a bandage on her cheek to protect the gash. He was pretty certain there would be no scarring from that wound.

"All in all," the doctor had told him, "she's a lucky woman. It was a glancing blow, rather than a direct hit, and that probably saved her life. It was the fall that broke her ankle, not the car."

***

"Are you in pain?" Gil asked as they drove home.

"Some, but it's more of a dull ache," she answered. "They've got me on Percocet for the first week at least, one tablet every four to six hours. After that I'm to use Ibuprofen if I need it. The doctor feels that I won't however. He seems to think that my threshold of pain is pretty high."

"The doctor says you're to stay down for at least a week. I've hired a nurse who will be at our home every weekday, Monday through Friday. He wants you in bed with your leg elevated to reduce the swelling."

"I don't want a nurse," Susan protested.

"Now that's smart. You can't walk; you have to stay in bed, but you don't want a nurse. She's coming anyway, whether you want her to or not. She'll arrive starting tomorrow at 8:00 and stay until I get home each afternoon. She will be more than a nurse. She will prepare meals and run your errands. She will keep house. I figure that I can take care of you over the weekend. Hopefully within a couple of weeks, you will be able to do most things for yourself, but if not, the nurse will continue. And once you're up, you're going to have to use crutches to keep the weight off your leg."

"I repeat. I don't want a nurse. I like my privacy. I can take care of myself."

"You want your privacy so that you can drink." He glared at her.

"And so what if I do? Do you have something better for me to do? If I'm lying in bed for hours, I'm certainly not going to entertain myself with soap operas."

"Well, you're not entertaining yourself with booze, either."

She glared and he glared and they rode the rest of the way home in silence.

Love renewed

Rick's transformation from withdrawn to warm happened overnight. At least it seemed like that to Carol. He came home that evening acting more like his old self. Trey noticed it, too, although he said nothing; just kept looking quizzically at his father while they ate dinner. Later, as Rick helped Carol with the dish clean-up, she asked, "What's happened?"

"What do you mean?'

"You're different. You're my old Rick."

He smiled. "A few things have happened. One, I have thought about our conversation the other night and as much as I want you to be wrong, I realize you aren't. I have to get over our loss. The grieving has to end. Jeff is gone. But you and Trey are here. I love you both with all my heart. It's time I showed it." He smiled even broader.

"The other thing that's helped me snap out of this blue funk is that a major glitch in our new development has been resolved. We're behind schedule, but we're back on the right course. The pressure that I have been enduring has been relieved." He put down the pan he was scouring and reached out to Carol. "I am so sorry." He pulled her close. "This isn't easy – you know that. I'm not good at asking for forgiveness. But I've hurt you and I've been a jerk. Please forgive me."

"One thing I can't do is stay mad at you. I love you." She touched his arm, tracing a small heart with her fingernail. "I forgive you."

**

Grey skies in the Seattle area were traditional. Margy knew that and was slowly learning to accept the clouds. For some, the weather was a source for depression. They didn't affect her that way. Maybe she had fallen for Rick's chamber-of-commerce-sounding propaganda: *"I have traveled all over the world—to sixty-seven countries—and I've never seen anything more beautiful than Seattle when the sun is out!"* He was right. It was worth waiting for. If she was a housewife, confined to the house, perhaps her attitude would be different. She was free to come and go. She had her tennis and her swimming. But she didn't have Rick. Since meeting him at the Space Needle, he was all she could think about. She had been such a fool. Why did she allow her mother to talk her into that long-ago divorce?

Margy was caught in a web that she helped spin. And as she struggled, she was all the more ensnared. Margy wanted to reclaim her youth, not that it was "times of yore," but then again, when she was younger, she didn't appreciate it to the extent that she now recognized as most appropriate. And so, while reclaiming her youth, she did whatever it took to maintain her looks; retain her body. In the process of retaining (or was it reclaiming) her youth, she wanted the man who was once her husband, when she and he were teenagers. Or did she? That issue was not as clear to her as it should be. She wanted to possess him, that much was clear. He was definitely more exciting than her current husband, with more vitality, and in the process, was good for her youth quest. But she was uncertain if she wanted him at the price of her husband, and perhaps her family, too. And yet, she was getting older. There wasn't much time left for her to be adored for her beauty. Rick was most assuredly the key to her immediate happiness.

Margy was far from perfect. She was self-centered. She wanted what she wanted. She had the habit of getting her way. She was raised that way as a child and it was allowed to persevere throughout her current marriage. Her lack of perfection was her Achilles' heel. It had the capability of bringing about her downfall, for she was unaccustomed to defeat and denial. Her selfishness, born of a childhood where she was the "princess," had been tolerated by her husband, Jim, because he too idolized her. But this only reinforced her flaw. She was beautiful, and she knew it. Men stared at her and she loved it. She asked and she received. She wanted and she got. When she was indulged, she was happy, bubbly and delightful. When she was happy, bubbly and delightful, people enjoyed being around her. When she was denied, she was death warmed over.

Margy's face and figure turned heads; male and female. She was an incredibly beautiful woman who, at 38, didn't look it. She dressed for men—that is, if form-fitting dresses molding her voluptuous figure, fabric drawn tightly across her small waist, and a skirt ending just below the knee, giving clear access to beautifully shaped calves and tiny ankles were turn-ons for men. Her walk was fluid, slow, and with modest steps. Her posture was erect. When she sat, she always smoothed her dress, running the palm of her hand across her bottom as if in a caress.

Margy didn't think of herself as "the other" woman. After all, she was married to an airline pilot who loved her and provided for her bountifully. She had two children. She was one year younger than Rick; ten years younger than her husband.

Margy picked up the phone.

"Rick Stoner," Rick answered his office phone with his usual upbeat voice.

"Good morning, handsome," the voice at the other end said. "This is Margy."

"Margy?" He couldn't believe she was calling again, particularly after last time when he rebuffed her. "What's up?" He tried to act nonchalant.

"I just wanted to hear your voice . . . and to find out if you were free for lunch today."

"Margy, I don't think lunch would be a particularly good idea." He began to feel nervous, like he had too much coffee, only it wasn't the coffee.

"Don't be such a stick-in-the-mud," she rebuked him. "This would just be a couple of old friends getting together for an hour."

He tried to collect his thoughts. Then he came up with an idea. "OK. Sure. I can meet you. Where did you have in mind?"

"How about that wonderful sidewalk café in downtown Kirkland? I don't remember its name, but it is directly across the park from the marina."

"You mean Pardisio?"

"That's the one. I'll meet you at noon."

Two for tea; three for lunch

Rick surprised Carol who was in the midst of making their bed. Roxanne jumped up from her official post of supervising the bed-making task and wagged her tail rapidly because of Rick's unexpected appearance.

"What are you doing home?" she asked. "Is everything alright?"

"Yes and no," he answered, cocking his head slightly to the side and frowning as he always did when he was uncomfortable. "I need to tell you something. Then I need your understanding. Then I need your help."

She sat down on the partially-made bed and watched him closely.

He stood in front of her, making eye contact. This was not the time to appear shifty, he reasoned. "A few months ago, I got a call from Margy."

"Your ex-wife?" she asked revealing a hint of stress.

"Yes. She was in town looking for a home. Her husband had been transferred and she thought it would be fun if we met for lunch." He paused, watching Carol closely.

"Now, you're not going to like this, but I said 'yes.' We met at the Space Needle."

Carol's eyes started to well up with tears. "Why did you do that?"

"I can't give you a good answer. I've asked myself 'why' over and over ever since." He hung his head. "I guess I was just curious."

"What happened?"

"We reminisced a little and filled in our lives a lot. She's married to an airline pilot, has two children and stays at home."

"Was she pretty?"

"Not as pretty as you."

"Did you talk about anything else?"

"No, that was it. It was all over in an hour. She had to meet with a realtor and I had to get back to work."

"Have you seen her since?"

"Technically, yes. I saw her at church a few weeks ago, but I purposefully didn't talk to her. It scared me that she was there."

"How did she know where you went to church?"

"I don't know. The only thing I can figure is that she saw the article about Jeff's accident in the Times and got the information from there."

"Have you talked to her since?"

"Three times. She called when she moved here. I was brief; didn't want to encourage her. I had the feeling that she was coming on to me. In fact, I'm pretty certain that's why she was at church that Sunday." He paused again. "Then I heard from her a few weeks ago . . . and again today."

"She called today? What did she want?" Carol's eyes grew big and she was clearly agitated.

"She wanted me to meet her for lunch."

"What did you tell her?"

"At first, I told her it wasn't a good idea. But she persisted, so I came up with a plan. I told her I would meet her. I told myself that I would bring you along."

"You did what?" Her agitation had turned to tumult.

"I told myself that I would bring you along.

"I am not into *ménage a' trois*," she said scornfully.

"Carol! I hardly meant that, and you know it."

"Then what did you mean?"

"I meant that I want you to come help me put an end to this. You are my wife. You are the woman I love. I want Margy to go away. I don't seem to be having much success convincing her on my own."

Carol seemed to mull his request over in her mind, still frowning, still upset. "I don't think I want to see this woman."

"Do you want me to see her alone?"

"No!" Of that she seemed certain. "I do not!"

"Then come with me."

***

Margy's face brightened as she saw Rick approach her table, and then it turned into a scowl as she realized a woman was accompanying him. "Rick," she said. "I thought we were meeting alone." Then looking directly at Carol, "Who's this?"

"This is my wife Carol. I thought it was time you met her." He held out a chair for Carol as she sat down at the table.

"Margy, I brought Carol along to let you know that I love her and that I am not available. I brought her along because she is a part of everything I do. I share everything with her. I will not do things behind her back. I did that the first time you called and I have suffered emotionally for it ever since. She is the love of my life and I will do nothing to compromise her love. Somehow you have gotten into your head that we can rekindle our teenage romance. We can't. It was over years ago.

"I have wanted to tell you to stop pursuing me, but I am the kind of person who hates to hurt someone's feelings. I don't like to be rude. I don't like to be blunt. So I have let you continue. It hasn't been fair to you or to me. Finally, this morning when you called, I realized I had to do something drastic to bring this to an end."

Rick stood up and pulled Carol's chair out from the table as she rose. "Goodbye, Margy. Please go home and love your husband and your children. They deserve all your love."

He and Carol strode across the parking lot to their car, holding hands as lovers do.

Just checking

Rick was musing about his noontime encounter with Margy. The phone rang. It rang again . . . and again. The third time he heard it. "Rick Stoner."

"You busy?" It was Art.

"Sort of."

"I figured. You usually answer on the first ring."

"What's up, Art?"

"I just wanted to know if you've talked with Carol yet."

"As a matter of fact, I told her this morning. Then I took her to lunch . . . with Margy."

"You say what?"

"You heard me. I took Carol to meet Margy."

"What happened?"

"I told Margy that I loved my wife and that she needed to love her husband and that she needed to leave me alone."

"Then what?"

"Carol and I got up and left.

"Way to go, buddy! I'm proud of you."

"I'm proud of me, too." He paused for a moment, and then said, "Look Art, I have a full schedule this afternoon so I need to get back to it. How about we meet for lunch at Azteca on Friday and I'll give you all the details."

"Deal. Call me with the time and to confirm that you can make it."

Gil's problems deepen

"What the hell do I do?" Gil confided once again with Rick later that afternoon. "I am as miserable with Susan as I once was happy. Her drinking has turned her into a shrew and me into a madman. I can't stand the daily torment."

"How did she get started?"

"You know, I don't have any idea, at least, not for certain. We have always been social in our drinking habits. Never in excess. In fact, Susan would usually nurse one drink all night." Gil slumped in his chair. "The only thing I can figure is that my late nights here resulted in her looking for something to do with her time. And alcohol was her answer."

"She wouldn't be the first wife to get started this way."

"The problem is all we do is fight. As she attacks me with her insults, I attack her right back. She screams; I scream louder. She cries; I ignore. She tells me I never loved her. I tell her that I certainly don't love her now."

"So what are you going to do?"

"Stay away from home as much as I can, I guess. I'm about to go nuts when I'm there or even when I'm headed there." Gil stood up and headed for the door. "In fact, I think I'll go take a drive right now. I need to clear my head."

And he was gone.

***

"Rick, have you seen Gil?" Charlie popped his head into Rick's office. Jinnie's typewriter clacked loudly in the background as she worked feverishly to finish the cover letter for the United proposal.

"You just missed him. He was in here for a few minutes and then said he was going for a drive. Something about clearing his head." Rick chose to keep his conversation with Gil quiet. "He seems stressed," he added, but thought he should at least give Charlie a small heads-up that personal trouble was brewing.

"I hope it's not the project."

"No, that's not it. It sounded more personal."

"Well, when you see him, ask him to drop by my office. We need to go over his budget."

***

Victoria was back in town. She had called Gil shortly after he had arrived at the office that morning. She asked him to meet her at her hotel. This time, she was at the Olympic. "The Westin was full," she explained.

He hadn't been able to get her out of his mind since she called. That afternoon, when he told Rick he planned to take a drive, his plan was simple; take the bridge across Lake Washington and drive to her downtown hotel.

He knew she was his Lorelei and that he would end up on the rocks, but he couldn't help it. Maybe if things had been better at home, he could have resisted. But they weren't. It made no sense that Victoria cared for him, but who was he to question a gift; especially one that looked as beautiful as she did.

The drive time to Seattle was filled by his thoughts; impure thoughts; thoughts brought on by hunger for a woman's touch; a woman's love. He wanted her more than he had wanted anything in his life. He wanted her laughter, her quick intelligence and her calm self-confidence, her astonishing brown eyes and her tantalizing smile. He wanted every inch of her superb body. But who was he to think this was even remotely possible? He had looked in the mirror. He knew what he looked like.

Better still, he knew what he didn't look like. He didn't look like a man worthy of her attention. He didn't look like a man she would be interested in. Someone told him once that men look with their eyes and that women look with their emotions. Maybe that was it, but even at that, what emotion did he invoke in her?

He was impatient and decided to use the valet parking service. He hastily took the offered parking claim stub and headed for the hotel's revolving entrance door. Moments later, he was on the elevator heading for the 14th floor. Moments after that, he was standing at her door, heart pounding like a teenager on his first date.

He took several deep breaths before knocking. "Easy big fella," he heard himself say. He knocked the familiar, sophomoric "dum-dum-dum-dum-dum . . . dum-dum."

"Just a minute," he heard from inside; then the sound of a deadbolt being opened.

Victoria stood in the open door with a smile and outstretched arms.

"I've missed you," she said as he walked into her arms.

This should have been so easy to accept what she was offering, but it wasn't. Gil was as uncertain of himself now as he had been as a teenager. Even as her arms enfolded him, he felt he didn't belong.

"Victoria," he had to ask, "why me?"

"Why not you?"

"Because I'm who I am. Have you really looked at me? I am no Gregory Peck."

"I should hope not. He's too old. You're just right."

"Just right for what?"

"This." Her finger moved his chin down as her lips moved to meet his. Their kisses became demanding. His hands drew her closer, then trailed down, following the contours of her superb body. He wanted her so much.

He broke away from her and repeated, "Why me?"

"Instead of answering, she began to undress him.

"No, not now," he said. "This is not the time."

"It's the ideal time."

"I'm not in the mood."

"You're in the mood."

"I can't."

"You can."

"No."
"Yes."
"No."
"See?"

***

As Gil drove away from the Olympic Hotel, he reflected on what had happened over the past two hours. What he had experienced was the most magical time of his life. He was in a total state of euphoria. Then, with a start, he awoke from his reverie and realized what faced him. He was headed home; home to Susan; home to a night of bickering and strife.

Gil switched on the radio and turned the knob to KIXI-AM. Maybe music would distract him from what was sure to face him at home. Anne Murray was singing a recent hit. *That lady sure can sing*, he thought. Suddenly, the song stopped and a frazzled announcer said, "We interrupt our program to bring you this bulletin. A grizzly mass suicide has been discovered in Guyana, a small country on the east coast of South America. It was prefaced yesterday by the murder of Representative Leo J. Ryan of California and four others who were visiting the People's Temple and their leader, Jim Jones. It appears that Jones led 910 of his followers, including more than 200 children, in a mass suicide by poison. Details are sketchy at the moment. We will break in as soon as more are received. In the meantime, we return you to our regularly scheduled broadcast."

Lena Horne was in the middle of singing "I Got Rhythm." It was poor timing. Gil felt like doing anything but tap his feet.

***

The day after his meeting with Victoria, Gil went to lunch with Carl Munsen. They did this periodically. In the middle of eating his salad, Gil inadvertently divulged his unhappy home life. Munsen wanted to know more and when pressed, Gil revealed that it wasn't all blackness; he had met someone in Rome and that she was in town.

"How does that make things better?" Munsen wanted to know.

"Well, she seems to like me."

"Meaning?"

"Meaning I am seeing her."

"Wow, who is this babe? Do I know her?"

"No chance. She lives in Washington, D.C. and is only here for a few days. Like I said, I met her in Rome. She's the Research Manager for a trading company that's based in Hong Kong."

"Hot stuff! I didn't think you had it in you." Munsen smirked at what he assumed was going on. "Are you passed the kissing stage?"

Gil didn't answer, chewing instead on a piece of Romaine, but his silence told the story.

"Go ahead, be the gentleman, Brockton. I can read between the lines." Munsen asked no more questions, but his curiosity was aroused. He wondered if this research manager, whoever she was, was pretty. He figured it didn't matter. *Sex is sex when you're desperate.* But he made a mental note to find out more about this *broad. It could be useful one of these days,* he reasoned.

Chapter 11

The Deepening Liaison

After their tryst at the Olympic, Gil and Victoria met almost every two or three afternoons a week for brief *liaisons* in different Seattle-area locations. They feared detection and realized that it was smartest for them to meet in out-of-the-way motels in Renton and Federal Way and Bothell—places where it was highly unlikely that anyone knowing either of them would be. Gil wondered how Victoria could remain in the Seattle area for this extended time period, but accepted her explanation that she had earned time off for good behavior and she wanted to spend it with him.

"Are you trying to tell me you're in love with me?" he asked after another extraordinary love session.

She frowned. "I think I am. It hasn't happened exactly the way that I always dreamed it would. Girls have their fantasies." She took a tiny little nip on her lower lip. "I hope I'm saying this right. You don't mind, do you?"

"I'm delighted. I'm falling in love with you, too, but I find it hard to believe that you feel the same way."

"I love you," Victoria said softly, savoring it. "Let me show you what I mean."

"Again?"

"Again. You are up to it, aren't you lover?"

***

The following afternoon, Gil told his secretary the same lie he had told Susan. A sub-committee meeting of the Airlines Engineering Association was going to run through the afternoon into dinner. Since this was not an uncommon occurrence, his story was unlikely to be suspected. Besides, he strangely enough didn't care if he was caught. His marriage was over.

Susan had killed whatever feelings were left, and miraculously, Victoria had stepped in to fill the void.

How was it possible, he thought as he backed his car out of his reserved stall at Pierce and headed for Seattle, that a beautiful, young woman like Victoria found him attractive? He was twelve years older than she was; not a tremendous difference if he was 58 and she was 46, but a big gap for her at age 28. Gil's once athletic frame had converted into one of more substance, with a beltline that had moved inches below the waistline. His paunch or was it his girth, had grown considerably these last ten years. And as it expanded, his hairline retreated. Ah, but he was still man enough to grow a mustache. Perhaps that was his appeal. Or was it the way he revered her that she found irresistible? Whatever, she loved him. She had told him so. And she made his heart dance.

In fact, he said romantic things that he had never even thought before in his life. Only yesterday, he had told her, "You look more beautiful every day. Today, you look like tomorrow." *Where did that come from*, he wondered? *I'm an engineer, not a poet. At least, not until now.*

***

Traffic was light as he crossed the Evergreen Floating Bridge. But then, it should have been. It was only one p.m., three hours ahead of rush hour. Luck was with him as he approached the Westin Hotel where she had found a room to her liking. There was no "full" sign blocking the entrance to the garage. He drove in, quickly found a parking place, and entered the hotel. Bypassing the front desk, he went straight to the elevators. As he walked toward her room on the 38th floor, his heart pounded. They had made love several times now, but implicit in her invitation today was the promise of exquisite pleasures that could only come from the most intimate of intimacies. He pressed the doorbell and as if she were behind the door waiting for the ring, she opened it immediately. The door no sooner closed than they embraced, awkwardly at first, and then with passion.

Victoria drew away and walked over to the couch that faced her spectacular view of the city. Gil followed and sat next to her. "I sure wonder if you realize what a weakness you are for me." She bit her lip. "I've always thought that I was so self-disciplined; pretty much in control of my life. But you've changed all that. I can't count the times in a day that I think about you; wonder what you're doing, where you are.

Wondering if you're thinking about me. Feeling guilty because of your wife, feeling afraid because of the consequences, and yet, still wanting to be with you. I care about you so much." She didn't look at Gil and fell silent. He put his hand on her shoulder and gently squeezed. But he was silent too, thinking about what she had said.

Finally, he said, "Victoria, I don't want you feeling guilty. My marriage is finished. It was finished before you came into my life. And there's no guilt; there are no consequences." His hand turned her head so that she looked at him. "The other day, you told me that you loved me. I think you said that because I said it first. I understand. You don't . . .

"Wait, Gil," she interrupted. "You do me an injustice. It's true that I said 'I love you' after you first said it. But that doesn't mean I said it because you said it. I said it because your saying it first gave me the courage to say it second."

"Are you certain?"

"I'm sure. Now, if all this is settled, what's stopping you, Tarzan, from taking me, Jane, to bed?" She smiled. He gaped. They stood slowly as if in a trance and embraced once more.

"You're sure?" he asked.

"I'm certain," she said.

***

Victoria called for room service, ordering a large meal for one, enough for two. The glow of their lovemaking had not worn off. Gil was euphoric. It had never been like this. Never. She had brought him to heights only alluded to in books he'd read. She partially dressed for the arrival of their meal, slipping on tight jeans and a blue flannel shirt. She didn't button the top three buttons. It was sexy. The young man from room service clearly thought so, although he attempted not to stare at her exquisite body.

Gil ate to be in harmony with her, not to mention satisfying a hunger that bordered on ravenous. She watched this man, so much older than her, in amusement as she ate her salad. With his thickset frame, closely cropped hair and bushy eyebrows, he was the opposite of one she normally would be attracted to. Still, he had been sweet, innocent, and enthusiastic.

In a short time, she'd grown fond of him. It was dangerous, she knew. "Don't become involved." The warning had been clear. Yet he was so helpless and he trusted her so completely. He really seemed to be in love with her. Once before, during a similar assignment, she had gotten too close to the man. Her uncle had not been pleased.

"Victoria," Gil broke her reverie, "I've asked you countless times because I find it hard to believe a woman as stunning as you would pay special attention to me. Yet, you singled me out those many months ago in Rome. Why? To find out why I was staring at you?"

Victoria smiled. Before she could answer, Gil continued. "Women don't look at me, at least, not with interest. Curiosity, maybe. But not interest."

"There was a puppy dog look about you. One that begged me to pick you up and take you home."

"Thanks. That's a charming comparison."

"I'm serious. You're an attractive man. But since we're asking penetrating questions of each other, why are you here with me? I've seen pictures of your wife. She's very pretty."

The mere mention of Susan caused a mood shift. Gil stiffened, his eyes narrow, his nostrils flared. He sat back in his chair. "Susan was a pretty woman." His voice underscored the word 'was.' "She only turned ugly in the past year."

"What happened?" Victoria wanted to draw him out, to discover his strengths and weaknesses, to know him.

"When I fell in love with Susan in college, she was the light of my life. She was two years behind me. When I graduated from Oregon State and moved to Boston to attend M.I.T., she had transferred to Radcliffe to be near me. We were married at the end of her junior year. She left school and took a full time job to help pay for my education, sacrificing her degree so I could work on my doctorate. Those were the best years of our lives together, filled with love and compassion, without stress and false expectations. We knew we were struggling but we were doing so with a cause. My Ph.D. was going to lead to later financial success." He paused. "Are you sure you want to hear this?"

Her reply was soft and assuring. "Yes."

"OK. I was offered a job with NASA and a move to a home of our own in Virginia was perhaps the most exciting event we had enjoyed together. Susan loved her 'used' home. She called it that because it wasn't new; it had a previous owner. 'There are many advantages to a home like this,' she told me, urging that I agree to the purchase. 'The lawn is in, the trees and shrubs are planted . . .'"

"'And,' I added, 'the carpet's worn, the outside needs painting, the . . .'"

"'Stop it,' I remember her chiding. 'You know you like it as much as I do.'"

"Yup. But I like to see you grovel." It was like it was yesterday."

"We lived there for four years, replacing the carpet but somehow never getting around to repainting the house.

"The move to Seattle was traumatic; a major change for Susan, which was a surprise for me. It was as if someone had messed with her nest. Nothing was right. She seemed upset much of the time, yet she had a far nicer home than before, lived in a more elite neighborhood than before, and enjoyed advantages that came with a better paid husband. I didn't understand her problem and coped rather badly, I can see now. I was happy in my work and felt stress only when I went home. One solution was not to come home as early as had been my custom. I opted for that arrangement. It was more comfortable at work.

"Unfortunately for Susan, her days alone at home stretched into nights when I arrived late—'Sorry I'm late. I grabbed a hamburger on the way home.' Rather than rising out of her melancholy, she spiraled deeper. Just when she needed me most, I abandoned her. So she found a friend she could count on; one who was at her beck and call; one who filled her days and nights with warmth and a sense of well being. He was from Tennessee originally but had come to Seattle because she needed him. At first, I didn't even notice that I was sharing my home with a stranger; Susan kept him out of sight. But after a while, as her dependence grew, Susan was less inclined to hide her friend, her comfort, her refuge. And so it was that I came face to face with Jack Daniels and the realization that my wife had become an alcoholic."

He slumped in his chair. "It's been a form of hell ever since."

"I'm so sorry," she spoke with compassion. "Was your work that important?"

"Looking back, no, it wasn't. My priorities were all screwed up. But I wanted to change the world, or at least be viewed as a great engineer who made a difference."

"Did you?"

"Until recently, no. I was more on the fringe."

"What happened to change things?"

"Well, I can't really go into it, 'cause it's a secret." He blushed. "I don't want to make a big deal out of this, but the project is classified and I'm not allowed to talk about it."

"Gil, I don't mean to pry. I'm just interested in you." Her expression was one of fondness. "If you're involved in something special, I'll bet it's important."

Pride seemed to fill his soul as his chest swelled and his jaw set. "It is. It is important," he said emphatically. "I can tell you this, one day our fighters will be able to fly all the way to their targets without being detected, and it will be because of my invention."

"Gil, how wonderful!" She fingered a button on her shirt, then slowly unbuttoned it and the ones below until her shirt fell open, revealing her lush curves beneath. "I'll bet you can't get all the way over here undetected, with or without your secret system."

Later, when he had gone, she called her uncle. It was nine in the morning in Hong Kong, the beginning of a workday.

The trap is set

It was her best routine. The one that men always fell for. Her uncle's company was on the verge of failing, and with its failure would be the need for her to return to Hong Kong, permanently. Her quarry would never see her again . . . unless; unless he was willing to provide a product idea that Shek International could market to another company. Victoria would weep. She was good at weeping. Men became putty in her hands. She would move toward him, seducing him with her need to be held. Her sobs would subside, muffled by his chest as tears covered his shirt. "I don't want to go back to Hong Kong," she would whimper. "I want to stay with you." What resistance was left quickly faded, with her dupe eager to resolve her problem any way that he could.

And so she brought out her polished routine for Gil. They would never see each other again. They would never make love again. She sobbed. She wept. She cuddled. He succumbed. "Victoria, I'll do anything I can to keep us together. There is no one who means more to me. You are what I live for. You are what keep me going. But there is no new product that I could share with you . . . except . . ." and then he caught himself, realizing the classified nature of the PROPHET Program." . . . there's nothing that I have to share."

She drew back from him and studied his face. She could tell from the way his body tensed and from the way his voice sounded constrained that there was something; something that he wasn't telling her. Tears squirted from her eyes. "You say you care, but you don't. If you loved me the way you say you do, you'd find a way to keep me here."

"Victoria, that isn't fair. I *do* love you. But there is nothing I can share with you. We are only working on one new product, the one I mentioned the other day, but it's highly classified."

***

Terror might have been an accurate description of Gil's emotions when he returned to his office at Pierce. How could he take his design and give it to someone else? He couldn't even do it if it wasn't classified. He walked to his four-drawer file which was securely locked. He fiddled with the built-in combination lock, nervously twiddling the tumbler. Right ninety-one, left one revolution, stopping the second time at forty-nine, right again to . . . He couldn't bring himself to dial in the third number. He rapidly twirled that dial to negate the action he had started. He sat down at his desk, put his elbows on the surface, cradled his face in his hands, and wept. He didn't want to lose Victoria, but he couldn't betray his country, his company, and his creation.

Blinded by passion

Tears rolled down Victoria's cheek when Gil told her the next night that he couldn't give her the secret. She was so practiced at this. "You say with your lips that you love me, but you act quite the opposite." She made no attempt to wipe the tears. "I have never asked anything of you. I have given you everything of me. But now, when I need you, you refuse me." She turned away from him and sobbed. "Last night, you said you would help. I relied on you. I believed you. Now, you tell me it was a lie. You will let my uncle's company fail. You will force me to return to Hong Kong. It wasn't love that brought us together. You used me."

"No, you're so wrong. I didn't use you. I love you. There is nothing more precious in my life. I would give my life for you. It's just that what you ask is far greater than my life. It is the life of my company," he shook his head as if counting the full cost, "the life of my country."

"You don't believe that for a moment, Gil Brockton," she rebuked him. "You have told me more than once that the way to bring peace to the world is for all sides to have the same weapons of offense and the same weapons of defense. This is your chance to practice what you preach." She stood and walked to the window, looking down on the night scene of the city. The monorail moved north toward Seattle Center. Cars headlights and taillights told the story of life being directed by a system of law and order. The traffic lights turned red; the traffic lights turned green. And the cars followed the dictates of an unseen bureaucracy.

"You're no better than one of them," she pointed down at the sight below. "You're afraid to break the rules. And because you are, we'll never see each other again. My uncle has instructed me to return home tomorrow on the afternoon Northwest flight through Tokyo."

"You can't mean it. What will I do without you? You can't go." Desperation filled his voice.

"I have no choice."

"But there must be something we can do."

"We? What could we do? Everything was decided when you said you wouldn't help."

"Maybe I can," he said, "but I need time."

"My uncle said I had no more time. I must obey him."

"Please. Tell him I need more time. I have to figure out how to do this. It isn't that simple. If I am not careful, they're gonna know that I did it."

***

This had been the most difficult day of his life. Her uncle had given her five more days. Then, she was to return to Hong Kong. There would be no further extensions. If he didn't come up with a solution, she would go away from him and take with her the exquisite joy that he had known only too briefly.

He shook his head. This wasn't happening. *Victoria*, he cried from within, *I live for your smile, your voice, and your touch. Someday, maybe I'll be strong enough to live without you, but not today. Not tomorrow either.*

***

She told him not to call until he had something of importance to share with her. He knew what that meant. He was to deliver the plans for PROPHET or he would never see her again. The loneliness of being away from her was almost beyond bearing. A vital part of him was missing. Being with her was fervor, a festival of life.

***

Gil looked for Rick but learned that he was out of the office. He had to talk to someone he trusted. He saw Carl Munsen in the cafeteria and asked if he had time to join him for lunch. He did. He didn't want to be overheard so they drove to a nearby Burger King and went through the drive-in.

"I have got to talk to someone I can trust," he told Munsen. "I am over my head and need some council." He opened his burger and checked for ketchup.

Munsen frowned as he bit into his cheeseburger. "Define 'Over your head.'"

"Do you remember that woman I told you about last week?"

"Sure."

"Well, I am in love. Victoria is the most beautiful and most wonderful woman I have ever met. And she loves me, too." He stared at his hamburger, not eating.

"So what's the problem?"

"Her company is about to fold unless . . ." He couldn't continue.

"Her company is about to fold unless what?"

"Like I told you before, they are a trading company. They buy products from one company and sell them to another. She says that she needs something from me or she is going to be forced to return to Hong Kong."

"What do you mean by 'something'?" He chewed vigorously on his cheeseburger.

"She wants the design to PROPHET."

"Are you serious?"

"Yeah, I'm serious. She says that by the time her company sells the design to another company, it will be old technology."

"You know that isn't true."

"It could be. The state-of-the-art moves awfully fast."

"You're not going to do it, are you?"

"I don't know what I'm going to do. I love her and can't stand the thought of her not being in my life."

The two men looked at each other, neither speaking.

Then Gil spoke. "I can't do this, obviously, but I am torn up inside. I don't want to lose her."

"What kind of company is this that sells company secrets?" Munsen probed a bit more. His cheeseburger was gone; his right hand was in his pocket jiggling coins.

"Maybe you've heard of them – Shek Industries."

"Nope. Sorry. You said before that they are based in Hong Kong?"

"Yes, that's their headquarters, but they have an office in D.C., too."

There was more silence as the two men puzzled over this revelation.

"Look, Carl, I don't want you telling anyone about this. I just needed a sounding board. I knew what the answer was, but I had to say it out loud to someone."

"Your secret is safe with me, Gil."

Chapter 12

Moles

1979. A nuclear near-disaster was averted at Three Mile Island, Pennsylvania; an American Airlines DC-10 crashed in Chicago, killing 272 passengers plus three on the ground; the Seattle Supersonics defeated the Washington Bullets, 4 games to 1 and were crowned NBA Champions; the U.S. Embassy was seized in Tehran, Iran; the Soviets invaded Afghanistan; Ronald Reagan announced his candidacy for President; and the Pierce Terrain Avoidance Radar was compromised.

Yu-Chan Shek visits Soviet Embassy

At ten thirty on the morning of February 9th, a phone call was made to the Soviet Embassy in Washington, D.C. It was routinely recorded by the FBI for later evaluation. The conversation that followed was not routine and was evaluated within moments of its completion.

Adamski, as he was called by his FBI listeners (because he was the first unidentified male voice they ever recorded), answered the phone but was unable to get the caller to identify himself or to explain the reason for his call. "Sir, I need to know who is calling."

"Ah, it is not good that I use my name." The accent was Chinese.

Adamski told the caller to hold the line; that he needed to find someone to take the call.

"Vladimir Gregoric speaking."

"Ah, I need . . . ah, it is not appropriate that we talk on the telephone. Do you understand?" The Chinese caller was uncomfortable.

"Yes, I understand. Would you like to visit the Embassy?"

"Ah, that would be best. I have something I think would be interesting to you."

"Yes. Interesting, is it? Could you come at lunchtime today?"

"Yes, ah, um, I could. Would that be the best time?"

It was now ten thirty-five in the morning. Agent Lydon had little time to get the word out to the photo unit at the National Geographic Building to make certain they photographed every Asian person who approached the Soviet Embassy between this notice and two in the afternoon in case he was late. And so it was that fate brought Rick and Yu-Chan Shek together in front of the Soviet Embassy during the lunch hour. Neither of their lives would ever be the same again.

Rick "*bumps*" into Yu-Chan Shek

Embassy buildings around the world are sources of refuge and protection to their citizens. They are sanctuaries and citadels, dispensaries of diplomatic rhetoric and immunity, font of intelligence and espionage. The Soviet Embassy, a three-and-a-half story building of gray stone and brick on Sixteenth Street, was built in 1910 as a town house by Mrs. George M. Pullman, widow of the railroad sleeping car tycoon. She never lived in it. In November 1913, it sold to the Imperial Russian Government.

If it weren't for a forest of antennas on the flat rooftop and the continual flow of people coming and going, it might have been mistaken for a genteel mansion of a well-to-do recluse. Its entrance is protected by a large, black-iron fence, its first-floor French windows sealed by louvered metal shutters, and its dark first floor windows barred by wrought-iron grilles. Seeing inside the embassy is impossible. Watching the entrance is comparatively easy. As a result, it is under constant surveillance by FBI counterintelligence agents. Photographs are methodically taken of people who enter and leave for future uses as identification should the need ever arise.

Yu-Chan Shek's approach to the Soviet Embassy was routinely recorded on the morning of February 9th. It was an unusually sharp picture, considering the focal length of the camera that was necessary from the FBI watchpost in the National Geographic Society Building. If it had been the usual grainy quality, it wouldn't have drawn the attention that it did. As it was, several agents examined it, not so much for recognition purposes as for appreciation of the new, high-speed color film now available from Eastman Kodak. When the photo was shown to

Agent Jim Windham, he was taken more with one of the two men in the photo than the photo itself. He quickly reached for the phone.

National Geographic Society

As often as Rick Stoner had visited Washington, D.C., he had never taken the time to visit the National Geographic Society. A three-day airlines' meeting at the Capital Hilton gave him his chance. He particularly wanted to purchase a world map for his office. When he emerged from the building, he not only had a map safely rolled and protected in a cardboard cylinder, he had a book on polar bears for his son, Trey, who was writing a school report on the arctic. He crossed the street and headed down Sixteenth toward his hotel. If he moved quickly, he figured he could be back with thirty minutes to spare before the afternoon meeting began. He suddenly realized he was passing the Soviet Embassy, that tiny bit of Soviet territory in the heart of the U.S. capital city. He stopped to study this bastion of what he found so reprehensible. Nikita Khrushchev's words of twenty years before, when he had pounded his shoe on the table at the United Nations and had proclaimed the Soviets would bury the U.S., still haunted him. *"No way, José,"* he mused. *"This is one country you'll never defeat!"*

He turned abruptly to walk back toward the entrance to see if he could observe more of the building. As he did, he bumped into a Chinese man who was hurrying toward the front door. Rick's book and map dropped to the sidewalk. So did the package carried by the other man. It was Rick's fault and he apologized as he reached for the three packages. "I'm sorry," he said. "I wasn't paying attention." The man seemed upset, almost angry, but said nothing as he retrieved his large envelope and scurried quickly toward the door. Unbeknownst to either man, an FBI camera captured their encounter on film.

East meets East

The door opened, exposing a small, fragile man with a fringe of gray hair circling a bald head. He peered at the visitor with eyes behind steel-rimmed glasses. "Da?" the Soviet said.

"I have an appointment with Vladimir Gregoric." Yu-Chan Shek seemed furtive and fidgeted with the package he was holding under his arm.

"Is he expecting you?"

"Yes."

"Come this way." Shek was led up a large marble staircase to an office on the next floor. His Soviet guide paused in front of a massive door, knocked sharply and entered.

A large, burly man moved from behind a desk to greet his visitor. "Mr. Shek?" he inquired.

"Mr. Gregoric?"

"Please, sit down," and he motioned the nervous man to a chair next to a fireplace. "What is it that brings you to meet with me?" The Soviet wasted no time in getting to the heart of the matter.

"I have something I wish to sell."

"And it is?"

"The design for an American collision avoidance radar."

"Is it in that package?" Gregoric pointed at the parcel now resting in Shek's lap.

"Just the summary description. I am not so foolish as to bring the entire document." Shek's composure was restoring itself. He was, after all, a feared business trader in the world of commerce. Negotiations were not unwelcome.

"And why do you think we would be interested in what you have?"

"Don't toy with me, Mr. Gregoric. If the Americans deploy this radar on their strategic and tactical aircraft, they will be capable of defeating your anti-aircraft defense system. But if you have the design, too, you will be able to develop countermeasures to overcome it. That's the way military evolution goes."

"Assuming you have what you say you do, what do you think it is worth?"

"It is worth more than I am asking."

"Maybe so. That would depend on how much you are asking."

"I want fifty million U.S. dollars." Yu-Chan Shek sat back in the overstuffed chair and smiled at his Soviet counterpart. "There will be no negotiation." He said. "If your government does not want the technology, I expect the People's Republic of China will. He handed his package to Gregoric. "Here. Give this to your people. Let them decide if what I offer is worth the price I am asking. You have one week. After that, I will make contact with the PRC in Hong Kong."

Shek stood, bowed slightly to his host and moved toward the door. He turned as he was about to leave and said, "I am staying at the Conrad

Hilton, room fourteen-fourteen. If you choose to call, merely say 'Deal,' and I will know what that means. If we have a deal, I will want the money deposited in my Swiss account that same day. He slid another piece of paper across the table. It had numbers written on it.

Remember, you have exactly one week to decide. I leave Dulles International to return to Hong Kong seven days from today."

He closed the door and walked down the staircase and out of the embassy.

FBI meeting in Washington, D.C.

The Washington Field Office had twenty counterintelligence squads. The squads, each consisting of up to thirty agents, were evenly divided between those focusing on Soviets and those who tracked spies from Soviet bloc countries, the PRC and the rest of the world.

Special Agent Wayne Peterson was a member of an elite secret squad of agents who focused on the best and most aggressive spies in the business. His special assignment was to track Soviet spies in the Western United States.

The only other time he attempted to find the FBI's Washington, DC Field Office on Half Street, he struggled. He knew that he went east on the Southwest Freeway, with the Washington Monument on his left, past apartment houses and marinas along the Washington Channel of the Potomac River, and that eventually he needed to head south on South Capital Street in the Anacosta neighborhood. There was a motel ahead where he was to take a right, then a quick left onto Half Street. A block away was Hoover Playground. *What a tribute.*

He found what he sought, through stubbornness and a smidgen of luck. It sure didn't look like the home of CI-3, the FBI's top counter-intelligence squad. This house was so secret that only the CIA, the NSA and the Soviet spies knew about it.

He presented his credentials at the front desk and waited for his escort. Never mind that he was a member of a similar elite squad of agents. No chances were taken, nor should they have been.

Peterson met with Paul Nickols, head of the counter-intelligence squad and two of his deputies. To his relief, they offered him a cup of coffee – his first of the day. Maybe that would alleviate the dull headache that was nagging him. Either that or it was the onset of a migraine. He hoped the caffeine would do the trick.

"We're pretty certain there was a drop made outside the Soviet Embassy yesterday." Peterson took a quick sip from his coffee cup. "If we hadn't been experimenting with a new Kodak film, we probably wouldn't have caught the transaction, at least not with the clarity we received." His audience was nodding their heads as he reviewed the facts that were known. "But it turned out that one of our agents recognized one of the people involved. Went to college with him, I understand."

"Do we know what he dropped?" Nickols seemed impatient for the bottom-line. His grouchy disposition had preceded him so Peterson was not surprised at his push for the facts.

"No sir, we don't, yet. But we did record a conversation between a person with a strong Chinese accent and Adamski of the Soviet Embassy. It was secretive and evasive. Our conclusion was that something of importance was being offered to the Soviets. Then a short time later, a Chinese and an American appeared to be involved in an exchange of papers right outside the Embassy."

"Who is Adamski?"

"We haven't figured that out. That's a name we gave him because he has never identified himself on the phone. We know he is highly placed in the Embassy based on the conversations he is involved in, but we have never heard his voice outside the Embassy."

"Most likely KGB."

"That's what we figure."

"Wasn't this exchange rather clumsy?" Nickols asked.

"It wasn't textbook, if that's what you mean, sir. The problem is that professionals are predictable. Amateurs are unpredictable. With the professional spy, we pretty much know what he's going to do in response to certain stimuli. Not so with the guy who's in it for sport. We have no idea what he'll do under most any circumstances." He smiled with the analogy he just thought of. "It's like handball. Which way the ball bounces is up to the way it hits the wall. And you usually don't know that until the moment of impact. Being in the right spot at the right time sure helps."

"So where do you propose we go from here?"

"We plan to perform an in-depth investigation of the man we have identified. In fact, it is already underway."

A Soviet mole

Colonel Josif Stepanovich Gromov was an Army Intelligence Officer in the GRU, the military counterpart of the better-known, more feared KGB. He was a fervent, contemplative man; a dedicated Communist throughout his adult life; dedicated that is, until he attained the military status that permitted him to move within the coterie of Soviet elite. There he saw the drunkenness, the debauchery, and the iniquity that he had been taught were the unique attributes of Western civilization. But because of his elevated capacity within the GRU, he had made several trips to the West and had not found it distinctively corrupt. He was bewildered, then angry. He had been deceived. This deception was not enough for him to betray his country. It would take more.

***

Josif Stepanovich Gromov was born in the beautiful city of L'Viv in 1926. He was a handsome man, not quite six feet tall with a sturdy frame. His appearance was more like someone from Leningrad, looking more Scandinavian than Ukrainian. His father was an outlaw, a soldier in the civil war seven years before as a White Russian against the Red Army. His father died the year he was born, having been in failing health since the war.

Following a normal Soviet education, with some encouragement to excel because of above-average intelligence, Gromov was commissioned into an armored tank regiment, and six months later, accepted into the Communist Party. He was a World War II hero, receiving both the Orders of the Red Banner and the Red Star. When the war ended, he continued his army career, attending the Military Diplomatic Academy, an advanced school for career intelligence officers. After ten years of loyal service, he was promoted and sent to Karachi, Pakistan as an assistant commercial attaché at the Soviet embassy. The commercial aspects of his job were a ruse, of course, but most governments played the same game. In truth, he was part of the GRU, providing a critical ear in the subcontinent. Gromov didn't remain in Pakistan long. Three months after arriving, he had a violent argument with his immediate supervisor who was KGB and was returned to Moscow. Rather than tarnishing his career, this incident actually enhanced his stature. His return to GRU headquarters was greeted with a promotion, not a demotion. He was made senior officer of the Chief Intelligence Directorate, a position that gave him access to many important military and state secrets. It gave him an impressive office in GRU Headquarters, overlooking Arbatskaya Square. It also gave him a black mark with the KGB. And as Gromov knew, the KGB had a long memory.

In 1972, Gromov decided to begin providing information to the West. He contacted Stanley Papps, U.S. Commercial Attaché at the American Embassy in Moscow. He and Papps had first met in Pakistan sixteen years earlier. The meetings then had been social, and so they were in Moscow. Spies knew each other, respected each other.

Three elements prejudiced his decision to betray his country. First, there was the corruption in the Kremlin which was blatantly obvious to him because of his own stature in government. Second was his strong fear that despite Brezhnev's declared interest in a treaty banning nuclear weapons, his internal Soviet policies were leading the world closer to a holocaust. Finally, he was frightened that the almost-certain discovery his father had fought against the Revolution would destroy him.

Gromov's first attempt to forsake the Motherland was a dud. He cautiously contacted an intelligence officer in the British Embassy. The effort was for naught. The Englishman wasn't buying. Seems a Soviet-turned traitor who ended up being a double agent had recently burned him. Besides, he couldn't believe that a GRU colonel would become an informant. No, it was too easy.

That was when Gromov tried his luck with Papps who had only recently been assigned to the U.S. Embassy in Moscow. Papps was Russian-speaking, neither without error nor without a distinct American accent, but good enough to make his needs known in a state-run store or to receive directions on the subway. When they had known each other in Karachi, in the early days of their two zealous careers, each had established a wary, but respectful regard for the capabilities of the other. But the relationship had never blossomed because of Gromov' premature departure.

Their next meeting was by accident. Gromov, fresh from the rebuff by the British, had been assigned to represent the USSR at an American Trade Exhibit in Leningrad. Papps was the U.S. coordinator of the month-long exhibition. It was during the later stages of the event that Gromov revealed his intentions that he had certain information he wanted to share with the West.

Stanley Papps did not look like a spy, at least any that Gromov had ever seen. If anything, he looked like he belonged in a classroom, lecturing students on the molecular makeup of grapefruits. He had a scholarly appearance, augmented by half-glasses that always hung on the end of his nose. He combed his graying hair across his head in an attempt to hide his premature baldness. His chubby face complimented his chubby body. Definitely a college professor if you didn't know better.

Two days later, Gromov provided Papps with an envelope. Its purpose was only to validate his intentions by sharing a small but important secret, heretofore unknown by the Americans. The ploy worked. Papps passed along the offering to Washington and was instructed to serve as the conduit for anything else the Soviet sought to share.

Four months later, Gromov went to Paris, heading up another Soviet trade delegation. His job was twofold; to engage in industrial espionage, and, as a member of the GRU, to watch the other members of the delegation. No one had the assignment of observing him. He met with Papps again at the Regina Hotel directly across the street from the Louvre. Papps was concerned with discovery and asked that Gromov participate in all trade delegation events during the day, while at night undertake a crash course in the procedures for communicating with the West.

For the next three years, Gromov was the West's primary source for the highest level Soviet military secrets on rocketry and missile development. Then, as quickly as the flow of information started, it stopped. Gromov told Papps there was more, but he was concerned that he was close to being discovered. Rather than expose himself needlessly, he was going underground, like a mole. It was obvious that being a GRU officer and a CIA spy exerted awesome contradictory pressures. Working for Soviet intelligence, he risked detection by various Western counterintelligence agencies. As a CIA agent, he faced the KGB and GRU security systems. It wasn't a morality issue or shame for what he had done, for he believed sincerely in his actions. Someone had to stop the madness in the Kremlin before the world was destroyed. If both sides shared the military secrets, neither side would have an advantage. Perhaps it was a morality issue, after all. He was more horrified of the consequences of his government's actions than those of his. In becoming a traitor to his country, he felt he had become a patriot of the world.

The CIA watched Colonel Josif Stepanovich Gromov' activities closely. Was he at risk? Had the KGB discovered his father's past? Had KGB or GRU discovered his spying activities? Everything they could observe appeared normal. Gromov continued with his normal functions, and traveled to London, Paris and Berlin as often as he had in the past. He participated in trade delegations to Rome and Ankara. No, he seemed secure. But the flow of information had stopped.

Then, as suddenly as it had stopped, it started again. That is to say, early in 1979, a message was received from Gromov saying that he would be flying to Berlin in two days and had critical information that must be shared. He would be at the usual place Friday evening at six o'clock.

Mole learns of PROPHET design

Colonel Gromov's hands shook as he held the documentation. Without any question, the GRU had uncovered an American secret of enormous proportions—a terrain-avoidance radar, undetectable from the ground. Its concept was ingenious. Its implication was frightening. With such a system, American bombers could penetrate Soviet defenses at low altitudes, travel to their targets without fear of detection, and escape without destruction. Within hours of receipt, the design had been translated and copied; distributed to elite scientists and engineers whose sole function was to dissect and then defeat the system. Within hours of his discovery, Gromov had contacted his CIA counterpart, arranging a meeting in Berlin.

Meanwhile, at KGB headquarters

Komitet Gosudarstvennoi Bezopasnosti, the dreaded KGB, had its headquarters in the Lubianka Building near the Kremlin on Dzershinsky Street. The First Directorate of the KGB was divided into six main divisions. The first was that of the Foreign Division that controlled all secret agents and assembled the results obtained by the vast networks worldwide. It was in this division that the intense, but secret investigation of Gromov was sequestered.

***

"I don't know how it escaped our attention, Comrade General, but Colonel Gromov's father was a traitor who fought against the revolution in 1919. The year Colonel Gromov was born, his father died and his mother remarried." Dmitri Tizyakov was a gaunt, red-faced man, with thick glasses and a prissy manner. His method of delivery lacked the impact one would expect from a KGB colonel.

"What was his father's name?" The old general squinted at the investigator.

"Oleg Alexandrovich."

With strained emotion, General Andrei Vedeniapin clenched his teeth together, then sighed. "Oleg Alexandrovich. The Ukrainian White!"

"You knew him, General?"

"Of him. I never knew him. He served under General Anton Denikin. He was a brilliant, but misguided, military strategist. Had his army been larger . . ." his voice drifted off. "But it wasn't. And he was a traitor to the revolution. We never found him after the fighting ended in 1920. We always assumed he had been killed during the retreat into Estonia." General Vedeniapin stared out the window, silent for the moment. "I know Colonel Josif Stepanovich Gromov. He too is a brilliant man. But it is difficult to believe that he is the son of Alexandrovich."

"We are certain of our facts, Comrade General."

"I suppose you are. So, with this blot on his record, it seems that all his activities bear scrutiny."

"Close surveillance began a month ago, General Vedeniapin, when we first learned of his father's treachery."

"Anything to report?"

"Only suspicions. We are digging deeper."

"What are his functions with our military neighbors?"

"Analysis of all data on the Americans' new top secret airplane."

"Where is he right now?"

"He's in Berlin."

Discovery revealed

The call came in just as Agent Tom Chase, a sandy-hair man in his late fifties, cleared his desk and reached for his coat. He was already late and his wife wasn't going to be pleased with this delay. He toyed with the thought of letting the phone ring, but there was something about a phone that demanded his attention. As a child, he had been told a phone could not ring more than three times. He had grilled that same ethic into his children. Phones were permitted to intrude. They were not allowed to be ignored. "Chase," he said brusquely into the phone. He awkwardly pulled on his suit jacket with his free hand.

"Chase, this is the Code Room. We've just decoded a Soviet communiqué that I think you need to see. It's 'Code Blue.' In fact," the nameless voice continued, "I would have called you in from home to see this one." The man didn't have to tell him that 'Code Blue' meant a breach of national security.

"I'm on my way." Chase's heart was pounding. Once before, he had received a top priority message. It was the day before the Soviets invaded Hungary.

***

The problem in meeting a mole for the first time is being certain the person you think is the mole is in fact the mole. This man had not contacted an American agent in three years. CIA Headquarters in Washington wasn't even certain until two days ago that he was still willing or able to perform for them. Karl Kilchert had served in Berlin since 1972. He knew his territory well. He knew his job even better. He understood the importance of receiving the information being brought out from Moscow. He didn't know what the information was. But it was significant enough to cause a mole to resurface.

The contrast between West and East Berlin was a ringing endorsement of capitalism. West Berlin was much like other northern European cities, modern, bustling, geared for business during the day, and frenzied with excitement at night. Office building skyscrapers, five-star hotels, palaces, museums, concert halls, parks, art galleries, nightclubs, beer gardens, sex stores, and of course, *The Wall*.

In stark contrast with the West, was the Deutsche Demokratische Republik with its "showpiece" East Berlin which in truth was a blatant dichotomy. Compared with its three-hundred foot wide boulevard, Unter den Linden, spacious Marx Engels Square and trolley cars running on shining tracks, were the bullet-scared buildings mere blocks away that served as glaring, yet outrageous reminders of a war thirty years distant in time. The lie of communism was there to be seen for those not blinded by chronic myopia. What amazed Kilchert was that East Berlin lived on, tolerated by a people who had to know better. What amazed him even more was that there were people dedicated to preserving this utopian delusion.

He strolled casually along the Ku 'Damm, Berlin's famous promenade, the busiest street in the entire western zone. There was no rush. He was thirty minutes ahead of schedule. On the other hand, he wanted to be settled in the rathskeller long before his contact arrived.

He entered the bar and sat at a table that provided the best vantage point. He scanned the room. It was smoky and noisy. The noise he could handle. The smoke clogged the air and gave him a headache. His eyes teared and burned. He was certain TriDelta hadn't arrived yet. It was too early. He sipped on his beer.

Movement by the entrance drew his attention. This could be his man. He certainly dressed like a Soviet. Kilchert watched the newcomer inspect the room slowly, then move toward an empty table. He was shorter than Kilchert had pictured in his mind. He couldn't have been more than five feet five. He was stocky, muscular, with no neck. 'He even looks like a mole,' Kilchert thought. 'All he needs are buck teeth.' In a charade of futility, the man had combed his remaining gray hair across his otherwise bald head, plastering it in place. It looked stupid. Maybe this wasn't TriDelta after all. Another man entered the rathskeller. He, too, looked around the small room, seemed to pay particular attention to the short, stocky moleman, then moved to a table across the room where he enjoyed a panorama of what went on. Kilchert decided to move cautiously. From all appearances, the man he had come to meet had drawn a small crowd.

"Have you ever been to Dubuque?" Kilchert was startled by a man sitting at the next table. That was the question to be asked by the mole. The speaker had a strong, intelligent face, brooding dark eyes, and a muscular body for a man in his sixties.

"No, the closest I've ever come is Cedar Rapids." He gave the official response. The Agency had selected "Dubuque" as the key word because of a sound-alike Russian word, "Dubok" that meant hollow tree, a hiding place for secret documents.

"It appears I guessed correctly, at least in part," the GRU colonel said in remarkably good English. "You are an American, even if you aren't from Iowa."

More pleasantries were exchanged for the sake of appearances with the ultimate result of Karl Kilchert joining his new acquaintance over a pitcher of beer. Ten minutes later, the man he originally thought to be the mole left the rathskeller, shadowed quickly by the other man who obviously was following him.

An hour later in hushed tones midst a cacophony of background noise, Kilchert and Gromov discussed the matter that had brought them together. "This is difficult for me," Gromov said with sadness in his voice. "You see, it is possible to love your country while hating its system. I love my country. I am a traitor only to its system."

"I guess I'm lucky," Kilchert rejoined. "I love my country and at least I like its system."

Gromov appeared to be sad. "What I am about to do is punishable by death. In the past, much of what I gave would have found me counting trees."

"I have absolutely no idea what you mean by that last statement."

Gromov brightened a little. "That is a Russian peasant expression dating back to czarist times. Anyone counting trees had been deported to Siberia."

"So what is it you are about to do?" Kilchert decided it best to move through this interview quickly. The risk of discovery was too great.

"I have absolute proof that the Soviet government has the plans for the Top Secret American Collision Avoidance Radar being developed by Pierce Electronics." He added the U.S. company's name as added proof of his knowledge.

"What do you mean, you have the plans?"

"We have all the schematic drawings."

"How did you get this information?"

"From a Chinese broker in Hong Kong. They sold it to our embassy in Washington."

"How did the Chinese get it?"

"It is our understanding they obtained it from someone high up in the Pierce company."

"We will need to see the proof," Kilchert said.

"Da, of course. I have everything, but I am concerned how we will make the exchange."

"I like to use 'cut-outs'" Kilchert said.

"Now it is my turn. I am not familiar with that term. What is a 'cut-out'?"

"A cut-out is an agent used as an intermediary for security purposes. Jones passes papers to Smith who gives them to Brown. Smith is the "cut-out." Jones and Brown never meet or know each other's names." Kilchert watched to see if Gromov understood. "We have been seen together tonight. There is always the chance that we are being observed. We will not meet again. This protects you. This protects me."

"Good. I fear this all the time. The 'Sosedi' are everywhere. That is what GRU people call the KGB—'the neighbors.' It is not a term of endearment." He pursed his lips and raised his eyebrows. "How will I know this Mister Smith?"

"He will know you."

"And we will meet when and where? I must be at the East German Ministry of Defense headquarters tomorrow morning. Can your man get into that sector?"

"That's where he lives. His name is Heinrich. He is a colonel in the East German military."

"But I know this man."

"As I said, he knows you."

Assassination

His gun looked like anything but a gun, not much more than an aluminum tube, really, weighing less than eight ounces, just over six inches long, and three-quarters of an inch in diameter. Hermetically sealed to the tube was a plastic ampoule containing liquid poison. The poison lacked color and was odorless, an invisible fine mist when fired by the weapon. He had never used this strange weapon. There would be no practice. He was a professional, and professionals get it right the first time. He read his instructions carefully. The poison must be fired directly into the victim's face at a range of no more than eighteen inches. Further away and the effectiveness of the poison would be affected adversely. He wondered how he could be so precise. What is he was twenty inches away? Would he fail? What if he got too close? Would the overdose be detectable? He read on. When the poisonous vapors are breathed in, the arteries carrying blood to the brain become paralyzed, followed by death within ninety seconds. Within minutes, the poison will wear off, leaving no trace of the killing agent. An autopsy will reveal death by natural causes, a heart attack.

Norbert Krug knew there was risk. There had to be. If his victim could breathe in the poison, so could he. He assumed the idea was to hold his breath. That certainly was his plan. Assassinations always seemed to be spontaneous, sometimes brought on by the passion of the moment. Rarely were they planned in advance. And that added risk to the assassin because of greater chance of error; miscalculation of the smallest detail.

Krug received his assignment Thursday morning—his victim, an East German colonel returning to Berlin that afternoon from a visit to Moscow. His premature death must occur no later than Saturday afternoon. Krug was to decide where and when. He already knew how.

He stood in the crowd that was meeting the flight, and easily recognized Colonel Heinrich. The military uniform helped, to be certain, but the sheath of photos he had received made identification positive. He easily followed the unsuspecting colonel to the East German Ministry of Defense headquarters where he dutifully reported his return to the country. From there, the trail seemed aimless; a government store selling cut glass from Czechoslovakia, an indoor food market, a tobacco shop, a stroll across Marx-Engels Platz. That evening, Colonel Heinrich, now dressed in civilian clothes, drank alone at a rathskeller. Krug sat at a table across the room, studying his quarry. He puzzled over what this man had done that warranted his death. All day Friday, Krug followed Heinrich, trying to establish a pattern of his movements, hoping for a clue of where he might be Saturday. Luck was with him. As he stood outside a government building, pretending to read a newspaper, Colonel Heinrich emerged in the company of a Soviet officer. "Tomorrow morning, then," Heinrich said. "I will meet you back here at nine o'clock."

"My office. Be prompt."

The colonel grunted at the admonishment but raised no objection. The two parted as they reached the street.

Krug hurried into the building to carefully study its layout.

Saturday, he watched Heinrich get off a streetcar and start his walk toward his nine o'clock appointment. Krug moved quickly ahead, into the building. Then, as Heinrich entered, Krug began to climb the circular staircase directly ahead of him. He was certain this was the route Heinrich would follow, since there were no offices on the ground floor. From the sound of footsteps behind him, he was correct.

At the first floor landing, he turned. Snapping his fingers together and feigning the look of a person who had forgotten something, he started back down the steps. As he passed closely by the officer, he took a deep breath, and without looking at his victim, fired the gun directly into his face and continued down the stairs. He heard his victim stumble, then fall, but he didn't look back. He couldn't afford to be involved. He walked out of the building, turned right and went directly to a nearby canal where he dropped a cylindrical tube into the water. Only then did he wonder about what seemed out of place. The color of the uniform seemed different. No matter. It was too late. The deed was done. He would receive his reward from Moscow, and then melt into the background. This was not a job he enjoyed or cared to repeat. Suddenly, the taste of sour bile erupted, burning his throat and tongue.

The next day, the newspaper reported that a Soviet colonel had died of a heart attack. Colonel Josif Stepanovich Gromov's body was being returned to Moscow with full military honors. There was no mention of an East German colonel who also died. Strange, Krug thought. Why the cover-up?

FBI learns of compromise from CIA

Tom Gates was routinely updated on all Sino-Soviet issues, the theory being that it was easier for him to receive too much paperwork than not enough. He could always shred what was unnecessary. And so it was that he learned of the possible compromise of the stealth bomber terrain avoidance radar project. Ordinarily, a courier would rush information like this to him. For some reason, this day it arrived through normal channels, so it only received his casual examination. Something in the title caught his eye as he shuffled papers. "TAR Compromise," it said. *What was that all about*, he wondered?

He opened the document, bolted upright from his slouched position, and headed for the office of the director.

Within minutes, a team was formed to begin the investigation process. The Soviets knew about a top secret, terrain avoidance/collision avoidance system being developed by Pierce Electronics. A Soviet informant died before being able to pass the corroborating evidence, but from the preliminary information he provided the CIA, there was no question of its veracity. Although the FBI knew nothing about the system, the fact that such a project had been compromised appeared to affect national security.

Calls were immediately made to the Pentagon, informing them of the situation.

Chapter 13

A Secret No More

Compromise revealed

"Senator Lundy . . ." His top aide caught up with the senior senator from Minnesota just as he was about to enter the Senate dining room. "Sir, Knox from National Security just left my office. Stealth has been compromised!" The tall Texan paused, undecided if he should reveal more in the corridor or wait for the sanctity of the senator's office. Perspiration beaded along his hairline as he gulped air to compensate for the ordeal of his run.

Just as he began to apologize for interrupting lunch, the senator held up his hand and said, "Tim, after six years on my staff, I know you well enough to realize the significance of your news. Let's head to my office," and with that, the two turned and moved swiftly toward the Dirksen Office Building.

Ten minutes later, behind closed doors, Tim Zwingle, a thirty two-year old Houston native with Harvard undergraduate and law degrees to his credit, began briefing his boss on the compromised classified program that had been uncovered involving Pierce Electronics. "They're a Seattle-based supplier of a terrain avoidance system for the Stealth bomber. It was a complex scheme, Senator . . . a three-country operation." Zwingle referred repeatedly to his notes. "There's a company in Hong Kong that traffics in buying industrial secrets and selling them to the highest bidder. National Security calls it a 'Chinese Laundry'." He paused so the irony of the title would not escape notice. It didn't. The senator's expressive eyebrows raised and a small smile played across his lips. "The FBI thinks they got hold of the information on the Pierce system from a seller within the company. At first, the Chinese didn't realize the military implications of the device. But when they caught on to what they had a hold of, they didn't look for the highest bidder. They contacted the Soviet Embassy and told them the price they'd accept."

"Was the disclosure complete?" Senator Lundy looked worried.

Zwingle checked his facts to assure his accuracy. He looked up and recited mechanically: "It appears that every schematic, from the power supply to the leading edge tracking of the radar altimeter to the phased-array radar system itself was handed over. If the Soviets ever wondered how we planned to come in at treetop heights, flying mach one, they'll wonder no more!"

"Son of a bitch!" He glared at Tim, but the aide knew that Senator Lundy's anger was not directed at him, only at his news." He rarely killed the messenger.

***

The defecation hit the rotary blades in the Pentagon moments later when General Alfred A. Bouren, Class of 'Forty Seven at West Point and Chairman of the Joint Chiefs accepted a phone call from Senator Elias T. Lundy, the chief purser of the Pentagon's purse strings.

"Lee, good to hear from you," the general employed his best diplomatic voice.

"General," Lundy set the tone of what was to follow, "we've got a major problem that compromises Stealth and every other attack bomber in our fleet." A hand covering the phone deleted the general's expletive. The senator continued. "My car has been ordered. I will be at your office within the hour. I request that those of your staff who can be mustered be available for a classified briefing upon my arrival."

Tim Zwingle's agitated voice could be heard from his office, tracking down John Knox at National Security. "I don't care who he's with. He and the file he discussed with me need to be at the office of the JCS within the hour. He's to be prepared to fully brief General Bouren, his staff and Senator Lundy."

***

John Knox's report was succinct and technical. "The heart of the new Pierce Terrain Avoidance Radar system, some people call it PROPHET because of its ability to see ahead, is their revolutionary radar altimeter, their innovative computer-controlled, forward-looking, terrain and threat-avoidance phased-array radar system, and the ingenious way that they have integrated these systems together. A radar altimeter is particularly important for flight safety during covert operations. Yet, even the low-power transmission of standard radar altimeters adds to an aircraft's detectability. The Pierce altimeter was designed to decrease that vulnerability with a spread spectrum transmission. Radar altimeters have traditionally operated at four-point-three gigahertz. The benefit of this signal is that it penetrates foliage and gives the pilot's precise altitude above ground level. There are also some altimeters that use fifteen-point-six gigahertz transmissions that don't penetrate the treetops. The philosophy here is that for low-altitude flying, the pilot needs to know height above the nearest obstacle rather than the height above ground level. The Pierce design allows its altimeter to continue with a four-point-three gigahertz transmission, but modulates the phase of the transmitted signal to obtain height above obstacles.

General Bouren interrupted. "How does this make the altimeter 'quieter' than any other?"

Knox checked his notes. "General, from what I read, the covertness is achieved by sequentially spreading the transmitted, four hundred milliwatt signal, plus or minus one hundred Mega Hertz about the four-point-three gigahertz center transmission frequency. The transmitted beam has been narrowed and the power management system has significantly constrained the output energy to further reduce detectability."

"Do you know what you're talking about?" Senator Lundy interrupted.

"No sir."

"Good. I was afraid it was just me."

"The altimeter's low susceptibility to discovery is clear," Bouren's years as a combat pilot showed through. "But how does the forward-looking radar avoid detection? I'd think that any ground search radar would spot it."

"Well, sir, for one thing, every time the enemy activates his radar-directed systems, it makes them vulnerable to our aircraft's anti-radiation missiles, so they have a tendency not to turn them on too much. And if we fly at night, they're severely handicapped if they switch to optics, TV and infrared."

"I understand that, Knox, but when we turn on our radars, I think the General's question was, 'what prevents our aircraft from being seen?'" Senator Lundy's reentered the mainstream.

"For the most part, Senator, our aircraft fly under their radar coverage, so we're invisible during those times. We combine extremely low altitude flight with high speed and lateral four degree per second maneuverability. Added to this is an incredibly low radar signature of the radar and the aircraft itself. The only sense that we haven't addressed is hearing. And if they hear us, we're already past them."

"It's like pulling hen's teeth." Bouren was becoming annoyed with what he perceived as evasion. "Look, Knox. It's clear how we can avoid their active radars. But that's not the only electronic detection technique at their disposal. They have passive radars too. All they have to do is sit there and listen for someone else to transmit. What prevents these radars from identifying our radars? Do you know or don't you?

"General, that information is not part of my file. My perception is that the frequencies used by the forward looking, phased array radar are fundamental to the radar's low profile. But I don't know the specifics. All I know is that they are extremely difficult to detect."

"Thank you, Knox." Senator Lundy nodded toward General Bouren. "That's what we thought. We'll find someone else who can explain it to us."

"Let's find something that you do know," Bouren said. "Or more specifically, what is it that the Soviets know, how did they come to know it and how badly compromised are we?

Knox took another look through his file before responding. "The Pierce Terrain Avoidance System is no longer a national secret. As best we can determine, all critical design details are in the hands of the Soviets. We don't know exactly how they got them, but suffice it to say, there's an unmistakable footprint to Pierce Electronics. And if the leak was at Pierce, the FBI is rather certain that it was their Vice President of Marketing, Derrick Stoner."

"What makes him a suspect?"

"Few people at Pierce were privy to the whole system. In fact, few people at Pierce knew about the whole system. There were only six of them. The President, the Vice President of Engineering who came up with the design, three design engineering supervisors, and Stoner. You see, the ingenious thing about the concept was that Pierce was only responsible for designing its specialty; the radar altimeter. The other crucial portions of the system were designed by outside consultant firms; none of which knew about the others. They all thought they were doing one portion and that Pierce was doing all the others. Inside Pierce, there was no reason to even suspect what was going on as long as the six people maintained secrecy. And actually, the three engineering supervisors only worked on smaller portions of the system. So in actuality, there were only three people able to compromise the full system."

Knox signaled that there was more as he paused, drew a deep breath and exhaled. "Stoner travels a lot; overseas, mostly. He goes to Hong Kong and was there less than a week ago. It's circumstantial, without question. But it's enough to show that he had opportunity. And guess what, he flies between Seattle and Hong Kong every few months or so. We don't know that he is involved, but it seems likely that he is. And the clincher is that Stoner was born in China and speaks fluent Mandarin and pretty good Cantonese!"

"The FBI has taken a hard look at every one of the other five Pierce employees. There is no better candidate. The President is rock solid. It makes no sense whatsoever that the Vice President of Engineering sold his own secret. And the other three have had virtually no occasion to make such a contact, nor can we find any motive that would make them nominees, particularly since it appears they aren't privy to the entire system."

"How did we determine that this radar system had been compromised?" Tim Zwingle asked.

"A mole in the GRU."

"I want to believe all this, Knox, but you worry me," Senator Lundy said. "You say that we only found out about this compromise yesterday. How on God's green earth did you put all of this information together in less than 24 hours?"

"Believe me, sir, we are not that quick under normal circumstances, but it just so happened that the F.B.I. was investigating Pierce Electronics, or more specifically this Stoner fellow. He had been observed making a presumed "drop" outside the Soviet Embassy. He was recognized by one of the agents who went to college with him. At the same time, a tail was placed on the Chinese man who was also involved in the "drop" which allowed us to determine his corporate affiliation. Thanks to the Air Force, we were able to establish what project Pierce was working on that would prove interesting to the Soviets. It was their PROPHET system.

"Then the word came that it had been compromised. It was just a matter of putting the remaining pieces together."

Lundy shook his head in appreciation. "You may not know what makes this system stealth, but you sure know how to figure other things out quickly. Good work."

General Bouren stood up, assuming his trademarked erect posture. "Gentlemen, let's take a break. And get Phillips in here. He's in DDR&E and knows the Stealth cold. We need to know more."

***

Harold Phillips from the office of the Director of Defense Research and Engineering began his briefing to the JCS thirty minutes later. "The radar is completely redundant. It's a modular system that uses five hundred electronically scanned antennas, half on each wing, sophisticated software modes, and advanced low-probability-of-intercept techniques that match the fighter's overall stealth qualities.

"The radar operates in the K_u band—12.5 to 18.0 GHz—using 21 separate modes for terrain following and terrain avoidance, navigation system updates, target search, location, identification and acquisition, and weapon delivery. These radar modes are unique in their low-probability-of-intercept design.

"This system greatly diminishes the effectiveness and range of radio frequency intercept sensor systems that attempt to detect and track an aircraft by locating the source of radar emissions.

"The antennas are installed in under-wing cavities starting about eight feet outboard on each side of the fuselage centerline. Matched to the fighter's low radar cross section, each antenna has an unobstructed view down, forward and to the side. The antennas are electronically steered in two dimensions, and feature a monopulse feed design that enables 'fractional beamwidth angular resolution'."

Bouren moved to the end of his chair. "Hold it, Phillips. What the hell is fractional beamwidth angular resolution?"

"General, I was hoping you'd know. I haven't the vaguest idea."

"Good, I'm not cracking up." Bouren sat back in his chair. "Go ahead."

Phillips didn't skip a beat. "Ultimately, the system will be redundant with two complete systems—ten line replaceable units per shipset—with all but the multiple antennas cross-strapped so any LRU can assume duties for either or both radar units if necessary.

"The radar transmitter is liquid-cooled. Packaged with its own high voltage power supplies as a single unit, the transmitter employs a gridded traveling wave tube RF amplifier. A forced-air-cooled receiver/exciter that generates RF waveforms, amplifies, detects and down-converts signals received from the antenna, and performs pulse compression of digitized signals for improved range resolution. A fully programmable radar signal processor (RSP) extracts target and other information from received signals, then provides those data to aircraft avionics in useable formats. A high speed, special purpose computer programmed in machine language, the RSP has a throughput of 7.1 million complex operations per second, and a two million, 24-bit word, 50 megabit bulk memory.

"The radar data processor, a military general purpose computer programmed in Jovial, serves as controller for other aircraft radar units. The data processor has a throughput speed of 2.5 million instructions per second, and a one million, 16-bit word (16 megabit) bulk memory.

"All radar units communicate over a dual data bus, and are hardened to withstand transient radiation and electromagnetic pulse effects. The vibration environment to be experienced at low altitude is especially severe because the aircraft has a much stiffer, less flexible structure than is typical for a large aircraft."

Bouren snorted. "And now, the Soviets know all this. And on top of that, they probably know what the hell fractional beamwidth angular resolution is."

Meanwhile, at 1110 Third Avenue, Seattle

Special Agent-in-Charge Roy Hanover of the Seattle Field Office gathered his counterintelligence group together. He signaled the last member of the team to enter the conference room to close the door. "This morning, we received an urgent action that's been assigned to us by Washington. Espionage activities have occurred, appearing to involve Pierce Electronics of Kirkland. The Soviets have acquired classified information on a Top Secret project they are working on for Wright-Patterson Air Force Base. We are to investigate what took place, determine how these clandestine intelligence activities occurred, and who was involved.

"The guess from Washington is that it started out as *Economic espionage*, and that somehow it escalated from there."

"What's the difference between espionage and economic espionage?" Agent Wayne Peterson wanted to know.

Hanover glanced at the paper in his hand. "Economic espionage is defined as foreign power-sponsored or coordinated intelligence activity directed at the U.S. government or U.S. corporations, establishments, or persons designed to unlawfully and clandestinely obtain sensitive financial, trade, or economic policy information; proprietary economic information; critical technologies; or to unlawfully or clandestinely influence sensitive economic policy decisions. This theft, through open and clandestine methods, can provide foreign entities with a treasure of proprietary economic information at a fraction of the true cost of their research and development, causing significant economic loss." He put the paper down. "Washington thinks this is the way that it happened, initially."

Peterson chimed in again. "Do we have any details?"

"A complete dossier is being couriered to us as we speak. It should be here late this afternoon. Until then, I just wanted all of you to have this heads-up. Once that file arrives, we are going to be busy; very busy."

He signaled that the meeting was over, then motioned for Agent Peterson to wait. "And Wayne, since you seem to be so interested, start gathering information on Pierce. By this afternoon, I want to know everything there is to know about them—principals, key personnel, company history, products, reputation, annual sales, whether there is a union, financial condition, and more. Like I said, this one is marked urgent. Everyone from the National Security Advisor to the Chairman of the Joint Chiefs in interested. We are in the national spotlight. It's time we put all our training to good use."

"They didn't teach me this in Cassidy's Alley."

"They didn't teach us a lot of things at Cassidy's Alley. It was just a bunch of facades replicating a typical small town primarily used for FBI and DEA New Agent Training. There was no such thing as clandestine training. That, you learn on the fly. The most I learned were low risk techniques like *dumpster diving*, looking through trash to obtain sensitive information not properly disposed of."

"When were you in Quantico?"

"The summer it opened—in 1972. I was in the second class to go through. Eleven weeks in the sun at that Virginia Marine base was enough for me. I think I must have set some sort of record for all the Cokes I drank. Man, it was hot!"

"Training at Cassidy's Alley improved a little after you left. We were taught to use commercially available listening devices like police scanners to tune in to the frequency of a wireless microphone being used in the corporate boardroom from several miles away. They labeled these techniques as 'social engineering.' We also learned that conversational extraction of information via telephone or face-to-face at conferences and trade shows has proved to be a sure and safe method of gaining information without detection."

"I'm getting a strong feeling that you should be my right hand man on this investigation. Interested?" He looked at this short agent, wondering if his diminutive stature was the cause for his tenaciousness.

"You had better believe it." Peterson stood erect, trying to look every inch an officer of the law.

An encounter with Customs

Rick moved rather easily through the Customs line up. Certainly faster than normal. The agent had him open one bag, asked to see two items he had declared, said "thank you," signed his form and motioned him on toward the terminal. Rick was exhausted from the ten-hour flight. He called on what reserve strength remained to lift his bags one more time to head toward the arrival hall and the waiting Carol. This had been a quick trip to Hong Kong and Bangkok. Thai International was considering a retrofit of their altimeters and Cathay Pacific wanted a face-to-face discussion before proceeding with their newest contract. Rick was the one they wanted to see. Rick had extended his visit one day so that he could meet with the Pierce representative. He was glad to be home.

Two men in business suits approached, cutting in front of him. One was short; the other was rather tall, reminding Rick of the cartoon characters, Mutt and Jeff. Both presented official-looking badges and asked Rick to accompany them to a nearby room. "We're with U.S. Customs and just have a few questions to ask you."

This had never happened to Rick before, and while anxious to move on, he regarded it as an interesting adventure . . . until he remembered the two rings of Carol's which he had taken to Bangkok to have missing stones replaced. He had forgotten to declare them when he left the USA, and in a sense, he was smuggling them back into the country because of this oversight. He didn't feel guilty, but he wasn't exactly calm either.

"Mutt" was in his thirties, a short, overweight man with brown eyes and brown thinning hair. His manner of dress was sloppy, a tie suspended short about three inches above his belt and a body odor that made Rick want to keep his distance. How did this man achieve the success he so obviously had? Maybe he married the boss' daughter. Maybe he was into blackmail. It had to be one of the two.

The room was tiny, barely big enough for the three of them, plus Rick's luggage that rested on a shelf that lined one wall. It reminded him of a dressing room in a clothing store. The interrogation was lengthy, not the few questions promised. The short agent did all the talking, implying misconduct but never accusing. "This is not just a random search," he said. "We have observed your frequent trips to Asia and feel there is something strange about them." It was obvious from his probing that he felt Rick was guilty of something.

Rick decided that he had been a Doberman pinscher in a former life. He had the look about him of an inquisitor, a Spanish variety. He held Rick's Customs declaration. "I want to see *everything* that you've declared," he said. "Then, I want to see everything else."

Except for Carol's two rings that were in his hip pocket, wrapped in a handkerchief, Rick had been meticulously thorough in recording every purchase, even the golden chains that he had purchased for a dollar from the Thai merchant in the Bangkok Floating Market. He had whimsically labeled them "junk jewelry," which in fact they were. He knew that his nieces, aged 6 and 8, would enjoy playing "dress up" with them. The agent took the paper sack that held the "junk" and bounced it in the palm of his hand. He extracted the necklaces and examined them. "Gold?" he asked.

The question was ludicrous, and in an attempt to break the tension that filled the room, Rick replied, "Gee, I sure hope so. I only paid a dollar for them." The agent looked contemptuously at him, took the sack and left the room to weigh the treasure.

The tall member of this vaudeville team talked for the first time. "I'm sorry my partner's been so rough on you," he said, trying to put Rick at ease. Rick remembered hearing about this kind of routine. The IRS reputedly used it, with one agent the "bad guy" and the other the "good guy." When the "bad guy" left the room, the "good guy" became a friend, an ally, a counselor. And the accused, fearing what might happen, turned to his newfound friend for advice on how to get out of his predicament. If this were what they were hoping for, Rick wasn't buying. His best ploy was to follow their lead, answering their questions and volunteering nothing. Yet, the temptation to ask for advice about Carol's rings was great. He certainly couldn't ask the Doberman. But he held off.

As this ordeal dragged in time toward an hour, Rick worried about Carol whom by now had no idea where he was, but probably assumed he had missed the flight. "My wife is waiting for me in the arrival hall. Can I get word to her, tell her what's happening, and that I'll be out sometime?"

"Sorry. We can't do that," was the reply from the 'friend.' "This shouldn't take too much longer."

The door opened and the first agent returned. Knowing that the contents of the bag were confirmed junk, and still seeking to restore normalcy to the proceedings, Rick said expectantly to the agent, "Gold?" He smiled, hoping for a reaction in kind. He received an angry glare instead.

The agent said, "That's it, except one last thing." Rick was excited that it was almost over. "I want you to empty all the contents of your pockets onto the shelf."

***

What amazed Rick was that his explanation of the rings was accepted without question. And within ten minutes, his bags were repacked and he was on his way. So what was the big deal? Why the harassment? Had they gotten the wrong guy? Or was his interrogation curiosity like they initially said it was? Amazed or not, he was out. What didn't amaze him was that Carol was no where to be found in the arrival hall. A quick telephone call home revealed that she had given him up for lost and was enroute home, not knowing what else to do.

"Tell your mother I'll take a taxi," he told his son Trey. "I'll be there in half an hour."

Adventure with Customs recounted

Rick was at work the next morning, ready to put in at least a full morning before calling it a day. While he always recovered quickly from time zone changes, the 16-hour change he had just encountered usually took a couple of days.

Charlie came into his office for a rundown on the trip. Rick was brief and to the point. It was a good trip. Thai International was certain to buy; Cathay Pacific was content. And their Hong Kong representative was fully briefed on the latest developments at Pierce.

Then, he told the story of his adventure with Customs the day before. "It was weird, Charlie," Rick said. "They grilled me, then stuck me on a skewer and flame-broiled each side." He wiped mock sweat from his brow. "I don't know what they thought I had, but they had to be disappointed when they didn't find it."

Encounter reported

"There was nothing to implicate him, sir." The FBI agent Tom Gates called his boss, Special Agent Phil Edwards, in Washington D.C. who first learned of the TAR compromise. "We searched everything when he reentered the country. Even found two rings he was smuggling in a handkerchief. But there were no technical papers related to the project, no payment checks or drafts, no large sums of cash. We even checked some chains he had in a sack to see if he had converted money to gold. Except for those rings, the guy was clean."

"OK, Tom," the chief responded. "We had no reason to think this was gonna be easy. Anybody involved in selling national secrets isn't necessarily stupid. But it would have been nice if we'd been lucky. Keep on the guy. That includes searching his home when the family is gone. He's the best suspect we've got." The line went dead.

Chapter 14

The Plot Thickens, The Knot Tightens

"There is a Mr. Roy Hanover here to see Mr. Strang." The Pierce receptionist called the company president's assistant from the lobby. She listened and then turned to the visitor. "Mr. Strang is in a meeting. Did you have an appointment?"

"No, but please inform him I am here on a most urgent matter. I must see him this morning."

"May I tell him what company you represent?"

"Just tell him I am with the government." He hesitated for a moment and added, "Tell him this is official business."

***

"Good morning, Mr. Stoner," the company's new receptionist said. "Mr. Strang would like you to meet him in his office right away. He said it was urgent."

"Oh brother!" Rick muttered under his breath. "I'll bet the Ramsey deal has gone sour!" He thanked Joan for the message and headed for his office. As he emerged, minus his coat and briefcase, he passed his secretary. "Jinnie, I'm going to be with Charlie for a while. Something's come up. Would you call Ed Blakely and postpone our nine o'clock meeting until I get back to him? And would you smuggle a cup of coffee into Charlie's office somehow. I need it to get the day started properly."

With that, he disappeared into the President's office. "Close the door, Rick," his friend and boss said. "We've got a problem that doesn't need to be shared." No coffee was going to penetrate that door. If that was an omen, Rick didn't like it.

The two men sat facing each other in the overstuffed easy chairs. Rick wished he could relax and enjoy the comfort, but his built-in alarm system had him nervous and tense. This was more than the Ramsey deal gone sour.

There was silence for a moment while Charles Strang nervously drummed a pencil on the arm of his chair. He stopped abruptly, breathed heavily, and then said in a monotone totally lacking emotion, "The full technical disclosure of PROPHET has been leaked to the Soviets."

"You've got to be kidding!" Rick heard himself say. "Who would do that?" He could come up with the dumbest questions during times of stress.

"We don't know . . . yet!" The monotone was gone. Charlie's cheeks were flush. "But the FBI's on it. I have every expectation they'll nail the bastard." His jaw went tight. "And when they do, I want him!"

Rick stared at his boss in disbelief. Pierce's radar system was not only going to revolutionize the industry, it was the heart of the Stealth bomber project. More than that, it was going to transform the company into a giant in the industry. The thought was mind-boggling. Sales were destined to be astronomical. The project was so secret that until two weeks before, only six people at Pierce knew the program even existed. But somebody . . . (who?) had destroyed everything. Rick opened his mouth to speak, but was speechless.

Charlie filled the void. "For openers, don't tell *anyone* what I've just told you. You're the only one I want involved. Don't tell Gil. I don't think there's any chance he's involved, but somebody is. And I don't want that person knowing we're on to him. I'm telling you because I need someone I can talk to." His eyes penetrated Rick's soul. "I need an ally. You're my friend. You're elected."

Rick sat up straight. "You've got it." Then, frowning a little, "What happens next?"

Charlie walked to the window and stared outside. Turning away from the window, he said, "The FBI has to think that one of the three of us did it. I know that I didn't. I know you well enough to be certain you didn't. And it makes no sense that Gil did it. But their investigation is certain to center on us. So, what happens next? I don't know other than I expect it won't be pretty."

Charlie turned back to the window, staring pensively into the woods that surrounded his side of the building. "For the sake of the company, we act as if nothing has happened. The FBI will handle everything. We can only hope they know what they are doing."

He was still staring out the window as Rick left.

Suspicions

Rick thought he was losing his mind. Charlie said to act like nothing had happened, but how could he? He could think of nothing else. Who could have done this? No one in the company would have had reason. One by one, he methodically examined each person with access to the system—enough to compromise its integrity. There were only three, and he was one of them.

It made no sense that Rick would suspect Gil of treason. It made no sense that Gil would be the one to betray his own secret, much less his country. But who else was there who knew the whole TAR system? Again, just three of them—Charlie, Gil and Rick. That was it. Everyone else only knew pieces. Rick knew that he could eliminate himself from the list of suspects. He was virtually certain that Charlie could be eliminated. That left Gil.

He probed his mind for clues that might implicate Gil's treachery. What would have motivated him, if he were the one? What would have caused him to do this?

The drive home

Rick sat in his car in the Pierce parking lot, his shoulders hunched, his chin almost on his chest. He couldn't believe what Charlie had told him at the end of the day . . . that he was the FBI's primary suspect. Charlie had told him to go home and get a good night's rest, like that was possible, and that they would talk again in the morning.

Rick sighed deeply and then reached for the keys that he had placed in the ignition fifteen minutes before. He couldn't sit there any longer. He was already late and he knew that Carol would be worrying. He pulled slowly past the few remaining cars in the lot, his headlights casting strange reflections as they moved over the puddles from the afternoon rainstorm. The trees along the drive looked differently under the cover of darkness. "Just like people," Rick thought. "Same, but different appearance. I wonder which is giving the right impression."

The drive home was pure agony. He wanted to cry, but he didn't know how. He had cried only twice as an adult. Once, when his grandfather had died. Once when his son had died. Those events had been gut-wrenching, heart-rending experiences—things that tore him apart from the inside. This feeling was different. It bordered on despair and abject fear. It wasn't the sort of thing that produced tears. It brought about panic. Rick had a childhood premonition of being accused of a terrible crime which he hadn't committed. In his dream, it had been murder, but this reality wasn't far from the other. As a child, he had imagined his distress and the anxiety of knowing his innocence while being accused. He couldn't come to grips with being incarcerated for a crime he hadn't committed. He thought about the hundreds of others who probably languished in prison though they were innocent of the felonies that sent them there.

But now his nightmare had come true. He could be accused. He was innocent. And he didn't know what to do about it. As he drove up the street to his home, he pushed the transmitter for the automatic garage door opener. It didn't work until he pulled up his driveway. "Figures!" he muttered. He waited as the door completed its cycle, then drove into the garage. Carol was standing by the stove, stirring the ingredients in a pan. She barely glanced at him as he entered the kitchen. "You're late," she said without a trace of humor. "Your dinner is ruined."

"Honey, I'm sorry." His voice was quiet, with a sound of defeat that caused Carol to turn and study her husband's face carefully. "This has been the worst day of my life. I don't think I could force food down anyway." He walked over to her, kissed her lightly on the lips per custom, and then walked toward the bedroom. He dropped his briefcase beside his dresser, removed his coat and tie, hanging them both up as also was his custom, and sat down on the bed. Carol followed him into the room and closed the door behind her. Roxanne whined from the hallway, wanting to be inside with her masters.

Carol sat alongside Rick and gently rubbed his back. Her voice soothed him as her hands moved to withdraw the tension from his body. "What's wrong, honey? I've never seen you like this." He moaned as she massaged a tight muscle in his shoulder. "Is it work?"

He sighed another deep sigh. "Charlie has sworn me to secrecy. I am to tell no one. But you're not no one. You're my wife. We are one." He sighed deeply again. "Our top secret project has been compromised and I think the FBI thinks I did it."

"What did you say?" Carol looked at him with a bewildered expression on her face.

"I said, 'The Soviets have the plans on PROPHET and the FBI thinks I'm the one who gave them to them.'"

"I don't understand." Carol was truly puzzled at this point. "How could they think you did such a thing?"

"They have no proof. They just know that I had the opportunity. And there is no one else who fits that description as well as I do. There are only three of us who know all the details of the design. There is no way that they believe Charlie did it, and it makes no sense that Gil did it. So that leaves me. They have a picture of me in front of the Soviet Embassy in Washington, D.C. I'm handing something to a Chinese man. They know that I travel to Hong Kong with some regularity, that I speak Chinese, and that the Soviets got the plans to PROPHET from the Chinese.

"There is no motive for my doing this. No money has changed hands. But there is this other evidence—Rick used his fingers to make the visual symbol for quotation marks around the word 'evidence' – that links me.

"And I'm scared." He collapsed on the bed, putting his head in his hands. "My whole world is crashing down on me."

Carol quickly put her arms around him. "Honey, it's going to be all right." She spoke the comforting words that women have used with their men for centuries. "They're going to find out who did it, and that it wasn't you." She stroked his hair, trying to bring calm to her man.

Then, revisiting something he had said, "What were you doing at the Soviet Embassy?"

"I was in Washington for an airline conference. At lunch one day, I had gone to the National Geographic Society to buy a world map for my office and a book on polar bears for Trey. It was an easy walk from the hotel. On my way back to the hotel, I walked right past the Embassy. I stopped to look at it and then bumped into a man who was about to enter the grounds. He was carrying a package and so was I. Both of them fell to the sidewalk. I picked them up, gave him his and we went our separate ways." He sat up and straightened his shoulders. "That must have been a smoking gun for the FBI. It's part of their proof—he made his quotation hand gesture again—that I am a bad guy."

"What can we do?"

"I'm not all that certain. But the one advantage I have is that I know I am innocent. That's one less person to investigate. The problem is, it only leaves Charlie and Gil and I can't believe either of them is the guilty party."

Then, after thinking for a moment, he added, "The thing that doesn't make sense is that in my gut I feel somehow Gil is the one involved."

The tightening of the knot

The secret didn't last long. The next morning, the Pierce facility had become an official crime scene. FBI agents swarmed everywhere, taking over conference rooms, searching offices, interviewing employees, transferring documents to waiting automobiles.

At the beginning of the work day, Charlie gathered all the Pierce employees into the cafeteria and told them of the compromise. He told everyone he expected their full cooperation with the government. He asked that they continue with their activities as best they could, but he knew it was going to be difficult. Still, he explained, the company needed to produce work in order to survive—and their individual performances would determine Pierce's success in doing that.

Then he introduced Special Agent Roy Hanover who was in charge of the investigation. Hanover said that his people would try to be as non-disruptive as possible, but they knew they would be causing some problems because of their proceedings.

Rick begins his own investigation

Rick didn't care. He had to see if there was any validity to his worst suspicions. He walked into Gil's office and closed the door behind him. Gil looked up startled. "Why did you do that?"

Rick sprawled in a chair. "Gil, everything we've worked for is over. The Air Force has shut down our program and the FBI is crawling all over this place. What I don't understand is how the secret got out? Who would have done it? What was the motive?" Rick was plainly disturbed. "Was the idea to hurt Pierce? To get back at the government? Was it for money?"

Gil stared blankly at the wall. "Maybe the person, whoever he was, did it for love?" Gil was not the romantic type and his remark was out of character.

"What??" Rick asked. "That doesn't make any sense!" he stated emphatically.

Gil's face was flush and he acted nervous. "What I mean is, maybe the person didn't think things through – didn't stop to think what he was doing, or at least to consider the full consequences."

"How could a person give away secrets like these without knowing the consequences?"

"I didn't say this was the answer. I'm just guessing like you."

"The thing that really troubles me is that by my reckoning, there are only three of us who knew enough about the system to compromise it. And none of us had any reason to be the perpetrator."

"How can you limit it to three? There are others."

"No others who know the whole system. We purposely broke everything up into pieces, not to protect it from something like this, but to assure our competitors didn't get a jump on the development. So we can't logically point to anyone beyond our inner circle. The only thing that makes sense is that one of us did it. And that makes no sense at all."

The two men stared at each other.

"Well you can drop the number from three to two, then. I didn't do it." Gil shuffled papers together, nervously slamming them down on his desk. "And I resent the implication that I did."

Rick stood, realizing that he was going nowhere with this conversation. "Charlie and I have as much reason to be defensive as you, Gil. Only that isn't where we are coming from. We are contending that it couldn't be any of us; that there must be another answer. So pointing the finger at someone else proves nothing unless you have justification. Which you don't."

As he returned to his own office, Rick felt that he had accomplished little, although he did feel that Gil's reactions were strange for someone without complicity.

Chapter 15

Free At Last, Free At Last

It should have been easy. Gil's twenty-two-caliber handgun was loaded and lay on the coffee table in front of her next to the now empty bottle of Bourbon. Living no longer made sense. It had become an endless stupor. "Drunk last night; drunk the night before. Gonna get drunk tonight like I never got drunk before." The old college tune ran through her mind without letup. She wanted to end her life. But she didn't. Each time she reached for the gun, her hand trembled so much she couldn't grip the handle, much less lift it to her head. And so the weapon continued to lie harmlessly on the table's shiny surface.

How long had she sat there in the family room? Hours, undoubtedly. The early afternoon sun had been streaming through the picture window when she first brought Gil's gun in from its hiding place. The bottle had been half full. Now it was dark and the bottle was empty. It wasn't clear to her when her resolve for suicide became a scenario for murder. Probably as the effects of the whiskey began to wear off. No matter. For the first time, she realized she was not the cause of her anguish. She had not done this to herself. She was the victim, not the perpetrator. He was the one who left her alone, night after night. He was the one who took her for granted. He was the one who showed her no romance. It wasn't her life she should be taking. It was Gil's. If Gil was punished, her suffering would end.

She rose unsteadily from the couch, picked up the gun and returned it to the holster under the bed. Then she went into the kitchen to make a pot of coffee. She wanted to be sober when she confronted Gil . . . whenever he decided to come home. Besides, she had strategy to devise.

At two a.m., when Gil quietly entered the house and climbed the stairs, he saw light under the door of the master bedroom. He groaned silently to himself, figuring that either Susan had passed out from her latest attack on the bottle, or worse, was still awake, ready to do battle with him. He debated sleeping in the guest room, but decided against it. Maybe the living room couch would be better. He had to get as much sleep as possible and dealing with her was not the best way to get it. Still, it was better to deal with her now than later.

He cautiously opened the door to the master bedroom.

The instant before he died, he saw Susan sitting up in bed, her legs pulled up in front of her chest, her two hands clasping an object on top of her knees. Then the object exploded.

As Susan squeezed the trigger of the twenty-two, she saw the look of pain and disbelief on Gil's face. She thought dispassionately that he must have been having one of his headaches. She fired again. Gil collapsed onto the bedroom carpet, a bullet in his brain and another in his chest.

At last, Susan was free. "Free at last. Thank God Almighty, free at last." Yet another tune began to play in her mind as she got out of bed and pulled a comforter over her husband's still body. She didn't want him to be cold.

The word gets out

The news of Gil's murder hadn't circulated the Pierce office yet. It had happened too late to catch the evening news and the media was only just becoming aware of the tragedy. But Rick and Charlie knew. Charlie had received a call from the police around three in the morning and he had called Rick.

As Rick approached his office the next morning, Jinnie came up from behind and said, "Gil called shortly after you left yesterday afternoon and wanted to set up a meeting on the Lockheed proposal first thing this morning. He said it was essential that certain items be resolved." Looking down at her notes, she continued. "I told him that as far as I knew, your schedule was clear until ten o'clock. He said, 'Good! Book him for an hour between nine and ten.' Is that okay?"

"Jinnie. You don't know, do you."

"Know what?" She looked concerned.

"Gil was murdered last night."

Rick searches Gil's office

His job was simple, yet incredibly complex. All he had to do was find the person or persons responsible for betraying the secret, determine how the secret was shared, extricate Charlie and himself, and hopefully Gil from suspicion, and exonerate their names in front of their peers. And he probably had to do it before the week was over. Piece of cake, he thought facetiously.

No one saw Rick unlock the door and enter Gil's office. Since Gil's death, his banty-rooster secretary had been reassigned, at least temporarily, until his replacement could be chosen. She was helping in Personnel. He closed the door quietly, secured the lock on the handle, and began his search. His heart pounded in his chest. The problem was, he had no idea what he was searching for. He felt like the boy he had described at the National Sales Meeting so long ago; the one who was walking down a country road with a rifle over his shoulder, who didn't know what he was hunting because he hadn't seen it yet. What was worse, Rick didn't even know why he should suspect Gil. But he did. And if his suspicions were correct, then maybe there was something in this office that would implicate him. He moved over to Gil's four-drawer file and opened the top drawer.

Twenty minutes later, except for the bottom drawer which was locked, he completed his meticulous search of the cabinet and moved over to the desk. He sat in Gil's chair and quietly opened the center drawer. As he began to empty the contents onto the top of the desk, he heard voices approaching the office. He froze, not moving a muscle. It sounded like Carl Munsen and Phil Talbot. Someone tried to open the door. "Damn!" he heard Carl exclaim. "Who the hell locked this door?" The knob rattled again but didn't turn. Rick exhaled as he heard them moving away. But he knew they would be back. They wanted something in Gil's office and the need for a key would be quickly overcome. He hurried to put the desk drawer back in order, stood up and scanned the room for evidence that he had been there. He moved to the door, opened it, and left. No one was in sight. No one saw him exit. He closed the door, then remembering that it needed to be locked, started to open it again when Munsen and Talbot walked up behind him. "What do you want in there?" Munsen asked. Rick was startled, and without a good excuse.

"I'm looking for a copy of our technical proposal to Boeing on the Seven-Three-Seven. My copy has disappeared." It wasn't much of an excuse, but it was something.

"How did you get that door open?" Milt asked.

"It was unlocked."

"Not two minutes ago, it wasn't," Milt replied. "We tried the door twice." He acted suspicious. "How did you get a key?"

"I didn't. The door was unlocked."

The three of them entered the office. Rick went over to Gil's bookshelf, located the technical volume he said he was looking for and left. He stayed near enough to the door to listen to Carl and Milt talking.

"That door was locked. I know it was." Carl was adamant. "He has a key. Now what I want to know is, why does he have a key?"

"Maybe we're making too much of this, Carl," Milt said.

"So, does your chief nemesis have a key to your office?" He jangled the coins in his pocket vigorously.

***

Chapter 16

Confrontations with the FBI

Apprehensive, Rick sat in the chair across from the three FBI agents and studied the faces of his real life antagonists. It was not a serene feeling.

"We haven't yet figured out how you did it, Stoner, but we know you did." Special Agent Wayne Peterson spoke in a monotone, yet with fervor. "It's just a matter of time until we put all the pieces together."

Rick recognized Peterson. He was the 'moleman' from Customs who searched his luggage at the airport. The FBI was accusing him of selling the design of PROPHET. He found it hard to breathe, as fear built up inside of him. What he didn't know was that if the FBI had enough evidence to arrest him, they would have placed handcuffs on him before the interview and advised him of his rights—to remain silent and to have a lawyer present. But because they lacked probable cause to arrest him, they had no legal obligation to give him any advice. He was strictly on his own, to surmise what he wished; to fear the worst. And his interviewers did nothing to dissuade him from his fears.

Instead, they added to them when Agent Peterson said, "Mister Stoner, you have the right to an attorney if you so desire." Just like on TV. He was going to jail. He'd better exercise his right and call his attorney, even if by doing so, he implicated his possible guilt. He was about to ask for a phone when a new obstacle was placed in front of him. "However," the FBI spokesman added, "your attorney will have to have a 'Top Secret' security clearance in order to inspect the classified information you know about." Rick was going to have to tough this one out on his own. He didn't know such a lawyer.

Peterson and one of the other two agents excused themselves, leaving the room without explanation. Using the "good guy, bad guy approach... again," the remaining agent, Roy Hanover, the man assigned as case officer, said, "I doubt you gave the Soviets everything you know. I'm not sure why you did what you did, but I don't think you were out to hurt the country." His eyes bore in on Rick, with just a hint of friendliness. "However, my superior in D.C. feels differently. He wants a full, open investigation that will include interviews with your family, your friends, and the people you work with." Rick was shattered at the thought. His reputation and his career would be bankrupt, even if he could prove his innocence. The agent continued. "I've succeeded in getting him to hold off if we get your cooperation."

Rick was a successful businessman, accustomed to pressure. Why was it that all the blood vessels leading to his brain were constricting? He couldn't think straight. "Look, I don't know how you zeroed in on me, but I'm not your guy." He tried unsuccessfully to keep his voice from quavering. "I'm a loyal American," he said with all the emphasis he could muster, while removing his shaking hands from the table. "I'm also loyal to my company." He was recovering a little poise. "There is no way I would compromise either by giving away secrets to our terrain avoidance system."

"Who said anything about a terrain avoidance system?" There was an accusation in the question.

"We're working on no other Top Secret project. Besides, I was told that there had been a leak and that the system was compromised." Rick stood his ground. More poise.

"Who told you that?" The agent was clearly disturbed that there had been a leak in the leak.

"Charles Strang told me. I'm his sounding board. We're friends as well as business associates."

***

Charlie Strang was clearly angry as he glared at the small audience of FBI agents in his office. "Just because I choose not to use profanity, doesn't mean I don't know the words," he said. "I vehemently denounce any possibility of Rick's duplicity in this. I don't care what the FBI suspicions are. You're after the wrong guy." His face was scarlet as his fist slammed onto his desk. "It's a bunch of crap! Rick is a great husband and father. He is a leader in our church. He's a top salesman and honest manager. He's well liked by virtually everyone here at Pierce. Then, suddenly he's suspected as 'the leak'—no longer a decent guy, but a probable spy." He stood up abruptly and walked to the window. "Rain on you!!" he said to no one in particular. "You're wrong."

"We understand your loyalty, Mr. Strang, but there is no one else within Pierce who had the opportunity, who was seen in front of the Soviet Embassy in Washington, who traveled to Hong Kong with regularity, and who speaks Chinese fluently. Furthermore, none of your other employees had either the motive or the incentive."

FBI agent Kyle Swinford spoke calmly, matter-of-factly trying to diffuse the tension in the room. "Can you give us another name to broaden our investigation?"

Charlie shook his head slowly from side to side.

Search for *real* traitor continues

Rick had never been so frightened in his life. Sure, all the evidence against him was circumstantial, but the indications of his involvement were so strong. At first he thought that he should demand a lie detector test. Then he was afraid that his fear would result in corroborating his guilt, rather than proving his innocence.

It didn't make sense. He knew everyone on the project who had any intimate technical knowledge, at least enough to compromise PROPHET. No one outside Pierce could be the traitor. And even thinking the "T" word was unthinkable.

None of those few would betray his country. He examined each man's personality and traits meticulously. His job was easier than the FBI's because he had two less people as candidates. He knew his own innocence, and for sure, he could rule out Charlie Strang. He knew Charlie well enough from work and church to know that his warts were merely blemishes. The man was without serious flaws. He chuckled almost sarcastically at the thought that he had any worth dwelling on.

OK, that ruled out two of them. What about Dirk Bogert, Tom Mathis and Pat Frankel? *What about them*, he thought? *All three of them are brilliant, hard working, have never been away from the office on business. Bogert and Mathis are both devoted family men.* While Rick had only known them for a few years and certainly didn't know their pasts, there was no hint that their presents were suspect. He let his mind wander over encounters with them. He could think of nothing that raised mistrust. *Three more down?* He thought so.

He moved on to his part-time friend and occasional nemesis, Gil. This project was his baby. He fathered the idea. How in the world could he have been the perpetrator? He pushed away from his desk and stood up. I need a break, he muttered. Time for coffee.

Jinnie saw him emerge from his office, coffee cup in hand. She stood up. "I'll get it for you," she said.

"Thanks, but I need to stretch my legs." The stern look on his face was troubling but she decided against inquiry.

Rick bypassed the fresh brew in his department and instead walked down the stairs to the cafeteria. He nodded to people as he passed them, but none spoke to him. He wondered if they were afraid to talk to him or if they didn't want to. No matter. He had things to do and was in no mood for superficial chatter.

Coffee in hand, he went back to his office without speaking to anyone. He tried to shrug it off, but it was obvious that the suspicion surrounding him had resulted in his informal excommunication. Jinnie was on the phone as Rick approached, so he whispered, "I don't want to be disturbed unless it's Charlie, okay?"

She was nodding her agreement as the door closed behind him.

Rick returned to his thoughts about Gil. While it didn't make sense that Gil could have been culpable, he had not been a man without troubles. He had seemed paranoid about his position within the company, he had been unhappy at home, he had been struggling with the final design . . . there were several things that made him a nominee. But logic ruled them all out. There was no reason to suspect his patriotism; there was no cause to challenge his company loyalty. Gil's troubles be damned, Rick concluded, it couldn't have been him either. The list was getting shorter. Whimsically, he thought, *Hey, maybe it is me.*

The examination resumed. And two hours later, he was no closer to sorting things out than when he had begun the process.

***

Rick brought his finds or lack thereof to Charlie. It was six o'clock and most of the staff had gone home. He felt certain they would be able to talk uninterrupted. Sure enough, Charlie was still in his office. Rick knocked, walked in and closed the door.

"What am I missing?" Rick asked as he collapsed onto his boss' couch. "If the Soviets have the schematics, they got them from us. No one else could be the source."

"You're assuming I didn't do it?" Charlie pushed his chair away from his desk.

"Yes, just like I know I didn't."

"So that leaves zero candidates."

"Yup. But who had the motive, the opportunity, and the audacity? I mean, Charlie, we're talking about a traitor. This isn't anything like accepting a job from Honeywell and taking proprietary data with you. This is selling secrets to the enemy."

"Hey, wait a minute," Charlie said. "What if this person didn't sell the secret to the enemy? What if the person gave it to a competitor? What if the intent wasn't nefarious, at least in the military sense, but just unscrupulous in the commercial sense? What if the person was planning to take our data to another company and something went wrong with the plan?"

"That could be, but intent aside, the bottom line is that the real enemy has the secret and one of us did it."

"That's right," Charlie said, "we keep coming back to the same conclusion as the Feds. One of us did it."

"And they're convinced it was me," Rick said meekly. "I didn't have the motive, but I had the opportunity."

"So now what?"

"Well, I'm sure not going to sit around and wait to be hung," Rick said resolutely. "And they don't seem to have the incentive to find anyone else."

"Well, before you do anything," Charlie said, "I think we need to turn this over to God."

Rick closed his eyes momentarily. "You're right. It is so easy to leave Him out of the process, as if He can't help and that we have to do it all on our own." He looked at his boss and the man who served as chairman of the board of his church. "Charlie, would you pray for me?"

"Lord, forgive us for not involving You except when all else fails. Sometimes I wonder who we think You are—or more correctly, who we think You aren't. We've got a situation here, Lord, one that needs Your help because we are in over our heads. Show us what to do. Give us direction. Give us Your wisdom. Oh, God, we are at Your mercy. We pray all these things in Your Son's most precious name."

Charlie stood up and walked over to Rick. "This will be resolved. You will be exonerated." He put his hand on Rick's shoulder and squeezed with affection and assurance. "In the end," he said, "the good guys win."

"Promise?"

"I promise."

It was no better at work

Rick had just entered a stall in the men's room when he heard Ollie Hunter and Gary Hennigan come in. They were heavy in conversation, so Rick remained quiet although he needed to speak to Hunter about the in-process Boeing proposal.

Hennigan was saying, "Rick's about to be buried."

"Interpret."

"Every sign points to him as the one who stole the PROPHET design, and the FBI figures he's the informant."

"Bullshit!"

"Hey, I know that, but they're talking evidence. Like countless trips to Hong Kong, pictures of a drop in front of the Soviet Embassy, meeting that Chinese spy, the whole nine yards."

"You're kidding."

"Nope. That I know for certain. Heard it from Carl."

"Carl doesn't count as a real source. He hates Rick's guts."

"Does that invalidate his data?"

"Probably not. But it holds it suspect."

"I hope so, but he sure sounded like he knew what he was talking about."

Hennigan didn't sound convinced. "I have the distinct impression that the facts are beginning to get in the way of the true story."

"Listen, I figure that if Munsen's mother had smothered him in his crib, no jury in the country would have convicted her. I figure he has been this obnoxious since birth."

"Now, I buy that part. He is totally without class. He seems to think that his speech is salty whereas most people find it profane and crude. There's nobody else like him here at Pierce and I haven't a clue why Charlie keeps him."

"Maybe he will be gone one of these days."

"Can't come soon enough."

***

Rick didn't emerge from the men's room until several minutes had passed. He didn't want to take any chance that Hennigan or Hunter would see him, and he needed time to compose himself.

He went straight to Don Stearns' office. He valued the opinions of his new second-in-command. After being told what had just occurred, the younger Stearns said, "Rick, don't concern yourself with Carl. He's a friend of no one. He lights up a room just by leaving it." His words were intended to be reassuring. "And, as you've noticed, he has an unsettling way of aligning himself with the strongest wind."

"But Don, some of what he says is true. I do travel to Hong Kong a lot. I have walked past the Soviet Embassy in Washington, D.C."

"Held any clandestine meetings with Chinese spies?"

"No."

"Don't dwell on this. Carl's a troublemaker with his cap set on creating a stir. As long as people listen to him, he's in the limelight."

Search for evidence

Rick was in Gil's office, rummaging through a bookcase, still not knowing what he was looking for.

"Looking for something?"

He turned. Margaret Catton, Carl Munsen's vintage secretary was standing in the doorway, arms folded across her chest. Her perpetual scowl and squinty eyes had always challenged him. "Yes, but it doesn't concern you," he countered.

"Traitors always concern me," she retorted.

"Spoken like a true American, Margaret," he said. "Guilty until proven innocent. Now, if you'll let me continue, I have work to do." He resumed his search of the bookcase.

"I will not," she said, raising her voice.

Rick stopped and looked at her. "Margaret, the last time I checked, I was an officer of this company, and you were a clerk. Has something occurred that I'm not aware of?"

Rick moved toward her as she slowly retreated. He gently but firmly guided her from the office and closed the door behind her.

Five minutes later, he aborted his search, finding nothing even remotely suspicious.

FBI review

"We've got our man," Agent Kyle Swinford looked his boss, Roy Hanover directly in the eyes, "only we can't prove it." He made a face and pounded a fist into his open hand.

"Are you certain he's the one?"

"Couldn't be anyone else."

"Have you looked at anyone else?"

"There's no need. Rick Stoner is the guy."

"You had better be right. We don't want to hang this guy out to dry if he's innocent."

"He isn't."

"This kinda reminds me of Christopher Boyce and Andrew Daulton Lee, except there were two of them, not one.

"That happened just as I graduated from the FBI Academy two years ago, but I don't remember the details."

"Well, these two long-time friends got into the espionage business selling spy satellite drawings to the Russians. It wasn't the money that drove them. They just were disillusioned with the USA. In fact, Boyce figured that it wasn't his fault he was born an American, so why should he feel any loyalty. He got a low level clerical job with TRW's Defense and Space Group. He worked in Classified Material Control, but didn't have access to Secret or Top Secret information. A couple of months later, he got a Top Secret clearance and suddenly was privy to information that made him angry about the government. Selling secrets was his way of punishing the government for what he felt was wrong."

"And your point is?"

"My point is that maybe Stoner is upset with something that he considers wrong. Maybe it isn't money-driven. Did he serve in Vietnam?"

"Nope. He was deferred. Had a physical disablement."

"Was he involved in any radical protests?"

"Not that we have found out."

"Well, if he's your man, there's something lurking there. You just have to find it."

"That's precisely what I intend to do."

Meeting with Charlie Strang

"Rick, this whole episode has gone beyond my wildest imagination." Charlie was solemn, choosing his words carefully. "There is no question in my mind about you and your integrity. I know you're innocent. I know you will be proven so." He spoke slowly, devoid of emotion. "But, and it's a big but, this whole issue has become too divisive within the company. Many of our folks are convinced you have to be guilty. This may be America, but in your case, you're guilty until proven innocent."

"So, the bottom line is I'm fired?"

"Hardly. The bottom line is you're on leave with pay until further notice. Go home, get some rest. Let the FBI settle this. That is their job, after all."

"Charlie, based on the way they've treated me, I'm not so certain they know how to do their job. It's obvious they have no other suspects and it's obvious they aren't looking for any. There is no way I can go home and rest. Somebody has to look for the traitor. I nominate me."

"Rick, that's nuts. What do you know about criminal investigative research?"

"Nothing. My only advantage is my unwavering dedication to exonerating me. On that score, I have everything to lose; absolutely everything if I don't prove me innocent."

"Where will you start?"

"I've already started. I've ruled out all but one of the possibilities."

"Who?"

"I don't want to say. I don't want to taint him unfairly. I know how awful that is. Once I'm proven innocent, there will be still be some who will never believe it. The brush of guilt paints a wide swath. I will always be guilty in their eyes. So if I'm wrong and he isn't guilty, I don't want to paint him with the blemish I've been painted with."

"Where will you look?"

"Unfortunately, the only place I can look is here at Pierce." He looked at his boss. "And you've just kicked me out."

"I put you on leave of absence, but I've got an idea . . . suppose you come in after hours? And suppose I help you? Think we can make a winning team?"

"We have since the outset of our relationship."

"Well, let's start the process now. Tell me what you have."

"There is no obvious culprit," Rick said. "No one makes sense. There is no one I know who would gain from doing something like this."

"Maybe so, but obvious or not, someone did it."

"I know. That's what's driving me crazy. But we can start with this knowledge. I didn't do it, and you didn't do it. So that narrows the field." He paused, rubbing his nose as he sometimes had occasion to do when thinking. "And because we can't figure out motive, I've been concentrating on who had the opportunity."

"You know, that's a point well taken," Charlie said. "There were three of us who had the opportunity. The other guys were only working on thin portions of the design without access to the whole."

"Right, while they had the security clearances for the whole, they didn't have the need-to-know as far as Pierce was concerned. They were purposefully sheltered from knowing the entire system."

"Let's count," Charlie said.

"There's you, me and Gil."

"Is that it? What about Dirk Bogert?"

"He never had access to the random frequency generator or to the programmable radar signal processor."

"Well shoot, no wonder they have zeroed in on you," Charlie declared. You are the one who's traveled to Hong Kong; you are the one who speaks Chinese. Furthermore, you are the newest member of the team." He sat glumly, staring out the window.

"Charlie, if it wasn't me, and it wasn't you, then it had to be Gil. Why would he have done such a thing? It was his concept – it was his design. All the glory and recognition were going to be his."

"For certain, but let's consider something else. His home life was a disaster. That means he was unhappy. Unhappy people do strange things." He paused. "You spent some time with him recently. Did you notice anything out of the ordinary?"

"Not really. Except for one morning in Rome . . ."

"What happened in Rome?"

"Well, I was starting to come out of my room to go jogging early one morning just as a woman emerged from Gil's room. She obviously had spent the night. Her name was Victoria Li. I recognized her as the Research Manager for Shek Industries. She is a stunning-looking woman, let me tell you. I thought it was strange that she was involved with Gil, but never said anything to him about it, nor did he ever mention it to me."

"Do I know Shek Industries?"

"Probably not. They broker deals between companies."

"Specifically?"

"They sell the technological property of one company to another."

"Where are they based?"

"Hong Kong."

The two men sat and stared dumbfounded at each other. "I've changed my mind," Charlie said. "I don't want you in here after hours. It's too risky. You're certain to be accused of wrong-doing."

"But Charlie . . ."

"No 'buts' about it," Charlie said. "If you are found gathering evidence, there will be the logical conclusion that you are gathering evidence to destroy it, not to offer it in your defense."

"What do you want me to do, then, sit on my hands?"

"No, I want you to counsel the investigator who I hire to do the real snooping."

"OK, but I want them to seek answers to dark questions by turning spotlights on them."

"Well said. There will be nothing overlooked, I promise you."

Agents take over

FBI agents swarmed over the Pierce building, commandeering two conference rooms, even stationing agents outside the two doors to prevent lingering in the nearby halls by Pierce employees. It was a hectic scene in one of the rooms as a steady stream of files was carried in for meticulous examination, and a steady stream of files were being taken out for return to their original locations. No one from Pierce was allowed to touch them. Every cabinet was secured and treated as potential evidence.

In the other conference room, exhaustive interrogations of Pierce employees were taking place. No one was too low on the totem pole. Everyone was a potential source for information. If it weren't for the inference that someone at Pierce was unscrupulous, it would have been a comforting feeling knowing that the FBI was thorough and turning over every rock. As it was, those being interviewed became huffy and defensive at the suggestion they knew anything about the theft of the Top Secret material.

Hump Marryatt was one who really got his back up, making no bones about his loyalty to Rick and to the absurdity that Rick could have had anything to do with the compromise.

"I know you're just trying to do your jobs," he spoke with intensity, louder than normal, "but I resent your implication that Rick was involved." He glared first at Roy Hanover who was his chief attacker, and then at Wayne Peterson, who was Hanover's right-hand head-nodder. "I get the distinct impression that he's the only one you're looking at, and that's just downright stupid."

"Mr. Marryatt," Hanover said calmly, almost condescendingly, "if you don't calm down, we might start thinking you had something to do with this."

The rest of the interview was more subdued. No information of quality was obtained from Marryatt who clearly knew nothing and had no involvement.

***

Later that day, Carl Munsen was the chosen interviewee. He was more anxious to please, or as he put it, "be helpful." His short-sleeved shirt revealed a Black Panther tattoo on his right bicep. Two yellow eyes peered eerily beneath the wrinkled shirt. Agent Hanover glanced at his personnel folder and noted Munsen's Army background. Enlisted. *Figures*, he thought. *Probably got the tattoo one night when he was drunk.*

"Mr. Munsen, what was the level of your involvement in the Pierce Terrain Avoidance System?" Hanover was not accusatory, but there was a serious tone to his voice.

Munsen squirmed and shoved a hand into his pocket. "Absolutely nothing. Like most of management, I was kept in the dark." His Boston accent was crude, suggesting a ghetto upbringing.

"Surely, as Production Manager, you attended some briefings."

"A couple, but they were just so much snake oil." Munsen shifted nervously in his chair as his fingers found some coins to jingle together.

"So, what's your take on this? How did Stoner pull this off?"

"Do you figgya he did it?" Munsen seemed excited by the news.

"Don't you?" Hanover was good at leading a witness.

"Something like this don't surprise me."

"Did he ever do anything that made you wonder?"

"Wonder about what?"

"I don't know; maybe that he was up to something nefarious or shady? Was he a loner? Did he stick to himself a lot?"

Munsen rapidly jangled the coins in his pocket while he thought. "I didn't pay much attention to who he hung with, or even if he hung out with anyone. Our offices were at opposite ends of the building and one floor apart. If he went to lunch with someone, I wouldn't know. I do know he traveled a lot, and usually was on his own then. I always assumed it was a money-saving attempt, but maybe it wasn't." His coins jangled even more rapidly.

It became clear to both agents that the rest of this interview would not yield any quality information. Carl Munsen did not appear to be in the know, so after a few more perfunctory questions, they let him go.

Charlie's fingers do the walking

Charlie sat back in his chair, laced his fingers behind his head, and stared at the picture on his wall, deep in thought. How would he find the right investigator? This was a subject about which he knew nothing. It seemed primitive, but maybe the place to start was in the Yellow Pages.

Charlie poured over Yellow Pages ads looking for investigators. Thankfully, there weren't too many choices – just three pages worth. One display ad in particular caught his eye: "Former Special Agent – U.S. Counterintelligence" with the added comment that the company specialized in "Industrial Espionage." He picked up the phone and dialed.

***

"I was not born to sit on my hands," Rick said to Carol as the two of them sat at the kitchen table while she shelled peas. "I read something the other day. It seemed to apply to me. It said, 'Dare to stand alone. Dare to win or lose.' I refuse to accept defeat. That denies my character. At the same time, I feel useless and impotent. I'm banned from the office. I can't do anything in my defense."

"I know," she said reassuringly, "but you have got to let the FBI do their thing."

"Their thing," he said vehemently, "is me. That's who and what they are doing. I see no evidence that they are looking at anyone else."

"Didn't you say that Charlie was going to hire an investigator?"

"Yup. But for now, the only thing that's good is that they won't be looking at me. Charlie will tell them to find another answer."

"Well, while you're waiting for them to find that other answer, could you maybe help me wash windows? You do the outside; I'll do the inside?"

"Are you trying to distract me?"

"Yes. Is it working?"

***

Two hours later, Charlie had met with Gary Nigretto, the owner of Nigretto Investigations and had hired him to find out all there was to know about Victoria Li.

The next morning, Nigretto called. "Mr. Strang, Miss Li works out of the Shek USA headquarters on Thomas Circle in Washington, D.C. She is there now and expected to be there for the rest of the week."

***

That evening, Charlie was on United's red-eye flight to the nation's capital.

Not to be one to put things off, Charlie checked into the Washington Sheraton, took a brief shower, shaved and dressed, grabbed a quick breakfast in the coffee shop and headed for Shek USA. He was waiting for Victoria Li in the lobby when she arrived at 9:30 a.m. The only thing the receptionist knew was that he had business to discuss with the Research Manager.

Victoria motioned him to a chair in her glassed-in office, carefully stowed her briefcase beside her desk and sat down. She smiled a devastating smile at him. "Mr. Strang, I apologize. I didn't recall that we had an appointment. Have I kept you waiting long?" Her brown eyes never broke contact with his.

"I've only been here for a couple of minutes, and no, you haven't lost your mind, we didn't have an appointment." He adjusted his tie clip, making certain it was secure. "I just flew in from Seattle this morning."

She seemed puzzled. "Then, how can I help you?"

"I want to talk to you about Gil Brockton." He watched her body stiffen and her eyes narrow.

"What about Mr. Brockton?"

"Well, for openers, I want to know what your relationship was with him."

"I don't think that's any of your business." She shifted nervously in her chair.

"On the contrary, Miss Li. Gil Brockton worked for me. His business was my business. And from what I have learned about your business, it can be your job to show an unhealthy interest in my business."

"I have absolutely no idea what you are talking about."

"Don't you?" He scoffed. "Correct me if I'm wrong, but doesn't Shek Industries broker deals between companies – selling the patented secrets of one to another?" He didn't give her time to answer. "How do you gain access to those secrets? It's puzzling to me that so many sellers would be in search of buyers. I know, for example, that my company would never consent to sell its proprietary products, nor would we have any interest in selling patents that we hold." She took a breath, preparing to respond. "Please," he said holding up his right hand, "I'm not finished."

"It turns out that a system we have developed for the U.S. government has been compromised. While carrying the highest security classification, its design is now in the hands of the Soviet Union. Someone stole that design, Miss Li. It appears that it was you." He sat back from the edge of the chair he had been occupying.

"I can't believe what I am hearing. You are accusing me of espionage." She didn't look so pretty now.

"I'll tell you what. It's only a matter of time before all the loose ends are tied together. When that happens, you're going to be in the middle. You're in this right up to the top of your pantyhose. Before I'm done, there will be no place for you to hide."

She stood up abruptly, rolling her chair forcefully back to the window. "Mr. Strang. I must ask you to leave. What little welcome for you there was has now been exceeded." She folded her arms across her chest and stared rigidly at him.

Charlie stood slowly, then left her office without saying another word.

He returned to the Sheraton, collected his belongings, checked out and headed back to Dulles International. On the off chance that his Washington business could be conducted in the morning, his secretary had made a reservation on the 5 p.m. non-stop to Seattle. He would make the flight with ease.

The next morning, he walked into Nigretto Investigations' office overlooking Seattle's Lake Union. He was quickly ushered into the conference room. Gary Nigretto and one of his assistants, Alan Boucher joined him a minute later.

Charlie slid a micro-cassette tape across the table to the two. "There's not a lot of condemning information on here, but when you listen to the tone of her voice; in fact, if you have an expert in stress analysis listen to the tape, I think you will agree with me that there is no doubt that she's involved." He paused before continuing.

"I want you to nail her."

***

The Nigretto agency gave top priority to the Pierce assignment. It was the highest profile case they had ever had. Success with this one would mean opportunities with others. Gary Nigretto took the lead but assigned his second-in-command, Dennis Land to assist. "We are assuming that Victoria Li is our gal," he told Land. "She plied the secret from Gil Brockton. That also means we are assuming Gil Brockton is our guy. For whatever reason, he provided the Li woman with the design."

"Why would a man steal his own design? I mean, he didn't steal it, but why would he give it to someone else? Do you suppose money was the issue?"

"It doesn't smell like money to me. No, I think there was something else."

"Like?"

"Like, that's what we have to find out." Nigretto shuffled through some papers on his desk until he found the notes he had taken during his discussion with Charlie Strang. "Here it is," he said. "Brockton virtually never left town once the project started. He made one trip to Italy to attend a conference and trade show in Rome. That's where he met the Li woman. But after that, he stayed in the Seattle area."

He sat back in his executive chair and adjusted his glasses. "Which means, if he met her again, it was somewhere around here." He pulled a photograph of Gil Brockton from his file and handed it to Land. "Here's what Brockton looked like. Get a picture of Li through our D.C. affiliate and see if you can't match these two at a hotel in Seattle or Bellevue. Check with doormen, room service, desk clerks—anyone who might remember them."

***

"We might as well sharpen up our resumes," Grady Morgan said. "And that worries me, because I don't know of anyone who is hiring secretaries these days."

"Grady, the company is not going down the tubes." Sandy McCray, Contracts Manager replied. "We have a strong product line and firm contracts that carry us out three years. We are profitable and will remain so."

"But the Air Force has shut down our contract with Wright-Patterson. Everyone said that was our future. And the word is that there will be mass layoffs."

"Grady, get a hold of yourself. Think. Why would we lay off people when all our production contracts are still intact? That doesn't make sense."

"Maybe so, but we're all in trouble because of what Mr. Stoner did. That's for sure."

Sandy's face hardened. She said, sternly, "Bite your tongue. I know that Rick couldn't be the one who did it. I've known him for a while. I spent a week with him in Hong Kong. He is honest, caring, thoughtful . . . and, well . . . wonderful. He is an incredibly loyal Pierce employee. All he could talk about was the future of the company, when he wasn't talking about his family. He was not a person who had just sold out his company and his country."

"Well, how could everyone be wrong?"

"Who's everyone?"

"Mr. Munsen, for one; Agnes Fristoe for another."

"Oh, you picked two dandies there. They have the loyalty of tomcats. Munsen would sell his mother for a promotion and Agnes gives the word 'hag' a bad name. Carl would bad-mouth anyone, but Rick in particular. He has disliked him from the outset. Agnes is just an unhappy old woman; anxious to make anyone look bad in hopes it will make her look good."

"I hope you're right. I've always liked Mr. Stoner."

"Trust me. On this one, I'm right. One of my jobs is to assess character. Rick Stoner is one of the good guys."

"I guess I just hope you're right."

"You don't need to worry about it."

***

Despite the effort for secrecy, word leaked out. It seemed to be a specialty of the press corps; to dig dirt. The call was not expected.

"Mr. Strang, I've been trying to reach you for a few days. Seems that you have a great filtering system at your office."

"Meaning?" Charlie was disturbed that the caller had made it through his secretary.

"Meaning I want to discuss a little item we're running in tomorrow's edition of the Times. I am looking for your comments about the F.B.I. investigation that is taking place at Pierce."

"Who is this?"

"Ken Egertson. I'm a reporter with the Seattle Times."

"Well, I have no comment about anything that is taking place at Pierce."

"I understand your reticence to talk, but surely you would like the opportunity to refute the allegation that your company has given top secret information to the Soviets."

"Mr. Egertson?"

"Yes?"

"If I say your facts aren't straight, your story will say 'Company President Denies He is a Spy,' right?"

"Unless you would like to confirm that you are, or make some other statement."

"OK, I do."

"Great. Say it slowly, please, so I can take it down. I'm not using a recorder."

"Mr. Egertson," Charlie said slowly as requested, "Is your wife having an affair with your editor?"

Egertson screamed into the phone, "What the hell kind of question is that?"

"Well," Charlie dragged out his words, "I have a reporter in my office from the Wall Street Journal. He is just finishing his interview with me on our latest contract with McDonnell Douglas. I am certain he would like to run a story that says, 'Times Reporter Denies Wife Having an Affair.'"

The line went dead.

***

It took two weeks, mostly because photos of Li took ten days to arrive. Apparently she had been in Hong Kong and wasn't available for surveillance shots. From that point forward, it was easy to confirm her frequent habit of staying at the Westin Towers in downtown Seattle. She was a stunning woman and quickly recognized. Brockton, however, was a little more difficult. But a man from Room Service did remember seeing a man in her room and he was almost certain that the picture of Brockton was the man he saw.

Detective work is akin to a chess match only backwards. You learn the outcome, and then try to figure out the moves that led to it. Li got the design from Brockton. Checkmate. Li met Brockton in her hotel room. Queen takes Knight. Brockton met Li in Rome. Rook takes Rook.

"I think our guy had to be desperate for love." Nigretto bit his lower lip as he talked his thoughts. "If I'm right, that could have been the chink in his armor. He was no match for a gorgeous Eurasian beauty who plied her wiles while making him think he was Mister Wonderful."

"We're going to role-play a little," Nigretto said.

Land smiled. He was only 32 years old and new at this business, but as an amateur actor with a few credits at the local Taproot Theatre, he enjoyed role-playing. "Which part do I have?" he asked, knowing what came next.

"You're the voluptuous, sexy Victoria."

"Ah, I get to touch my feminine side." His hands playfully pushed up what bosom he had. "OK, Big Boy, let's begin."

Nigretto laughed at this attempt at burlesque. "The only place these two could have met would have been at the trade show in Rome. We'll start at the Pierce booth. You've targeted the company and are looking for a patsy. You know from experience that engineers are usually introverts, so you seek them out." He motioned Land to begin as he pretended to fiddle with his computer.

"Excuse me, Sir. I've stood here, reading the signs on your booth and see that leading edge tracking is a key design feature of your altimeter. Is there someone who could explain what's so special about it?"

Nigretto stood up and walked over to Land. "As a matter of fact, I can. It's my design."

"OK," Land said, "that makes the connection. It doesn't take much of a genius to advance these preliminaries into a bunch of oohs and aahs and flattering compliments, followed by an invitation to dinner. Hell, she was probably the one who invited him. 'I have so much enjoyed talking to you, Mr. Brockton.' ('Please, call me Gil.') 'I wonder if you would like to join me for dinner.' What horny, shy, never-pursued-by-the-opposite-sex guy wouldn't succumb to a gorgeous, sexy woman?"

"Sounds like a valid theory to me," Nigretto said. "We know she ended up in his room for the night. This scenario would sure get her there."

"OK, we probably can skip forward a few weeks or months. Brockton is in his office and gets a call from Li. This is the first time he's heard from her since Rome. He figures it was a one-night stand, but her call totally disarms him. 'Gil, I'm here at the Westin in Seattle. I've thought so much about you. Is there a chance I can see you while I'm here?' He can't believe it. What should he do? Go home to an alcoholic wife or visit a beautiful woman who obviously desires him? That's a real no-brainer."

"Another valid theory."

"Yeah, but what doesn't make sense is how she would get the classified design away from him. Not many love-struck engineers are traitors to their country."

"The only thing that would make sense is that she turned him into an addict."

"Meaning?"

"Meaning he became enslaved to her charms and would do anything to prevent her from taking them away."

"That means they had several encounters. Two romps in the hay would hardly do it."

Both men stared at each other for a minute. Land chewed on a pen he had pulled from his shirt pocket. Nigretto returned to biting his lip.

"If she was smart," Nigretto resumed, "and she was smart, she chose her rendezvous spots carefully, in places where he wouldn't be recognized. And probably not the same place twice to prevent anyone from remembering them. They were an odd couple, after all. He was almost twice her age, a little paunchy and not particularly attractive. People would notice them."

"I think I need to broaden my search," Land said.

"That you do. But don't go too far a field. They weren't likely to go beyond Renton or Everett or Issaquah."

Another week of detective work yielded four more probable sightings and one absolute. All were at motels. One was on the Bothell-Woodinville highway, one was in Renton near the airfield, two were in Lake City, just north of Seattle, and the absolute was in Redmond. All were sleazy and obviously selected for the unlikeness that anyone knowing Brockton would be there.

***

It seemed best that their contacts be as clandestine as possible, so Charlie and Rick went to Gary Nigretto's office, rather than having him come to Pierce. Nigretto shoved a file folder across his desk toward his employer. "We've got pretty hard evidence that Brockton and Li were engaged in a torrid love affair." He let the news sink in. "This is a classic rich, older man squires around a beautiful young woman script. She wants what he's got and he wants what she's got. Usually it's a fair trade between consenting adults. Only this time, he wasn't rich. But he had something she wanted. The question is what? He was married. Not a lot of money. Not handsome. Old enough to be her father.

"From what we can piece together about her visits, she met no one else when she came to Seattle. She had no legitimate business reason to be in town. It's all circumstantial, but the only thing that makes sense is that Victoria Li was after the Pierce design."

"I agree with you," Charlie said, "but why did Gil give it to her? That part doesn't make sense."

"Well, we've role-played this and have come up with a strong possibility. Suppose you were hooked on drugs and your only supplier said he couldn't provide any more because he was out of money. Even if you weren't rich, wouldn't you have tried to figure out a way to get some to keep him in business?"

"But Gil wasn't hooked on drugs," Rick said.

"No, but he was hooked on love. What if our femme fatale said she couldn't see him any more because her company was going under? What if she said without a profitable sale, she would have to return to Hong Kong, never to see him again? What if she sobbed and wept and cried really big tears?

"What if she assured him that she would withhold the design for a year? What if she told him by then the design would be common knowledge and no one would know what he had done? An addict makes all kinds of rationalizations not made by normal people."

Charlie stared out the window at the TV towers atop Queen Anne Hill. Then, he said softly, "I don't see how he could have done it."

"That's because you're normal."

Meeting with Special Agent-in-Charge

Charlie picked up the phone and dialed 622-0460, the FBI's Seattle Field Office. When he was put through to Agent Roy Hanover, he said, "I want to meet with you in half an hour. I am headed back to my office and will be there when you arrive. I have information that you don't have. And I want you to have it." There was no question that this was to be a command appearance.

Forty minutes later, Hanover and his deputy Wayne Peterson were ushered into Charlie Strang's office. Once they were seated, Charlie's eyes bored a hole in the eyes of the Hanover. It was clear to him that the Government was not looking for new facts. They were content with what they had. In defiance to Charlie's state, Hanover's body language revealed how unimpressed he was with the summons to come to Pierce.

"I hired a former associate of yours to follow some leads that you apparently weren't considering."

"Who's this former associate?" Hanover squared his body in his chair. Charlie was gaining his attention.

"Gary Nigretto."

"He's a nobody. Never made it in our organization."

"Funny you would say that. He's come up with some solid evidence that Gil Brockton was the source for the leak."

"Kind of convenient, now that he is dead and unable to challenge your assertion, isn't it."

"Yeah. It sure is. It also happens to be pretty damn incontrovertible." Charlie's stare remained steadfast and then he added, "Incontrovertible unless, of course, you're dead set against hearing facts."

"Why do I feel we are in an adversarial relationship? I'm one of the good guys, remember?"

"Would that I believed that. But I have yet to see evidence that you are looking for anyone else, or even considering anyone else other than Rick Stoner. Instead, you are focused solely on him, so certain that you are right and that everyone who believes otherwise is wrong." Charlie drew a deep breath. "There is an old expression that I've heard since first coming into the business world. It says, 'When looking for a solution, it is always helpful to know the answer.' From the outset, you've figured that you have the answer which makes solving the case simple. All you've done since the beginning is shape the so-called evidence around your so-called solution. That puts us in an adversarial relationship."

"All right, what's your incontrovertible evidence?"

***

Within thirty minutes, the time it took to drive back to his office, Hanover was on the phone with his superiors in Washington, D.C. "We were wrong; all of us. Stoner is clean. He's not our man. I just met with the Pierce president, Charlie Strang. He laid out irrefutable evidence that someone else in the company is the one who leaked the plans to the Chinese."

"You have got to be kidding!"

"That's what I thought, but they hired old Gary Nigretto to do some snooping. He discovered that this guy was having an affair with a key official from Shek Industries—a Victoria Li. Had pictures, eye witnesses, and the whole nine yards. This company is in the business of buying and selling company designs. It sure looks like they are the Chinese connection. At the moment, it's all circumstantial, but there seems to be no way that these two aren't the ones involved."

"What do you recommend?" Christopher Barrett, Assistant Director of the FBI's Counterespionage Division in Washington asked.

"Put a tail on the Li woman immediately. We can't let her disappear into the Asian mist."

"Done. She won't slip through. We'll alert all the airports. I doubt she'll take a Greyhound, and driving a car seems to be out."

"I hate to be wrong, but it looks like I was this time. Guess I owe Stoner an apology."

There was a pause, and then Barrett said, "The Bureau doesn't apologize for doing its job."

Remorse

Remorse. That was what she felt. Total remorse. After the tears, there were no emotions. The devastation of her life was even now being accepted. Gil had been dead three weeks. He would still be alive if it hadn't been for her. Why had she allowed herself to become involved with him? Why had she been smitten with him? Her task was to beguile him, to charm him; not be ensnared by him. And now, that terrible revelation, the scandal that rocked the United States, the compromise of the secrecy-shrouded stealth bomber. It was in all the papers and on TV. Someone at Pierce was the leak, but she was the spy. The FBI didn't know it yet, at least she didn't think so, but she was the one they were looking for. It was only a matter of time. Fleeing to Hong Kong was an answer, but only a temporary one, she was sure. Eventually, the trail would lead to her. How had this whole thing happened? It was all so distorted. Her job was to ply a company trade secret, not a national top secret. Now she was a spy of a different sort.

***

Victoria was exceptionally bright. Her intelligence had always served her; had always kept her out of harm's way. More than once she had pushed the envelope in a relationship, but never this far. But then, she had never stolen government secrets before. Panic began to mingle with remorse. What if the FBI suspected her? She had always heard that they "got their man." What if they were investigating her right now? What if they had figured it was a woman, not a man who had obtained the design? Before, it had always been exciting to be involved in subterfuge. Now, there was the horrific knowledge that she had done something terrible and that the consequences were probably worse than she could even imagine. They executed spies, didn't they? And she would surely be considered a spy, wouldn't she?

***

Paranoia is not a pretty thing. Particularly when people honestly believe something or someone is out to get them. At first Victoria stayed late at her office, not wanting to be home alone. Then she reasoned that she was too vulnerable when she traveled home in the evening and that she was better off going home in a crowd. She started leaving around four o'clock. No matter when she left work, she always sensed that someone was watching her. She suspected taxis that seemed to crawl along the street, almost pacing her steps. She stole furtive glances at others walking beside her on the sidewalk. She feared she was beginning to lose her mind.

***

She could not remain in the United States. She had to get away. But where? If she was indeed being watched, they would find her anywhere. If the FBI was watching her, she wondered if she could even leave the country. Wouldn't they stop her when she tried to board an airplane? But what if she didn't fly out of the country? What if she drove or walked across the border? Passports weren't checked when driving into Canada. She could fly to Seattle, rent a car and drive to Vancouver, British Columbia. She had done it before. All they did at the border was ask for the reason of her visit, waive her on, and tell her to have a nice stay.

She called her travel agency, requesting a morning flight the next day out of Dulles to Seattle. Both United and Northwest had non-stops leaving around the same time at nine. She would arrive at SeaTac just before noon, local time. To throw any investigator off, after booking the flight on United, she reserved a room at the downtown Seattle Westin. She also reserved a car through Hertz. She had no intention of going to the Westin. She was heading straight to the border. But someone learning of her travel would think otherwise.

***

Things went smoother than she might have hoped. She was virtually certain that she wasn't followed. She only had carryon luggage so upon arrival at SeaTac, she went straight to the Hertz counter near Baggage Claim, signed the rental form and headed across the street to the parking garage and her waiting car. *Don't get too cocky*, she told herself. *Just because you can't see them, doesn't mean they aren't there.* She headed up Highway 99 toward the entrance to Interstate 5. At a traffic light just before entering the interstate, she slowed her car until the light turned yellow, then dashed across under the red light. No cars followed her and she was comforted into believing that if there was a tail, she had shaken it.

She passed through the downtown corridor without slowing and continued heading north, being careful to stay within the posted speed limit. The last thing she needed was to be stopped by the police. Traffic was light, thanks to the early afternoon hour and there were no construction delays. She kept a constant watch in her rear view mirror for suspicious cars. Every time she thought that maybe one was tailing her, it would turn on a right blinker and take an exit.

She approached the Canadian border checkpoint just after 3:30 p.m. and fell in behind the one car that was in her lane. It only made a brief stop at the Customs window before moving on in British Columbia. She moved slowly forward, rolling down her window as she did. "Good afternoon," a smiling, uniformed officer said. "What brings you to Canada today?"

"I'm going to visit relatives in Burnaby." It was true that she had relatives who lived there, but she had no intentions of going to their home.

"Are you a citizen of the U.S.?"

"No, I carry a British passport. I was born in Hong Kong." She had hoped that the questions would have been fewer. There had never been this many before.

"May I see your passport?" the agent asked.

She fumbled in her purse that lay on the seat beside her, then remembered that she had put the document in her carryon luggage which was in the trunk. "I'm sorry, officer. The passport must be in my bag in the trunk." She hoped he would tell her to move on; that he didn't need to see it.

"Ma'am, I'm going to have to ask you to pull over there to the left." He gestured toward an area where another Customs agent was standing. "I'm certain we will have you on your way promptly, but we do need to see your passport and I can't have you holding up the line here."

She rolled up her window, drove to the designated location, turned off the engine, and stepped out of the car. The agent walked toward her as she explained that her passport was in the trunk of the car and that the other agent had wanted her to present it. He shrugged his shoulders and backed up under the cover of the building's overhang. It had started to drizzle and he didn't care to get wet, apparently.

Her passport was right on top, in the zippered compartment. It started to rain harder and she hurried to hand it over for inspection and to get on her way. She hoped that rain was masking the perspiration that was flowing freely down her face.

It was only a cursory check. The agent seemed nonplussed about the whole thing, as if to say, *why bother me with this*. He examined it briefly, noted the places she had been, and handed it back. "Thank you," he said. "That's all."

"That's it?" she asked, somewhat incredulously.

"Yup. Everything's in order." He nodded and retreated to the office behind him, getting out of the rain.

As she pulled back into traffic and headed north on Highway 99, she decided to take a chance that the Fairmont Hotel Vancouver would have a room available for her. She had stayed there twice before and liked its ambiance. She remembered that it was on Georgia Street in the heart of downtown.

She was too far away from the border to see that the Customs agent was talking on the telephone.

She switched on the radio, feeling relaxed for the first time in days. Victoria had feared the worst; that there was an all-points bulletin out on her; that the Americans had asked the Canadians to hold her at the border. But obviously, no such requests had been made. She had made it out of the U.S. All she had to do was book a flight on Cathay Pacific and she would be on her way home. An old Beetles tune was playing and she happily sang along with the "Yellow Submarine."

An unmarked Canadian Royal Mounted Police car pulled in behind Victoria's car. She never noticed, because for her, the pressure was off. She had made it out of the U.S. safely.

Somehow, the entrance into Vancouver always confused her. She got lost twice trying to find Georgia Street, but once she crossed the Granville Bridge, she was reassured and ultimately pulled up to the hotel's front door. A bellman greeted her and told her to go straight to the Reservations desk; that her luggage would follow. There was a feeling of elegance as she walked across the marble floor of the lobby. She had forgotten the magnificent chandeliers that seemed to frame from on high the glass table with its beautiful bouquet of flowers. As she hoped, they had room for her--"A nice room, Madam, on the 14th floor." None of the suites were available, but she told the clerk it didn't matter; she only planned to spend two nights.

Shortly after settling in her room, she called the Air Canada ticket office and made arrangements to fly to Montreal the next day. She decided it was smarter to not fly directly to Hong Kong. If someone was indeed following her, that's what they would expect her to do. There was a morning flight that would get her into that Quebec city at 5:00 p.m., local time. She knew she was zigzagging back across the continent, but if anyone was following her, she wanted to make every move possible to throw them off. From Montreal, she would make arrangements to fly to

London and then on to Hong Kong. But she didn't want to tip her hand by making reservations more than a few hours in advance. And just to be certain she played the elusive game correctly, after making the flight arrangements to Montreal, she asked the hotel switchboard to put her through to the ticket office she saw just off the hotel lobby. She inquired about a Cathay Pacific flight and asked that they book her on the nonstop to Hong Kong two days hence. "Yes, Victoria Li. I am in Room 1422."

An hour later, she went for a walk, wandering into several of the nearby shops, mostly browsing, but making occasional small purchases. One purchase was a large handbag with zippers that allowed it to expand or contract depending on the contents she wished to carry. She put her purse inside and put the bag over her shoulder. This was her new look, like so many other women who seemed to carry unusually large loads.

At seven the next morning, with her large handbag filled with all her essentials, she stood outside the hotel, waiting for a taxi. She decided against taking her car. If it was still in the garage, it would be assumed that she was still at the hotel. Once away from the curb, when she couldn't be heard, she instructed the taxi to take her to the airport.

The flight to Montreal was uneventful and once again, she saw no one who appeared to be interested in her. It was looking more and more like she had made a clean escape.

Her seat companion on the flight had recommended that she stay at Le Centre Sheraton Hotel & Towers Montre on Boulevard Rene-Levesque West—a four-star hotel in the heart of downtown Montreal. Upon arrival, she called the hotel to see if they could accommodate her for the night. They had a room and would look forward to welcoming her shortly.

It might have been paranoia. It might have been idle curiosity, but as Victoria hung up the telephone, she scanned the baggage claim area wondering if anyone might be concerned with her. There was movement near a pillar and her eyes were drawn to it—the figure of a tall man wearing a black raincoat. He seemed to be studying her. As soon as she looked his way, he turned his head quickly in the other direction. She was used to men looking at her, but this one acted strangely. It wasn't a physical attraction; more like someone who was shadowing her. Immediately, her senses were heightened. Was she under surveillance after all?

She was frightened anew and spent the whole taxi ride to the hotel looking out the back window to see if she was being followed. If she was, she couldn't tell.

After check-in, as the bellhop was leading her to the elevators and her room beyond, she saw the man from the airport. He was sitting in the lobby, hiding behind a newspaper, but there was no mistaking that it was him. His black raincoat was folded over the arm of the couch. And it was no coincidence. He was looking at her, just like before, only no longer hiding the fact. This was a downright stare. Now, fear permeated her whole body. She knew that she had been discovered and that she had no place to hide.

He didn't follow her to the elevator. Why should he, she reasoned? He knew she was in the hotel and he knew he could easily find her room number from the hotel registry. All the same, she kept glancing back down the hallway as she was led to her room. The young bellman was courteous and anxious to show her all the amenities his hotel had to offer. "Mademoiselle, would you like me to turn on the air conditioner?" No, she told him, everything was just perfect. "This is an honor bar," he told her, pointing to the wooden credenza that housed a small refrigerator. She whimsically noted that a cord sealed the two handles that opened the 'honor' bar. She might have been on her honor, but the hotel would have known she had been in it whether she told or not. "Is there anything I can get you?" he asked. "Ice?" No, she was just fine. All she needed was some rest. With that, he extended the hotel's best wishes for a pleasant stay and left. She double-locked the door behind him.

She walked over to the floor-to-ceiling window that overlooked the city. It was a commanding view, particularly as night fell and the lights in nearby buildings shimmered against the rain-streaked window of her room. The weather had turned colder with the onset of rain. It started falling on the way from the airport. The glass, though double-paned, did little to keep the cold out and she shivered as she stood there.

She sat on the edge of the bed. Her heart was pounding and she felt she could hardly breathe. The phone rang, setting her further on edge. No one knew she was here. Who? Maybe it was the hotel management. "Hello?"

"Miss Li?" A distinctly American voice exploded in her ear. She didn't speak. She couldn't speak. Air was trapped in her lungs.

"Miss Li, I know I have the correct room and I know that you are listening. My name is Special Agent Swinford with the Federal Bureau of Investigation. I need to talk to you about something of the utmost importance." She remained silent.

"May I come up to your room?"

Does the FBI have jurisdiction up here? Do they even have the right to follow me in Canada? Can they arrest me? She didn't know the answers to her questions, but it did seem as if the agent was acting with the utmost impunity.

"I'm very tired right now," she answered. "Perhaps after I have taken a nap."

"When would be a good time?" he asked.

""In an hour." She hung up the phone and walked back over to the window. The view of this spectacular city from her floor was wasted. She saw little except her own despair.

Tears? No, she couldn't cry. It would mock the life she had led. Serenity? No, she didn't deserve it, for it too would mock the life she had led.

She was in a bottomless chasm. Totally bottomless. There was only one way to escape.

She walked away from the chasm and into the bathroom. The bottle was on the counter.

First it was a twinge; then it was pain. There was heat and irritation in her throat and stomach. Then there was vomiting followed by cramps in her calf muscles. She knew that convulsions, dizziness, and delirium would probably precede a coma. Arsenic was not a pleasant way to die.

She hadn't taken a sedative because she wanted the pain. She didn't deserve mercy. She wanted to die without mercy.

Chapter 17

Disappearing Act

A critical flaw

"There is a critical flaw in the Pierce terrain-avoidance design," John Knox from National Security announced to General Bouren, Chairman of the Joint Chiefs at a hastily called Pentagon meeting.

"Meaning precisely what?"

"Meaning the information that the Soviets bought for $50 million is invalid." Knox sat back waiting for the information to sink in before proceeding. He watched the hardened veteran of two major conflicts shake his head slightly as if disbelieving. "That's the good news." Knox continued. "The Soviets can't copy it, or if they do, they won't get it to work."

"So where does this leave us?" Admiral Philip Jeffrey, Vice Chairman and onetime Commander, Naval Air Force, U.S. Atlantic Fleet, asked.

"Well, it leaves us with bad news too, 'cause valid or not, the insight they've gained into U.S. plans is the more damning of the two. Now they know we are working on this, and even though they won't be able to make the system work from the design they purchased, they will reasonably deduce that with time, we will make it work. Which means the countermeasures will start."

"How do we know the design is flawed?" Bouren pressed on.

"This morning, Pierce contacted the Air Force Project Office at Wright-Pat and told them. They said they had encountered a snag and couldn't get the system components to talk to each other."

"Is the problem just a glitch or something that has them buffaloed?"

"There are buffalo chips all over the design floor."

Lost at sea

Rick was on his way home in the car when he heard the first report on KIRO Radio.

"We interrupt our broadcast for this breaking news bulletin." Rick reached over and turned up the volume. "Intercontinental Airlines reports the apparent loss at sea of its Flight Zero-Zero-Six with two hundred eighty seven passengers and a crew of sixteen aboard. No listing of passengers will be made available until next of kin have been notified. Intercontinental did announce that the crew was Seattle-based and was under the command of Captain James R. Guerber of Mercer Island." Rick switched off the radio. He realized the pounding in his ears was his heart beat. Margy's husband was gone. Things were going to be tough for her. But he was not going to be the one to step in. She was going to have to handle this one on her own. That didn't stop the heartache he felt for her loss, however.

The report of the disappearance of Intercontinental Airlines Flight Number Zero-Zero-Six dominated the Seattle news, allowing only passing mention of all events, local and national. It was twenty days before Christmas and the Tokyo-bound 747 had been two hours from the Japanese mainland when all contact with it was lost.

Guilty as charged

It was first-degree murder. It had been willful, deliberate, and premeditated. She wanted to kill her husband, she intended to kill him, and planned the crime before carrying it out. But the District Attorney allowed the defense to plead the crime down to second-degree murder in exchange for no trial. He agreed it was a crime of passion, which he called a mitigating factor for his leniency.

Superior Court Judge Gerald Shuttleworth heard the plea in closed court. He asked Susan if she understood the charge and the significance of her confession. He then asked her to make her confession before him, for the record and his own satisfaction. Susan had been prepared for this, but stammered in hearing her own voice.

She spoke almost in a whisper. "I'm an alcoholic, your Honor." She starred at the Washington State seal on the wall behind the judge. "I planned to kill myself that afternoon. I wanted to die. Then something happened. I realized my misery was my husband's fault, not mine; that he should die, not me. So I stopped drinking and waited for him to come home." She paused and looked directly at Judge Shuttleworth. "When he walked into the bedroom, I shot him. I wasn't drunk at the time. I knew what I was doing and I guess I would do it again. I was not insane at the time, at least no more than any other person who commits murder."

The judge found her guilty of murder in the second degree, and after consideration, sentenced her to 30 years in prison, the minimum time allowed for the offense she had committed. If she served the entire sentence, she would get out of prison just short of her 75th birthday.

No one from Pierce attended the trial. Because of her calm resolution and lack of fight, the press chose to soft-pedal its coverage. The murder was sensational. The trial was not, and without the hype, it was hard to sell newspapers.

Chapter 18

Who Done It?

"I don't remember us ever being so far off in an investigation," Roy Hanover said. "I mean, we weren't even close. All of us were convinced Stoner was the guy. There was no chance that he wasn't guilty. Everything pointed to him. So when Charles Strang showed us the findings of his independent research, we were stunned."

Hanover knew that his invitation to meet with Christopher Barrett, Assistant Director of the FBI's Counterespionage Division, wasn't so that he could receive a commendation. The Agency, right up to the top, wanted to know what went wrong. More than that, they wanted to know how an independent investigator in Seattle, picked out of the Yellow Pages, had cracked the case when the FBI Field Office had not.

"The research that you allude to certainly sealed the case on that Li woman." Barrett spoke without emotion. "But how did you sort out the rest?" He was giving Hanover a way of escape.

"We discovered that Li was having an affair with Dr. Brockton."

"I know, but how did you find out about Munsen?"

"That was pure luck." Hanover figured that humility was in order. "We followed up with the hotels where Li and Brockton were seen together. We wanted to make certain we had the facts this time. No mistakes. We also thought we would do it like a lineup, showing a picture of a few people to see if Brockton would be singled out. We had one picture with Brockton, Stoner, and Munsen in it. At two of the hotels, they pointed to Brockton. But get this, at two others, they picked Munsen."

"Had you suspected him?"

"Not a chance. He was a duffus as far as we were concerned. He desperately wanted to be in on the know—but he wasn't. In hindsight, we should have detected his nervousness. He was an habitual coin jiggler.

We thought it was a tic; didn't pick up on it as revealing his being on edge."

"Just because he was recognized for renting motel rooms didn't mean that he was the one who sold the farm. What other clues were there?" Special Agent Phil Edwards joined in, leaning closer toward Hanover.

"Victoria Li provided all the information we needed. Before she committed suicide, she left a note confessing her part in this. She said that she had tried to get the design from Brockton but that she failed. He told her that he couldn't compromise his company and he couldn't sell out his country. And then suddenly, out of the blue, Carl Munsen contacted Li and said that he might have something she wanted. A few clandestine meetings in out of the way motels, and a payment of $200,000 later, and he provided the full design disclosure."

"How did he get his hands on it?"

"He got it from Brockton, only Brockton didn't know it.'

"You've got to explain that one." Barrett was fascinated with this.

Hanover shook his head and smiled at the simplicity of it all. "Munsen knew the combination to Brockton's safe. He was the one who purchased the safe and set it up for him. Apparently, Brockton never thought of changing the combination, so Munsen just went in after hours and helped himself to the design."

"What happened when you confronted him with this?"

"He caved. He was and is a weak individual. Morality, loyalty and honesty are not part of his code. He didn't even lawyer-up; just confessed. He's currently in detention at the Fort Lewis facility near Tacoma, pending trial motions. We are asking that he be tried in the Western Region, but we will see. From my standpoint, it doesn't much matter where he goes on trial. We've got him, and because he sold military secrets, we've got him for treason."

Exonerated

Government agencies are without the capacity of asking forgiveness. Perhaps it is a fear of liability, at least implied. The confession of Victoria Li, added to the evidence compiled by the Nigretto Agency, provided irrefutable proof that Rick Stoner was not the culprit the FBI had painted him to be. There were coincidences, no question about that, coincidences that suggested Stoner might be guilty. And there was nothing wrong in making the assumptions they did. When you get a strong lead, you follow it. Their error was prematurely concluding that there could be no other person to blame. They never really looked for anyone else. In mathematics, there usually is only one solution to a problem. But not so in police work. Many different paths need to be taken in order to arrive at the right destination.

The federal agents left the premises of Pierce Electronics as silently as they appeared.

Chapter 19

The Rest of the Story

1980. President Jimmy Carter announced the U.S. withdrawal from the Summer Olympics in protest over the Soviet invasion of Afghanistan; the U.S. Olympic Hockey Team won the gold over the Soviets in the Winter Olympics; an April 24th U.S. hostage mission in Iran ended in disaster when three of eight helicopters failed at the staging area and one of the remaining helicopters collided with one of six C-130 transports, killing eight and injuring five; Mt. St. Helens in Washington State erupted; Ronald Reagan and Jimmy Carter were nominated to lead their political parties in the Presidential Election; Ronald Reagan was elected in a landslide, carrying 44 states; and life changed dramatically for Rick Stoner.

USAF press conference

On August 22, 1980, a press conference was held at the Pentagon where for the first time, the actuality of an American stealth program was officially acknowledged and revealed. The conference was given by the Secretary of Defense, Deputy Director of Defense for Research and Development, and the Air Force Deputy Chief of Staff for Research and Development. Secretary of Defense, Harold Brown spoke first.

"I am announcing today a major technological advance of great military significance. This so-called stealth technology enables the United States to build manned and unmanned aircraft that cannot be successfully intercepted with existing air defense systems. We have demonstrated to our satisfaction that the technology works. This achievement will be a formidable instrument of peace. It promises to add unique dimension to our tactical forces and to be the deterrent strength of our strategic forces. At the same time, it will provide us capabilities that are wholly consistent with our pursuit of verifiable arms control agreements, in particular with the provisions of SALT Two.

"For three years, we've successfully maintained the security of this program. This is because of the conscientious efforts of the relatively few people in the executive branch and legislative branch who were briefed on the activity and the contractors who worked on it."

Rick laid the newspaper in his lap and stared blankly at the wall. Sure, he thought. They maintained the security of the program until his company compromised the whole program. Some security.

Brown's statement continued. "However, in the past few months, the circle of people knowledgeable about the program has widened, partly because of the increased size of the effort, and partly because of the debate underway in the Congress on new bomber proposals." *And partly because the Soviets know all about our terrain-following radar,* Rick injected. He read on.

"Regrettably, there have been several leaks about the stealth program during the last few days, actually the last couple of weeks, in the press, and there's been television news coverage. In the face of these leaks, I believe that it's not appropriate or credible for us to deny the existence of this program. And it is now important to correct some of the leaked information that misrepresented the Administration's position on a new bomber program." Rick had read enough for now. He knew the rest of the story, and didn't bother to read what Secretary William Perry or Lt. Gen. Kelly Burke had to say.

Instead, he reached across the arm of his easy chair to where Carol sat and took her hand. She looked at him and said, "What's this for?"

"I love you, and I just wanted you to know. God has blessed me in a special way. Why He chose to give you to me, I'll never know. He must have loved me very much."

He moved over to the couch and sat next to his wife, putting his arm around her. Roxanne got up from her pillow and nuzzled in between Rick and Carol as if she knew that a wonderful healing was going on.

Agape kind of love

It was incredible. Their lives had been restored. Rick and Carol had never been happier. It was all because of Carol, too. She knew how to love. She knew that love was long-suffering, patient, and kind. That love forgave and more important, that it forgot.

Funny, the ancient Greeks had a total of 25,000 words in their vocabulary. At last count, there were over 700,000 words in the English language. So how was it that the ancient Greeks had at least three words for *love*, while there was only one in English? In Greek, there was *Eros*—sexual love—"I love you for what you give me;" *Philia*—brotherly love – "I love you because you love me;" and *Agape* –Godly love—"I love you no matter what."

Carol had the *Agape* kind of love.

About the Author

Norm Noble has been writing professionally since 1963, publishing over 100 articles and booklets covering fields as diverse as marketing, sales, aircraft electronics, marine electronics, and energy management.

Following a successful career in the aerospace industry, where he managed international sales and marketing groups for major corporations, he was the owner of the NOBLE GROUP, a publisher of custom newsletters for corporations.

In 1989, his non-fiction book titled *Advertising Your Church Services* was published, and in 2004, he published his first novel, *In the Still of the Night*, a story of tragedy in the skies. An historical adventure novel, *Changing of the Gods*, about a con game in 66 A.D. Corinth, was published in 2006.

Norm has traveled extensively (up to 150,000 miles a year) and has spent time in 79 countries on six continents.

Norm and DenisAnn Noble have five children and 13 grandchildren, all of whom live within just a few miles of the Noble family home in Redmond, Washington. The Nobles are *rainbirds*, living in Arizona six months of the year and in Washington the other six months.

Norm Noble is a Deacon at First Baptist Church of Sun Lakes, a freelance writer for the *Arizona Republic* (Phoenix), president of the Desert Chordsmen Barbershop Chorus of Sun Lakes, Director of Rotary International's STRIVE program, a mentoring program for *at risk* high school students, and Director of Public Relations for the Sun Lakes Rotary Club.

Further details about Norm Noble and his work may be found on his website, *http://www.normnoble.com*